Strong, But Broken

Casey Power

Strong, but healing
Copyright © 2025 by Casey Power

Edited by Valerie Jones
Cover Design: Tori Epps

Dedication

There are two people to whom I want to dedicate this story.

To Mom:

What can I say? You were the one who taught me to love books. You encouraged me to read, and for so many nights, you read to me. You spent so much money on books, and poured countless hours into taking care of me and my brother. You told me to start checking out books from the school library because we couldn't afford to buy new ones every day, but you still always bought me books. You encouraged me to explore new worlds through stories, even ones you'd never read yourself.

Because of you, I learned to love writing, too. At first, I recreated the books I'd read, writing them the way I wanted them to go or the way I thought they should have turned out. You endured my horrible writing skills when I was ten, but still gave me your full support as I grew. I love you, Mom. I'm sorry it took me this long to finish something, but here it is—and it is because of you that it is here.

To Sydney:

Where do I even start? There would be no story, no Casey, if it weren't for you. You've held me up in my darkest hours, letting me just be myself. You've given me a reason to keep going by showing me that life is worth living, even when things seem at their worst. You're the STRONGEST person I know, and I feel like the luckiest person in this world to call you my best friend, especially since knowing you feel the same.

I'm sorry we lived 400 miles apart for four years; I will not lose you again. Wherever you go, I'll be right there with you. You're the Skyla to my Maggie, the Monica to my Rachel, the Christina to my Meredith. You're and will always be my person, my other half, my better half. This is for you, babes. It's all about use and everything we've been through. I love you.

Table of Contents

Introduction

Think of something that makes you smile without even trying. It could be a memory, a person, a thing, or even a scent. I want you to picture yourself holding it in the palm of your hand. Take all that warmth and happiness and lock it into your brain. Feel it and really let yourself be washed over by it.

Now imagine that thing —whether it's something physical or something more abstract—being crushed, shattered by your hand or something else. Then picture it breaking into millions of pieces, blown away, or destroyed. That warmth and happiness are replaced by sharp pain and numbness. That thing will never be seen again and will never make you feel the same as it once did.

That is what it feels like to be broken. That is what it feels like, battling every day with yourself. The pain, numbness. All that we are trying to achieve in this world is that feeling of warmth and happiness. We are all trying to be someone. We are also all trying not to be the person we are. We want to be the person with the picture-perfect life (happiness being the central theme). We want to be successful, which looks different to everyone, but it is still the same feeling of happiness.

This way of thinking is negative, but when you are born with a broken brain, your mind can sound like this. One thing is for sure: I know people who struggle with a broken brain do not ask for it. I know, personally, I would not wish this on my own worst enemy.

Having a broken brain isn't something we should be ashamed of. People with cancer don't hide or try to cover up their illness, and neither should anyone with mental health struggles. Yet, when someone loses their battle with depression, schizophrenia, PTSD, bipolar disorder, or an eating disorder, we often say they "lost their battle," but we don't mention what they were fighting against. However, when it comes to cancer, we're clear about what the battle was against.

People are afraid of what they don't know. Mental illness is a scary term, so in my mind, I always use the term broken brain. In the last decade-plus, many people have been fighting for others to realize that mental illness is a serious thing. The problem with our world is that accepting new ideas and wiping away old biases and thoughts is not something we like to do.

For example, there are still people who don't feel like African Americans or people of other races should have the same rights as whites. Some people disregard others who are the same sex or are transgender. There are even people who are still prejudiced towards women having rights. These are examples of how people still can't accept a new idea.

Mental illness is just as serious as any other illness. It may not look like a typical illness, but who sees the actual tumor on a cancer patient with the naked eye? What is being conveyed here is that mental illness is just as much of a killer as cancer. However, with cancer, there are people in remission, and with mental illness, there are people who survive. The difference is that cancer goes away, but mental illness does not.

Let those with broken brains have their story heard. Let their struggles and journeys be heard. You never know what good comes from hearing others' stories, especially those of struggling people. Let's say this girl who is telling you this story heard others' stories and voices. I'm here to show you that it's okay to be okay, but it's also not to be okay. I'm here to make these voices heard.

One broken brain to another. One warrior to another. To anyone who wants to understand and not be afraid, here you go.

Chapter One

The Plane

Maggie

The airport in Minneapolis was crowded as usual. When I was little, we didn't travel much, but my dad traveled for his job before he was confined to the hospital. The one time we took a family trip, Mom said it was for fun. In reality, it was just to run away from what had happened to our family. From what I can remember, it was not a happy vacation.

I remember walking around and looking at all these people rushing around. Knowing that each person was trying to get somewhere brought me some kind of comfort. Some were trying to get home, some were running from home, some were on vacation or returning, and some were trying something different. Either way, everyone in an airport is trying to get somewhere.

While in the airport, Mom and I were walking around the Minneapolis airport during a layover. Looking around, I was amazed at all the chaos and how smooth it was. Everything was running like a well-oiled machine. Everyone knew their place. My place was to stand next to my mother and hold her hand to stop the shaking.

When we got to one clearing in the airport, you could look straight up and see all these different floors. I remember pausing, letting myself take in all the layers. They reminded me of what it was like to get to know a person: layers upon layers: good, bad, ugly, pretty, sad, and happy. Everyone is different, and every layer of a person is different. That is why people are complicated. I concluded this by staring up at this clearing at twelve years old.

Now, here I stood in that same spot so many years later. Nothing had changed besides some rust on the railings and a painting job. The sun was shining brightly, and I cracked a small smile. My thoughts on people being complicated remained the same. All that had happened to me in these years solidified my thinking.

Colorado has been my home for the last nine and a half years. I decided to move here to go to college and stayed to get my master's here. There was no single answer to why I chose it. I remember many people at my high school graduation asking, and even now, there is no true answer. After all this time, it was time for me to return to my hometown, Bemidji, Minnesota.

Most people had never heard of it; it was a decent-sized town of fifteen thousand. It was about a hundred miles from the Canadian border, making it land in the middle of northern Minnesota. It got cold, bitterly cold, but summers were beautiful and mild. Being born and growing up here, I was used to the weather. I was used to the small-town feel, small mall, two McDonald's, etc. I was used to people traveling all over to come and see the Paul Bunyan and Babe the Blue Ox statues. I was used to hockey being the crowning jewel of this town, especially when it came to the college team in the city. I am used to people parking on the lake in the winter. I was used to seeing people leaving their cars running at Walmart during the winter. I was used to the kinks of living in the tundra of Minnesota.

I made my way to my gate, 3D, one of the smaller gates. It wasn't like Bemidji was a hot destination for travel in August. I was lucky that there was even a flight going into Bemidji; usually, there were very few flights. The flight to Bemidji wouldn't start boarding for another thirty minutes. I settled into a stiff seat near the glass. Our plane would be smaller, maybe holding thirty or fewer people.

I visited my home three times in the years I had been away. My siblings and father didn't want to have anything to do with me. On the other hand, my mother would find ways to see me, or I would meet her somewhere. My avoidance of my home was not my first choice, but rather everyone else in my family. However, things changed dramatically over the last year, and my return to Bemidji was more of a requirement.

When April came around, I told the school district where I worked in Denver that I was accepting a job back home. I have been a kindergarten teacher in that district since I graduated five years ago. I also put my house on the market, and it sold in early June at the asking price. Leaving behind the life I had built away from my family wouldn't be easy, but at least there would be one constant: Skyla James.

Skyla had been my best friend since middle school, and we had been attached at the hip since awkwardly introducing ourselves in the lunchroom. Her family had moved here from Rapid City, South Dakota; it was just her and her mother. Skyla and I ended up in Colorado for her undergrad and medical school. When Kensinger Memorial back in Bemidji called to offer her a fellowship, she didn't turn it down, especially since her mother had been diagnosed with cancer. Sadly, four months ago, Ms. James passed.

So, last August, Skyla moved back and began her fellowship while I remained in Colorado. It was a challenging year, but the FaceTimes and phone calls helped. She was over the moon when I told her I was moving back; I needed her just as much as she needed me.

Now, the main reason for my return was my father. Mitchell Kensinger was the physical therapist for the Minnesota Vikings for over a decade before he moved back to be with our family permanently. He ran the physical therapy wing at Kensinger Memorial until two years ago. My dad was one of two children from Jacob Kensinger, my grandpa, who inherited the hospital from his dad. My uncle, Frank Kensinger, the older of the two, was the hospital's chief and still was.

My mother was a pediatric surgeon and head of that department until about a year ago when she retired. She was very accomplished in her field of medicine. I was the middle child of three. My older brother, Calvin, was a neurosurgeon, and my younger sister, Anika, was in medical school on the West Coast.

In an entire family of doctors, I was the only one who opted out of that field. Strike one against me. Strike two was choosing to be a kindergarten teacher. Strike three was turning down my father's offer to pay me to go to medical school at Stanford. From that point, none of them wanted anything to do with me. My mother didn't care; she came to my classroom every year and was fascinated by what I did, which was a true mother's love.

"Flight 3708 to Bemidji will begin boarding ahead of schedule." The intercom said overhead.

When I informed Skyla that I had accepted the kindergarten teacher position at the public school, she found us a townhome. Last week, we officially got the keys and started unpacking and settling in. I had come back to Denver to do the last few things, such as closing on my house and signing some documents for transferring my teaching license, and then my life here in Colorado was gone, with just a few signatures.

The plane was ready to board, and I waited patiently in line as we scanned our tickets and were escorted down onto the tarmac into our tiny plane. I was one of the last to board, near the back of the aircraft. There were two seats on the right and one by itself on the left. No one was seated next to me, and I felt a wave of relief as I shoved my duffel bag above and settled in.

Taking a deep breath, I laid my head back and closed my eyes, preparing for this new chapter.

Jackson

I was among the first to board the plane, which is one of the perks of flying first class. The flight from Los Angeles to Minneapolis was quick, and I hoped the next leg from Minneapolis to Bemidji would be just as smooth. This trip was hopefully the last time I'd be flying for a while.

I'd spent my whole life in California—born and raised—and had never left the state until about four months ago when I flew to Bemidji for a job interview.

They offered me the job, and I accepted. Saying goodbye to everything I'd known in LA felt surreal, but I was ready to start fresh. The questions were inevitable. Why are you leaving? Why are you abandoning your family? But honestly, it was a challenge I was ready to take on. And I've always loved a good challenge.

To back this up, I was the only one in my family who had a degree; my mother had been working at the same restaurant since she was 16, and my father had died after I had been born in a car accident. I had two older sisters who were all married right out of high school to someone wealthy enough to support them.

The last three years had been challenging, and I looked forward to being somewhere different. My best friend from medical school had accepted the position of head of neuro at this hospital, so he was able to pull strings and get me there.

I had known Calvin Kensinger since medical school at Stanford. He was a few months older than I. He came from a family entirely of doctors: Anika was finally in medical school, and both of his parents were retired from the field. Calvin moved back to Bemidji about a year ago to help the hospital. I ached to be around my best friend, so he found a way, and here I was on this small plane to the middle of the Minnesota tundra.

Bemidji was a good-sized town, not small, but not massive. It had pleasant warmth, minus the negative fifty degrees and three feet of snow it could get. I already knew the hospital, as they were helping me find housing and letting me work part-time for the last three months to finish getting everything in order back in LA with my mom, who was taking this hard.

Being in the airport was a very overwhelming experience; the chaos was maddening. Everyone was unaware of what was happening because they focused on getting to their destination. Being in the airport felt like an escape from reality.

I settled into first class; the hospital had paid for my flight, so I enjoyed the perks. Someone caught my eye as I laid my head back as the last person boarded the plane. The first thing I noticed was her beautiful, golden-colored hair and the smell of vanilla as she whisked by. I felt warmth and a sudden draw to her as I secretly watched her shove her bag in the overhead bin and settle into her seat towards the back.

I was not a believer in what is meant to be and chances. With the card I had been dealt, there was no belief in that. I was also a person who had never let himself feel for anyone because if they got too close, they would get hurt. My oath as a doctor was not to do harm; letting someone in or letting me feel would be harmful.

Growing up and for the last few years, I had told myself not to let anyone in and get tangled in the mess of the person I was. I had come to terms many months ago that this was my life: work and myself. All that talk and work to get content went out the door when her blue eyes surveyed the plane before sitting down.

I felt as if a spark inside me came alive. It was a strange feeling, like striking a match for a candle. The warmth was spreading through my body as if I had been deprived. Biting the inside of my lip, I willed myself to focus on sleeping, but whatever this draw to her beat my will.

Maggie

"Hey," a smooth voice caught my attention, "this is my seat."

Caught off guard, "Oh," was all I could say before returning to the window.

There was no doubt that this man was attractive. He was tall with dark hair and dark eyes. He was fit and seemed to have a calm composure. What surprised me most, though, was how friendly he was. Just by looking at him, I could tell he wasn't from Bemidji. His skin had this subtle tan that stood out.

He settled into the seat beside me, fumbling around with the buckle. I felt my body relax as I tried to focus on the people outside the plane. He smelled like fresh mint, like he had freshly showered.

Usually, after all the shit that had happened to me, I would ignore him and go about my way, sitting in silence. I was a kid at heart, but there was no way in hell I could stand most people.

"I'm Jackson, by the way." He said, and I slowly turned to look at him. He wore a casual smile as he held his hand.

My eyes bounced back from his hand to his dark eyes before I took his hand. "Maggie."

I shifted my focus back to the window. "What brings you to the tundra of Minnesota?" Jackson asked, catching me off guard, that he wanted to continue to talk.

I turned my head, preparing to tell him we didn't need to make the whole small talk. As I looked at him, all that bitchiness or coldness inside me disappeared.

"I could ask you the same thing," I responded.

Jackson cracked a smile, "Well, I asked you first."

A small smile appeared on my face, "I was born and raised there, returning home. You?"

"I accepted a job at a hospital and will start full-time on Sunday morning."

I frowned, not liking where this was going. "Which hospital? Let me guess, cardio is your specialty?"

Jackson looked impressed. "General, actually, and Kensinger Memorial." I started to feel the barriers inside me go up. "Are you in the medical field?"

"No, I just grew up in a family full of them," I said dryly.

He looked generally intrigued: "Well, what is your area of specialty?"

I rolled my eyes. "You're a doctor; you will just laugh at what I do."

"I highly doubt that unless you are some social media influencer, then I might laugh." He teased me.

I stopped building barriers as his words again caught me off guard. "I am a kindergarten teacher. I majored in elementary education and then got my master's in early childhood education."

A look of confusion crossed his face. "Why would I laugh about that?"

"Why wouldn't you?" I suggested. "I don't do anything like save lives or cure people. I just babysit the bottom of the human food chain."

Jackson frowned. "That is what you think of your profession?"

I shook my head, "When your whole family is in the medical field, that is what you get told daily." I shrugged. "I wouldn't do what I do if I didn't love it."

Jackson looked just as young as me, maybe a few years older. He watched me silently as we took off from the ground and into the air. I loved the feeling of takeoff, but hated the feeling of landing.

"You're telling me, your family, none of them support you or have had your back?" He seemed generally concerned by this.

"My mom must be secretly proud of me. My brother and sister haven't talked to me in about ten years, along with my dad." I listened to how that sounded, making my family sound shallow. "They're not bad people; they just don't understand how I didn't want to become a doctor."

"If it makes you feel better, I am the only doctor in my family. None of my sisters or my mother has a degree. My mom works at the same diner she always has, and my sisters found themselves someone who makes enough so that they don't have to work." His cheeks flushed as he seemed embarrassed by sharing all of that. "What I am trying to say: on some level, I understand being an outsider."

I smiled sadly. "Well, I have learned to accept it for what it is." I glanced around the plane; everyone was sleeping or had headphones on. "Where is your family from?"

"You can't laugh when I tell you where I am from."

I shot him a look, "I highly doubt I'll laugh."

Jackson gave me a playful smile, "I was born in Santa Ana, outside of Los Angeles."

"California is nice, a little too warm for me, but it's not a place to be ashamed of."

"Unless you lived in the ghetto."

I pulled my knees to my chest and wrapped my arms around them. "Sorry."

"Why are you sorry? It is true; California has a certain beauty, just not where I am from."

"Curious," I started, "why general?"

"Why Kindergarten?" He shot back playfully.

I smirked at him, "I asked first."

His eyes searched my face for a second before smiling back at me. "Why the interest?"

My eyes took in his face, high cheekbones, and thin lips. In a perfect world, he would fit in just fine. Jackson, however, seemed to be hiding more below the ideal surface. That was maybe why I was interested. Or maybe because I generally was?

He was intoxicating and intriguing; I did not like the combination.

Jackson

Maggie was studying my face incredibly hard. She seemed to be searching for the answer. For me, I was taking every bit of her in. Her hair was long, falling to her mid-back. Eyes were an incredible shade of blue that was rare. She was thin but tall as well. Her lips were full, and her eyes were almond-shaped. There was no denying she was beautiful. When she smiled, oh fuck, that spark struck through my body all over again.

Beneath all of that, however, I felt as if there was so much more to her. I found it incredible that she forged her way into a career that she loved, and that her family was upset about her doing so. From what I remember when I was in school, without people like Maggie, there would be no people like me or anyone else. What she did affected the whole world; she made a difference. I watched her eyes; she seemed strong, but there seemed to be a lot of missing pieces beneath her.

"Curiosity," She raised her eyebrow, "So spill, why general?"

She was smart, no denying that. She seemed to be one who could see through any kind of bullshit. I could already tell she knew there was more to me.

"In my opinion, general is the king of all specialties. You must know so much, and the things you see and get to do will always be different than working in one area." I shrugged and smiled at her. "I know there are times when it is not as cool as the others or that I repeat many of the same procedures, but there is just so much more I feel you need to know. Plus, I get the chance to work with everyone."

She took in my answer, processing it slowly before she gave the slightest smile. "I always wanted to teach fourth grade; my fourth-grade teacher taught me to feel confident." Biting her lip, she looked away from me as she spoke. "If not for her, I would not have accomplished a fraction of what I have. So, going into the field, I thought that I would be just like her. Then, I was introduced to a kindergarten class, and they made me feel like what I was doing mattered.

"I guess growing up with generations of doctors, being told teaching means nothing, it makes you feel worthless. The light in a kid's eyes when they make a connection, the way they love you unconditionally, all of that is priceless."

Maggie smiled and pulled her knees to her chest. Then, I noticed she was wearing black leggings and a thin, long-sleeved blue shirt. She had no makeup on, and her hair looked naturally crazy.

The way she spoke of her family shaming her rubbed me the wrong way. "What, uh, kind of doctors are your family?"

She shrugged, "Everything you can think of neuro to peds. My best friend is a trauma fellow at Kensinger." She said calmly.

My brow furrowed. "I've been at the hospital part-time for a while; I bet I know her."

Maggie laughed, "Dr. James?"

It didn't take long until the piece came together. "The intense dark hair, cat-eyed bitch?"

Maggie's eyes narrowed: "Hey, now."

"No, not like that. She's just intense. Not a people person; I think she's spoken to me once with a simple grunt."

"Yeah, definitely not a people person, but she can turn it on when necessary."

Maggie's eyes drifted back out the window. "How do you handle being an outsider?"

"You just do. Skyla never cared what I did if I was happy. My mom was proud of me. You find those that support you and stick with them."

Maggie smiled sadly and kept her attention on the window. I decided to sit silently beside her. I feared that if we kept talking, more layers would unfold, and I would never see or speak to her again.

My biggest hidden fear is being alone. Even though I had convinced myself that being alone was better for me, I still let that fear consume me. Letting it consume me was better than fighting it.

Maggie

"So why Bemidji? I am assuming it is not a well-known town in the land of California." I gave him a small smile.

Jackson returned my small smile: "My best friend works there. He is the head of neurosurgery and the youngest ever. He is the one who was able to score me the job."

My stomach dropped, and I felt suddenly sick. Calvin. Of course, he would find a way to ruin my chance of being friends with Jackson. My anger was well-painted across my face because Jackson had stopped talking and looked concerned.

"Calvin Kensinger," I said his name as normally as I could. "Yeah, I know him. He's about a few years older than me."

Jackson didn't seem so convinced: "Not a fan?"

I shrugged and tried to play it off. "I mean, I grew up with him. I was never impressed, but I haven't seen him for a while, so maybe he's changed."

"It wouldn't shock me if he acted like a dick." He gave me a playful grin. "I mean, he can be a dick and act like he walks on water. Unfortunately, he can back up all the trash talk."

To keep my hands from shaking, I started using my middle finger to pick the outside of my thumb. I had little nervous habits like this, partially because it stopped my mind from going to the dark side.

"Enough on me, how about you: where did you end up after leaving the tundra?" Jackson noted that I was uncomfortable with this topic.

Focusing my eyes on Jackson: "I went to Colorado State for my undergrad and masters. I stayed in the area since, and I liked it there well enough." I chuckled softly: "Not cold enough for me."

Jackson's face was unreadable as those dark eyes searched my face. I felt my face flush, and I looked away into the endless sky. My insecurities surfaced: My hair was a crazy mess, I had no makeup, and I had a random selection of clothes from my duffel bag. Biting my lip, I had to remind myself that it didn't matter.

"Well, you most definitely would not like California." He teased me as I looked back at him. "There would not be many places you would like."

I rolled my eyes. "Not true. I liked Colorado well enough and would be okay in Washington or Oregon."

"Only three states. Your options are minimal."

I sighed, "Well, it doesn't matter. I am going to be in Bemidji for a while."

"Don't sound so excited." He said sarcastically.

"I am excited, just not fully prepared to be back around my whole family. My parents are the only ones who know I am coming back. My siblings would throw a hissy fit if they found out I was back." I took a deep breath. "I have Skyla, but her hours are crazy, so it will just be me and a glass of wine more nights than most."

Jackson nudged my shoulder, "Well, lucky for you, I am way more entertaining than a glass of wine."

I raised my eyebrow, "Oh, is that so?"

He flashed a wicked grin. "You'll just have to wait and see."

I smiled, "True, we will just have to wait and see."

We were close enough that I could smell his spearmint breath. My eyes fell to his lips and quickly bounced back to his eyes. It was hard to believe he was my brother's best friend; he seemed genuine. However, what do I know? I just met Jackson; he could be as cocky and stuck up as Calvin.

The silence between us was not awkward. There was more to Jackson than just a doctor who grew up in the ghetto of California. There seemed to be more secrets, but once again, everyone has secrets, including me.

Chapter Two

The Reveal

Maggie

In my free time, I have grown to love watching murder documentaries and police shows. These shows kept my mind from drifting off. The downfall of my love of these shows was that I grew paranoid, always aware of my surroundings. I could never fall asleep in cars or on airplanes, deathly afraid this would be the time I got kidnapped or stabbed to death.

It was a crazy fear to have, and maybe it would be better to avoid these shows, but it made me feel at ease to be aware. The good thing was that Skyla was as aware of her surroundings as I was. Now, her reasons were a lot different, but it still was another thing we had in common that seemed to make us both insane.

We were descending the plane when I discovered I had fallen asleep. I was curled against the wall with one of those thin airplane blankets. Glancing at Jackson, who had his head back and eyes closed, I curled my toes and stretched my arms.

"Hey, sleepy head." Jackson looked over at me and smiled. "You have hair sticking up." He reached over and brushed my hair down.

I was more focused on his natural movement of brushing my hair down. His fingertips were smooth and cold, which shivered my spine. Although this whole thing only lasted five seconds, the sensation froze my mind.

"You should see me after several hours of sleep on a bed." I joked and then regretted it as soon as I said it.

Jackson laughed, "I can only imagine." I looked out the window and was greeted with the vast blue lake of Bemidji. It brought back a hint of excitement that was only taken away by the sudden movement of the plane. "Hey," Jackson's hand grasped mine. "Are you okay?"

My eyes landed on our hands. "Yeah, I never liked the landing part." I gave a nervous laugh.

He gave my hand a tight squeeze, "Close your eyes,"

"What? No!" I took my hand back. "That makes it ten times worse."

Jackson smirked, "What's going to make it better?"

I sighed and kept my eyes focused on the airport coming into view. So many small memories flooded my mind: when I would go with my mom to pick up my dad from the airport, when Calvin went away for a whole summer, and I got to go with Mom and pick him up. Believe it or not, I missed his cocky self. The tiny airport had countless other memories, which made my heart sink.

I would be landing with someone to run to. No one would be waiting for me. No one was going to surprise me. No one. Skyla worked, and my mom was with my dad. This was normal in my life, but somehow I still hoped someone would show up.

Jackson

Maggie's whole-body language had changed since I grasped her hand, which was a bold move. In my defense, her hands were shaking with fear or nervousness, and to help my case, they stopped shaking the minute I touched her.

Her mind seemed to be in a whole different world. Her eyes filled with a layer of sadness. There was so much more to her, so many layers and stories, good and bad. Usually, my self-centered self wouldn't give two shits about someone, let alone a girl, but something about her was different.

It was all in the little details: the way she went along with the teasing, the smile, her eyes, the smell of vanilla, the way she picked her thumb out of nervousness, and her heavy attempt to keep herself together. Her hair seemed to glow in the sunlight, peeking through the window, and her skin looked soft and smooth. She seemed so strong, but the longer I looked at her, the little by little she revealed, and I could see where there were cracks.

Besides being outed by her family, something else seemed to have formed these cracks. She seemed to bring color to the world even with this slight imperfection. It was hard to explain, but she made everything feel at ease.

As we pulled into our gate, I feared I would never see her again. This thought sent panic and unease throughout my body. There was so much more to her, and I wanted to know. I wanted to know the details, I wanted to know the backstory, and I wanted to keep feeling the ease she brought. I knew that in return for learning all about her, I would have to reveal all about me, which was a scary thought.

She looked over at me and smiled, fuck me. Despite wearing so much clothing, I could only imagine what was beneath. Maggie seemed all too perfect at this point, everything from the way she smiled to the way she smelled to the way she made me feel; I was screwed.

Once we landed, I waited for everyone to go in front of us before I got up. Maggie grabbed her duffel bag and swung it over her shoulder. I kept my head down as I got to the first class and grabbed my bag. Maggie raised her eyebrow at me as I gave her an embarrassed smile. The dark-haired flight attendant gave me a friendly smile as I stepped out. Maggie kept her head down and avoided any eye contact.

As we walked side by side through the airport, neither seemed to have checked bags. It was drastically smaller than Minneapolis, not to mention LAX. There was hardly anyone bustling around, just a few men in business suits. Once again, it differed from where we had just come from.

I counted the seconds until she vanished, and I would never see her again. I tried to think of ways to ask for her number without sounding desperate or disgusting. She paused when we reached the front door and set down her duffel bag. She ruffled through the top layer of clothes and grabbed the keys.

Maggie looked up at me: "Well, this is where we part." She said with uncertainty in her voice. "Thank you for not making that plane ride suck."

She swung her duffel bag back on her shoulder. "You know," I started nervously, "if you ever want to take me up on being more fun than a glass of wine, let me know." I joked, sounding more like a cocky dick.

Maggie smirked, "Well, you're the stranger in town; you're the one who's going to need company." She reached into her pocket, pulled out her phone, and handed it to me. "Here is your way out to give me a fake number and never see me again."

Even though it was a joke, it still stung. Is that what she thought of me? It was something Calvin would pull, and she seemed to know him.

She must have sensed my dislike. "This is also when you put your number in and ask me out."

I cracked a smile at her. "Now I like that a lot better." I typed in my actual number. "Now, I promise I didn't give you a fake number. I will even let you try it out."

Maggie shrugged, "I'll take my chances and trust you. Plus, I know where you work, and I could just show up there and make a scene." She joked and held out her hand. "I probably should go, but hopefully, I will see you around?"

Her hand was so soft and warm. "The ball is in your court," she said, let go, and turned around. "Wait!" I said too quickly, and she looked back at me. "I never got your full name."

Her expression was unreadable, and she seemed to be debating inside her head. She closed her eyes, sighed, and held her hand again.

"Maggie, Maggie Kensinger."

Her hand dropped quickly, and she walked out without even looking back. I stood there, shocked. Unable to move or even comprehend what she just said. I just watched as she didn't turn back and walked out into the sun.

It took me a solid minute to finally make myself walk out those same doors Maggie had. The sun was glaring, making my eyes sting. As she had done in the airplane, I kept my head down and headed towards the back of the parking lot to my Nissan Rogue. I threw my bag into the passenger seat and turned my car on. I sat there, waiting for my car to cool down. My head was still trying to catch up on what information had been revealed to me.

I sat there long enough to where I was debating whether she had said Kensinger. As far as I knew, Chief Kensinger was the only sibling of Dr. Mitch Kensinger, who was Calvin's father. The chief did not have kids, nor was he ever married. Calvin just had a sister named Anika, so where in the fuck did Maggie fit into all of this?

While my head was swimming, I managed to pull out of the airport parking lot, pay for my parking, and find my way to the main road. There was no way Calvin would lie about having another sister, would he? Even with all this debating going on in my head, I managed to get to my hotel. I opened the door to my room and was greeted by the mess I left behind.

The curtains were drawn shut, the light barely peeking through. Everything I owned was around this room. The hospital gave me six months to find a place; in the meantime, they were paying for me to live in this hotel room.

Throwing my bag down, I fell back onto the unmade bed. Maggie's last name wasn't the only thing my mind was focused on. I was still trying to piece together how she made me feel. It was as if I were back on a drug bender, but in a good way. I craved her. I seemed not to have anything else on my mind but those stunning eyes.

The way Maggie had made me feel made me uneasy because this was not normal. I had kept my distance from people, especially women, not for the fear of being hurt but for the fear of breaking them.

Maggie

Jackson's reaction to my name was unreadable, but I was not about to stand around and debate this. I could not tell if he had put all the pieces together. Suppose if I had to guess, probably not. I did not exist to my siblings, father, or even my uncle, for that matter.

It still stung that Calvin didn't even have the decency to mention me, as we were the closest in age. He was only three and a half years older, and Anika was four years younger than I was.

When I was growing up, Calvin and I were close, but I was dead to him when I decided to shame the family. I was more than dead. I never existed.

My mother tried talking to them, pleading with my father that teaching was just as good as being a doctor. There was no convincing my father when his mind had been made up. It killed my mother that he hated me. She honestly didn't care what he thought; she still would see and support me. I know I was a huge tension point in these last years of their marriage, which added to making me feel like shit when they announced they were splitting up.

Driving from the airport to my townhouse took me about ten minutes. We lived in an area mainly consisting of newly built homes and freshly laid yards. Our house looked sterile as if no one had lived in it. Skyla had been so busy at work, and I had been spending the last weeks finishing up in the Denver area, that our house was lifeless.

As I entered through the garage, I was greeted with the fuck load of broken-down boxes. Skyla had been living on fast or hospital food, as the kitchen looked untouched. Everything inside matched what the outside looked like: unlived-in and sterile. The whole house had gray tones, and even our furniture matched.

The walls were lined with photos of Skyla and me on our different adventures. Our diplomas were proudly displayed on built-in shelves next to the fireplace, along with framed pictures of our graduations. On the other side of the fireplace, the shelves held all the books we had bought, read, reread, and just couldn't part with, always thinking we might want to revisit them one day.

After passing the front door, I went up the grand stairs (which were vast for no reason). A bathroom was at the top of the landing, and bedrooms were to the right and left. To the right was my bedroom: my bed was made, the TV was set up, clothes were put away, and my desk was neatly in the corner.

I tossed my bag on my bed and checked across the hall at Skyla's room, which, to my surprise, looked like it was lived in. The bathroom between our rooms was also set up; it looked like life existed there. I went back to my room and plopped down on my bed. I was tired and drained, even though I had slept a decent chunk of that flight.

There was no way I was going to call Jackson, ever. One of the main reasons was that he was my brother's best friend, but two, he didn't need to get caught in my tornado of depression. Skyla and my mother were already sucked into it, and it was excruciating for me to know they had to go through what I was going through, feeling just as helpless.

My first year of college was one of the most brutal years of my life. After I had announced my decision for a new major and was banned from the family, it set me on a path. If I had to guess, I probably have had depression since I was in middle school, but it was not diagnosed until college. In the last nine years, I have attempted to take my life twice, both very early on back in college. Instead of taking my life in the later years, I cope by slicing my arms with a razor. Not the way to handle it, but with my stubbornness, I refused to see a therapist.

So here I was, twenty-eight years of age, crippled with depression. This was one of the main reasons I kept my distance from people, especially guys. There was no need to get tangled in my messy web. No one deserved that. I hated that my mother and Skyla were in it, but they always reminded me that they would rather be in the mess than be visiting my gravesite.

I pulled up my shirt sleeve, and sure enough, my scars were there. I hadn't cut in about a year or so, not since everything went down with my father back here. I told myself this was when I needed to be strong enough to come back here and face them all.

Little did I know it would take more than strength from me to face everything here.

Chapter Three

The Return

Jackson

Towards the end of medical school and into residency, things started to get rough for me. I was barely scraping by in school, and Calvin and I were partying way too much with the bit of free time we had. However, what Calvin did not know was my slight addiction on the side.

For three years, I was addicted to pain pills, and it didn't matter what they were. If they made me feel good, it was what mattered to me. I would pop them like they were candy, but a lot of the time, to make it enjoyable, I crushed them up and snorted them. Since pain pills were so readily available in my hand, it wasn't hard to get them, and sometimes I would just steal them. No one would question a doctor with a prescription bottle of pills.

What got me to stop was my heart attack and my six-month stint in rehab back home. Lucky for me, I was back for one of my sister's weddings when I went into cardiac arrest. I was down for ten minutes, and when I finally became lucid enough, I was surrounded by my mom, sisters, and a doctor. The pills were found in my car, jacket, and suitcase. My bloodstream also indicated the amount I had in my system and the reason for my sudden cardiac arrest. My choice was simple: rehab or jail. I chose rehab and found myself sentenced to having to do weekly blood tests and meetings. The time I was gone, my mom told Calvin I had been down with Mono. To this day, I don't think he bought it, but either way, when I returned, he didn't ask me. He didn't even question my blood draws or my meetings every Wednesday night.

My mom and sisters are the only ones who really know what happened. I've been clean for over four years now. That whole thing where people say it gets easier? Well, it doesn't. What was hardest for me was the emptiness I always felt. I managed the emptiness by working all the time and having as little free time as possible. I did my best to avoid the pills, and at work, the urge was easier to ignore.

However, my thoughts were on Maggie. Somehow, my addiction vanished when I looked at her. When she spoke, the urge was gone; when she smiled or laughed, the urge disappeared. Her touch and voice seemed to heal my wounds. Maggie wasn't just some girl I had met on the plane. She seemed to hold power, someone who could heal with one look.

Shaking my head, I pounded my fist into the shower wall and groaned. Hot water was trickling down my back like multiple waterfalls. Showering was not helping my thoughts. What the fuck was wrong with me? I turned it off and let the cold air in the room pierce my skin. She was just a girl I would likely never hear from again. Some part of me still believed it all to be a dream, and there was a deep part of me that would wake up and be landing in Bemidji alone in my first-class seat. But it wasn't; she was real, and what I felt was accurate, which scared me more than relapsing. Because that meant someone could get close, someone could get sucked into my sticky web of suffering.

Kensinger Hospital was right on the lake, towards the north shore near the campus. It shone brightly on the miniature city skyline like a beacon of light. The hospital was ten times bigger than the local hospital and had better ratings and scores. Our death rate was one of the lowest in the Midwest region, and we were known for our trauma. All traumas north of Minneapolis were usually brought to us.

Calvin had insisted that I join him for dinner at his mother's house, and I was not about to pass up on a homemade meal. So, instead of taking time off to rest, I dressed in jeans and a polo shirt. I met Julia Kensinger a handful of times. Her presence made you sit up and get a little straighter. She was highly respected in her field and received numerous awards and recognition. She was the darling of the pediatric field. She was very intimidating, just like her husband.

As I got into my car, I rolled my windows down and headed to the west side of town. The sun was already set, and people were all out and about, tourists and regulars alike. The temperature had dropped a bit, and it still felt nice. The air was fresh and didn't smell like rotten fish or oil; it just felt clean. I was so used to everything being on top of each other, not trusting, and mostly not friendly. The famous saying of Minnesota is friendly; it is true.

The Kensingers lived on a vast plot of land on the outskirts of town. It was three or four miles out of town, but they were right on the border of state park land. It was easy to drive in Bemidji. I could drive around the whole lake and the town in thirty minutes or so.

I pulled into the gated property, the childhood home of Calvin and Anika Kensinger, hidden within the woods. The house stood tall and was all lit. It was so drastically different from what I grew up with. My childhood home could fit in this house at least ten times, just from looking at the outside. The house had a second story, a wraparound porch, and a porch swing. There were two giant sheds to the right of the house, not to mention the six-stall garage connected to the house.

Pulling closer to one of the garages, I parked behind Calvin's black Range Rover. I grabbed my wallet, stuffed it into my jeans, and headed towards the front. Calvin must've seen my headlights because he stood there, leaning against the side of the door in jeans and a button-up. His hair was perfectly tousled, which probably took him at least ten minutes to achieve.

Calvin looked nothing like Maggie or Anika. He had dark hair and hazel eyes, was a good few inches taller than I, and was more built than I. Calvin also screamed, confident asshole, the way he walked, talked, and even in the way he looked at others. There was not a single thing about him that reminded me of Maggie, which I still found hard to believe she belonged here.

"Hey, dickwad." He fired at me as I made my way up the stairs. "Took you long enough. Mom is ready to serve dinner."

It was intimidating to Calvin's friend, and honestly, I seemed to be the only friend he had. I don't think many could put up with his ego. Many days, I was not in the mood to deal with it either, but I was all he had. Also, he is all I have, so I guess there is a trade-off. A lot of the time, I would go with the flow with whatever he wanted to do. I know it made me look like a pathetic bitch boy, I was very aware of that, but I had given up on caring what people thought long ago.

I was a quiet and reserved kid throughout elementary and middle school. I stayed out of trouble, did my homework, avoided gangs and drugs, and was always home. By the time high school rolled around, my growth spurt hit, and I had developed a decent skill at playing basketball. I was no longer the quiet, nerdy boy; I had found my way to the top. Even while at the top, I still did my homework, avoided gangs and drugs, and was always home at my curfew.

My sisters, on the other hand, were wild, running around late into the night with various criminals and getting high themselves. I was the total opposite of them. Once they both graduated, barely, they did one semester at a community college, and they found their husbands. My two brothers-in-law made good money and came from wealth. Each of my sisters had some luck when choosing to go out to the bars, and some luck when my brothers-in-law had for scoring a trophy wife.

I was greeted with a fresh breeze inside the house. Everything was clean, warm, and rustic. I followed Calvin down a hall and into the formal dining room table. Windows lined the room, exposing the porch and the woods around it. A table long enough to seat fourteen was set for three and full of dishes. Candles were lit at the center of the table, and the lights above were dimmed, bringing a more comforting mood.

"Jackson," a woman's voice sang from behind me, "it has been so long. How have you been, honey?"

Dr. Julia Kensinger had a very smooth and sweet voice. She was taller than all my sisters and mother, and slender. She embraced me quickly, and she smelled of lavender. When I finally looked at her face, I saw how Maggie fit in this picture. Ms. Kensinger had those stunning blue eyes; her hair had more white streaks, but you could see hints of that golden color. When she smiled, it was like staring right at Maggie. There was no denying that Julia Kensinger was Maggie's mother.

"I'm good, Ms. Kensinger." I returned her warm smile. "How has retirement been treating you?"

She gestured for me to sit. "Whiskey man?" She asked as she poured herself a cabernet, and I nodded. "Get your friend a drink," her eyes narrowed towards Calvin, "retirement is boring. Never thought I would say I missed the hospital, but I do miss being on call and the high you get from being in that OR. Now," she settled in the seat across from me, "I don't miss the heartbreak or devastation of losing a child, that I am relieved not to have to endure that."

I smiled at her as Calvin handed me a glass of whiskey. "Do you have any trips planned? Maybe to go out and see Anika?"

Ms. Kensinger sipped her wine, "Maybe around the holidays, but I should stay put for a while." Her eyes shifted to Calvin. "How's your lovely uncle?"

Calvin settled in beside me, "Jackass as always."

Her eyes narrowed, "Let me guess, he's getting on you and not spoon-feeding to your every need?"

His cheeks flushed, "He needs to retire or, better yet, find something outside of the hospital."

Ms. Kensinger rolled her eyes and gestured to the food before us: "Jackson, I hope you like lasagna. It's a family recipe. Speaking of family, have you gone to see your dad lately?"

He glared at his mother from across the table. "Not since last week."

"Well, lucky for you, you won't have to worry about seeing him every week. Your sister moved back here to help with that."

Calvin froze and wore a look of confusion: "Anika?"

Ms. Kensinger frowned. "Try again."

"That's the only sister I have."

Ms. Kensinger glared at him, "Maggie moved back here per your father's request."

"Why would Dad want that cunt back?"

"Calvin Roger Kensinger," she raised her voice.

He gritted his teeth and shot me a look, "I have a pathetic younger sister."

Ms. Kensinger stood up. "Calvin has a younger sister, Maggie, who chose to be a teacher instead of a doctor, and there is nothing wrong with that."

"She took an easy way out. She embarrassed our entire family. All she is… is a teacher. A fucking kindergarten teacher. All they do is crafts and shit, how can that be fulfilling? How can that be challenging? She took the easiest job because she's lazy." He fired back in frustration.

Ms. Kensinger smiled wickedly, "As I recall, she's the only one who graduated high school and college with honors."

Calvin stood up, and I felt uneasy. "I am going to head to the bathroom," I barely was able to get out. "Down the hall?"

Both Calvin and his mother said, "Yes."

Sliding out of my seat, I exited the dining room and headed down the hall. I didn't have to go to the bathroom, but I didn't want to sit and watch the brawl between my best friend and his mother. Instead, I found myself in the back den at the end of the hall. There was one large window, but almost all the walls were covered with built-ins. There was a long couch, a coffee table, and a long desk in front of the grand window.

Looking around, I was amazed at all the books, including the sliding ladder that helped the reader reach the top shelves. This house was like a fairy tale, something you would see in those movies or read in books as a kid. My eyes finally settled on a display with many awards for Ms. Kensinger, but to my right was a massive display of the sister in conversation: Maggie.

There were multiple pictures of her: graduations, sports, summer vacations, and pictures with her siblings. Those eyes still shine in each photo, and her hair remained gold. Her smile was stunning despite her braces and awkward middle school stages. She and Calvin looked so happy together while they held Anika as a baby. I was still in shock at the cruelty that my best friend felt towards his sister.

"She's easily my smartest child." I whirled around to be greeted by Ms. Kensinger. "Maggie had the best grades, was hard-working, and creative." She smiled, and her eyes lingered on the pictures. "She is so unlike my other children, humble and kind. I'm not saying that Calvin and Anika aren't humble, but Maggie was the only one who was content with the little things. She loved her books, whereas Calvin always wanted expensive video games, and Anika wanted expensive clothes. Not Maggie, she was just happy with her books and cards."

My eyes caught the picture on the coffee table. Calvin was lying on the carpet while Maggie played doctor. They were so young. "Why does he hate her?"

"I wish I had a nicer answer," she sighed and settled on the couch. "He hates that she wasted her potential. He's jealous that she always seemed to outdo him in grades, sports, and the likability of others. He resents her for doing something different."

"Sounds like Calvin, but why does Anika hate her?"

Ms. Kensinger shrugged, "Got to follow in the footsteps of her brother and father."

"Better footsteps to follow than a teacher." Calvin spat from behind us. "Who turns down a chance to have her medical school paid for? Who wastes their life to be around six-year-olds all day long?"

Ms. Kensinger stood up, "Your teachers. Your college professors. Every person who helped you get to where you are now." She said coolly. "If it hadn't been for them, you wouldn't have even made it out of high school. Who was the one who got you out of your-"

"Stop now, Mom." He growled, clutching his fist at his side.

She grinned wickedly. "That's right, your kindergarten teacher, who cared enough to stay in contact with you."

Calvin slammed his fist down, "Would you just stop defending her? We all know she's mentally fucked up, not just for choosing a teaching career but for trying to"

"ENOUGH!" Ms. Kensinger yelled and then turned to me. "I'm sorry, Jackson. I can box some lasagna for you to take home, but I think this dinner is over."

"You are the one who brought her up." Calvin fired back. "You know what I have to say about her. You know that none of us wants anything to do with her. She's not my sister, not anymore. You know how we all feel, so don't put this on me ruining dinner."

Ms. Kensinger ignored Calvin. "Would you like any pie? I have strawberry rhubarb or apple, you can take as well."

Before I could answer, "Stop ignoring me." Calvin yelled. "No wonder why you drove Dad crazy, you are cold and bitchy."

Pain flickered in her eyes, "Out, out of my house." She growled.

"Your house?" Calvin laughed. "Please, you wouldn't have had half of these things if it hadn't been for Dad."

Ms. Kensinger shot up and got into Calvin's face. "You have no idea how hard I had to work. You have no idea what it is like to sleep in your car and dig through the dumps for food. All you have ever had is all the food in the world, a warm bed, and a large room." She was yelling at him, furious. "I worked to get my medical degree, and I worked my ass off to get the doctor in front of my name. I graduated from college and med school and had my pick of the litter regarding fellowships. So don't you EVER say I didn't earn what I have." She turned and looked at me, "I am sorry, but Jackson, I think it is best that you just leave."

Calvin's face was flushed and embarrassed. "Why would Dad change his mind to have her here?"

She had a somber look in her eyes. "You know why," she looked over to me. "I am sorry, Jackson. We will have to do it another time." She flashed a fragile, encouraging smile.

"Thank you for the dinner, Ms. Kensinger." I hugged her before excusing myself from the house.

Once I got in my car, I let out the air I didn't know I was holding in. Maggie Kensinger was real. My heart was racing. She was not just some stranger who lied about herself; she was real. I hadn't realized I had all these doubts about her until I saw all those pictures and heard her being discussed. She wasn't just a random girl or some dream; she was real.

I couldn't stop thinking about it as I pulled out of the long driveway and made my way back into town. She was real. She was somewhere here, in this town. I drove past downtown, and people were all still out and about, walking and admiring the lake. She was real, and she was here. I stopped at McDonald's across from my hotel and got something to eat.

Even when I headed back into the hotel, I desperately hoped to see her face—the chance to see her walk out of the bar and restaurant. I was drawn to her, but did she feel the same?

Chapter Four

Suicidal Fate

Maggie

Sleep was hilarious to me. It is essential to life, but it can also be deadly. Most of the time, people dream while they sleep. We hardly remember most of our dreams, but for some reason, nightmares seem to be what we remember. That still never stopped me from sleeping. Any chance I had, I was willing to take the gamble of waking from a nightmare. Sometimes, the nightmare was better than my reality.

I woke up to Skyla sliding into bed next to me. She looked horrible. She simply laid her head on my shoulder and sighed. She didn't speak or even crack a sarcastic comment. This meant she lost a patient today. Her hands were shaking, which meant she had lost a patient to suicide. I reached out and grabbed her hands. She looked at me in the dark; she had been crying the whole way home. I gave her a sad smile and laid my head on top of hers as she closed her eyes.

"How old?" I whispered.

"Ten."

"What happened?"

Skyla closed her eyes. "She hung herself." She whispered painfully. "Her family didn't believe she was depressed, and sure enough, she hung herself."

I sat up and looked down at her. Not only did Skyla have to live with the fact that her best friend was crazy and suicidal, but her high school and college boyfriend killed himself three weeks before graduation. I knew it still haunted her. Bentley struggled with the transition from high school to college. He struggled to make friends or make a life for himself in college. Skyla knew he needed help, but he reassured her he would be okay.

One Friday night, he had too much to drink and hanged himself. The only thing on his suicide note was: 'I am sorry, Skyla.' She went dark, ignoring everyone, not going to class, drinking herself to sleep, getting high on Molly, and refusing any help. She found herself locked away in her bathroom, ready to attempt to do it herself. All it took was one phone call; I will never forget it.

"Skyla."

Silence.

"Alright, what do we need to do? Scream and cry to each other. Do you need me to bring up happy memories to make you laugh? Or do we just need to sit in silence?"

Silence.

"Okay. Well, let's just lie here and breathe."

Forty-five minutes later, I listened to her breathe heavily and fight back sobs. "He's gone, Maggie. He is gone."

I frowned. "I know."

"I told him to get help. I told him there were options for him. I told him I would do anything to help him. All he said was I am going to be okay." She gritted her teeth. "I believed him. I truly believed we would have a life past this dark period. I believed he was going to fight hard to get himself out. I believed he was okay. I believed-"

Skyla sobbed and cried out. I immediately whipped my door open and found myself racing across the apartment; her door was locked like always. Calling her on the phone reassured me that she was still alive. With her door shut, I groaned, shoving up on the door, fucking with the knob. She was now screaming with pain behind the door. I rammed my body against the door, and it broke down. There was Skyla in the corner, sobbing with a bottle of tequila and aspirin.

I carefully walked over to her, kicked the bottle of aspirin to the corner, and kneeled in front of her. Skyla had horrible dark circles under her eyes, and they were swollen. She was still in the same sweats and t-shirt from the day she got the call. She hadn't showered in weeks, her hair had dry vomit stuck in it, and she smelled.

I brushed her hair off her face as she continued to sob. I used the back of my sweater to wipe her tears. Skyla was shaking violently, now more embarrassed about the state she was in. I slowly grabbed the tequila bottle and threw it onto her bed. Skyla sobbed louder and harder now. I pulled her into my arms and held her tightly. She tried getting out of my grasp, but I didn't break. She cried out to let go, but I ignored it and felt myself beginning to cry. I bit my lip down and ensured I wasn't loosening my grasp.

"Maggie, let me go!" She sobbed and screamed.

"No!" I managed to say. "No. We are going to sit here in silence, and I am going to hold you. Then we are going to shower. Then I am ordering food from the Italian restaurant you like, and you will eat."

Skyla's head pressed into my shoulder, and I could feel my heart breaking at the pain my best friend was feeling. Skyla's body started to relax as her breathing became slow, and her sobs subsided. I looked down and saw that she had fallen asleep in my arms. Her breathing deepened, and for the first time in a while, I smiled. She was okay.

I sat there, holding Skyla for three hours. When she woke up, she started to cry again, but this time, it was quieter. I gave her one last tight squeeze before helping her up. We both made our way to the bathroom. I started the shower and helped Skyla peel off the clothes that had been on her body for 18 days straight. She hopped into the shower, and I set out a towel, sat at the far edge of the tub, and held her hand as she let the water run down her. After a while, she finally let go of my hand to wash her hair and body. When she finished, she crumpled to the shower floor and pulled her knees to her chest.

"He's gone, Maggie." She said out loud. "He's gone." Skyla turned to face me as I nodded silently. She closed her eyes and leaned her head back on the shower wall. "It's not going to be easy, is it?" I gave her a shake of the head. "He's gone." She whispered once more.

Ever since Bentley's death, suicide has been a touchy thing for her. This was the first time in a long time that she had come across a case like this. I looked over at Skyla now: she was in sweats and a baggy t-shirt, her hair was in a crazy bun, and she smelled of the hospital. She was staring off into space. Everything about her was on autopilot while she found herself deep in thought.

"I think he would be proud," I said, sitting up. "I mean, you're a fucking surgeon. You were able to do so much, and Bentley would be proud. He supported you with whatever you wanted to do, including when you wanted to pole dance for a living."

Skyla glared at me. "That was a joke," she said coolly. "I just wish he were here. "She sighed, laying her head back down. "He would be happy that I came back here, though. He loved this place and his life here."

I smiled, "I know he did. We all did at one point."

"Things will get better with your dad. Your brother will always be dickface. At least you have me." She nudged my shoulder. "The best gift you could ask for."

"The greatest," I said sarcastically.

She rolled her eyes, "Bitch."

We laughed, "Well, I've got some news for you."

She furrowed her brow: "Bad news or good news?"

I flashed her a wicked smile, "Boy news."

Skyla shot up, "This calls for a bottle of wine."

In the blink of an eye, Skyla vanished and returned with a chilled bottle of white wine. She sat cross-legged on one end of my bed as she took a swig from the bottle. I smiled at her as she passed the bottle, and I took a swig from it.

For the next ten minutes, I explained my encounter with Jackson. It was hard to read her facial expression. I could not tell if she was pissed, excited, or annoyed. She did not interrupt me and let me blab on.

"The last thing I said was my full name." I took a swing from the bottle and handed it back. "I could not tell what he was thinking. I left before anything else could be said."

She seemed to be pondering her choice of words carefully. "Jackson Calsen is Calvin's bitch. And Calvin pretends like you don't exist." She was thinking out loud at this point. "How do you know if he believed you?"

"I mean, all I said was that my last name was Kensinger. He could think I am like a cousin or some shit."

Skyla narrowed her eyes, "Maggie, everyone knows your family bloodline. They know your uncle never married or had kids. They also know that there are only three Kensinger children. You're like the royal family of Bemidji."

"That's a little exaggerated." I took the bottle from her. "He could not think of anything at all. After all, I am just some girl he met on a plane."

She made a face of disgust. "Don't make it sound romantic, it sounds weird."

I rolled my eyes, "Either way, he probably doesn't give two shits anyway."

"I don't know," Skyla drank a long drink, "he's quiet for the most part. He is known for being Calvin's best friend. He keeps to himself and even eats by himself in the cafeteria."

"You eat by yourself." I pointed out, making her frown.

"That's different because everyone knows not to fuck with me." I smiled and shook my head. "Now, I am not going to lie, Jackson Calsen is fucking hot."

"You also find John Wick hot."

Once again, she glared at me: "You're just strange for not finding John Wick hot." I held my hands up as if I had been caught red-handed. "You know I am right; Jackson is way better-looking than your brother."

"You're also saying that because you hate my brother more than anyone."

"Fair point, but so do a lot of people." She smiled at me before drinking another drink. "In the end, I think it's best to say fuck it and leave it alone. If he is truly interested, he will take the time to seek you out and find you."

"Don't make it sound creepy like that."

Skyla shrugged, "What can I say: men are all creepy."

I rolled my eyes and smiled at my best friend. She was right in that department.

Chapter Five

The Bar

Maggie

Surprisingly, I completed a lot over the next three days. I met with my new boss, was given a tour, and was shown my new classroom. I spent a full 24 hours setting up and decorating my room. Then, with the help of Skyla, who had a day off, I finished unpacking and got everything in order around the house. Now, all that was left to do was prepare for multiple meetings and the first day of school.

Ever since talking with Skyla about Jackson, I had done my best to keep him at the back of my mind. A few times, I considered making my way to the hospital to see him or even calling him up, but I knew Skyla was right. If there indeed was any interest, he'd find a way. Calvin wasn't exactly a smooth liar, especially now that Jackson knew I existed.

My mother has been busy these last few days. She had to fly down to see her sister in Arizona for their annual sisters' weekend. Of course, Calvin never returned my text. The only thing left for me to do was go and see my father, which I dreaded the most.

I went out to my car, a black Honda Accord, which I bought back in Colorado when my first car broke down. It had been a decent car with four wheels and took me from place to place. I was never one for high-end vehicles. My parents gifted me a brand new Nissan Altima for my sixteenth birthday, which broke down about seven years later, but I loved that car.

My siblings were still my siblings, and I loved them to pieces, but they weren't always such self-centered people. Calvin and I did a lot together when we were younger. He loved holding my hand and dancing with me in the living room. We both played doctor on each other and even played school, and then Anika came.

My guess for this sudden change was dominance in the house of women, or that attention was not on him anymore. Many people love attention, and when they start not to get it, they do one of two things: seek it out elsewhere or act out. Calvin chose the latter.

The drive was close, maybe five minutes. The sun was covered by clouds today, which made it seem cooler than it was. I drove by downtown; of course, it was packed with people wanting to see the statues of Paul and Babe. As a kid, Calvin and I always begged our parents to go down there. My mother had a whole photo album designated for Paul and Babe's pictures. Once Anika was born, Calvin vanished, and it was just Anika and me in the last part of the photos in that album.

Pulling into the parking lot, I sat and stared at the front gates of the hell I was waiting to endure. I bit my lips and closed my eyes. *Cedar Hill Assisted Living Facility.* Squeezing my eyes shut, preventing tears from falling out, I took a deep breath. I smoothed out my cotton shirt and rubbed my hands back and forth on my thighs. My jeans were beginning to feel tight, and everything around me seemed to slow down for a minute—the words: assisted living burned holes in my body.

I exited my car and reminded myself he needed this more than I did. My father needed me to be the bigger person.

My father met my mother when they were at Dartmouth together. They were only a grade apart from each other. It was like love at first sight or some bullshit like that. They married not long after my mom was in medical school together. It wasn't until my father worked for the NFL and my mother, near the end of her fellowship at Kensinger Memorial, that they got pregnant with Calvin.

They had three children and thirty-nine years of marriage, and about a year ago, it all came crashing down. My father started to become forgetful, which turned into anger, and then he went missing for four days because he decided to wander. After he returned from his adventure, he drove to be seen at the Mayo Clinic. Coming back, he told my mother to divorce him after the doctors confirmed he had dementia.

It all seemed to happen so fast: the divorce, which my mother took hard, and then the rapid decline in my father's mental state. As children, no matter how fucked up your relationship might be, watching your father or mother diminish before your eyes is one of the cruelest experiences.

Calvin, Anika, my mother, and I were all sworn not to share his mental state. No one in the medical world or even in the town of Bemidji itself knew what happened to my father. The story was that he was traveling the world.

As I entered this hell, the lady at the front greeted me with the fakest smile. "How can I help you today?"

If people thought Skyla had a resting bitch face, they had never seen mine. "I am Mitch Kensinger's daughter. I am coming to see him." My voice was flat.

The lady gave me a sad smile. "Of course, he's in his room. Is it all right to visit there? It's hard to get him down here."

"Yes," I replied.

She smiled again, then asked to see my ID, making sure I was in the system to visit. The place smelled like a sterile hospital, a sharp scent that made my nostrils burn. I kept my head down, refusing to let my eyes wander. I didn't want to see others vanishing away day by day or watch loved ones crumple.

Sometimes, to make myself feel better, I convinced myself that the reason I didn't become a doctor was that I could not handle my emotions. That was far from the truth of my reason, but telling myself this comforted me. It made the real reason vanish and relieved the pain it brought.

In my freshman year of college, I told both of my parents that I had every intention of becoming a doctor. However, because I like to be a pain in the ass, I told them I wanted to go into psychiatry and specialize in forensics. Something completely different from my family. My dad was not a massive believer in the field, but he was happy I wanted to be a doctor. One of his closest colleagues was well-respected in the field and was willing to take me under his wing. Then, well, here I was, a teacher.

Don't get me wrong; I love my job. Over time, I found my true passion for teaching and realized that the medical field wasn't the right path for me. My job gave me a unique sense of purpose and helped me stand out from the rest of my family. I could do so much more and give it back to the world in a different way. Looking back, though, I wish my heart change could've been done differently.

Following this lady, I was taken to the second floor. This place was a beautiful building with excellent finishes. I wouldn't expect anything less from my father, who was always flashy. It's easy to be that way when you are born into it. His room was at the end of the hall, and the lady gently knocked on the door.

"Dr. Kensinger, you have a visitor."

Closing my eyes, I took a deep breath and entered the room. My father was sitting in a cushioned chair, looking straight out the window and onto the lake. I looked around his room. There was a picture of my mother and him from their 35th wedding anniversary, as well as many pictures of Calvin and Anika. Just as I was about to stop looking, I saw myself on the left side of the bed on that nightstand.

There was my high school graduation photo, college graduation photo, and master's graduation photo (all side by side in one of those three-frame things). Next to them, there was a bigger picture of my dad holding me when I was three, with me smiling up at him.

Tears rolled down my cheeks. It didn't mean he loved me like my siblings or forgave me. It just meant I still existed in his fading memory. Maybe.

My father had not even bothered to turn around to see who his visitor was. The lady had already closed the door to give us privacy. I set my purse down on the side table and braced myself for the reaction that could come.

"Dad?" I said dryly. "Dad, it's me, Maggie."

My father slowly turned his head to look at me. He had dark brown eyes, tan skin, and gray hair. He had lost so much weight that he may have weighed 120 pounds, and he was well over six feet tall. Those brown eyes looked lifeless, like nothing was there anymore.

I slowly walked over to the bench to his left. Those lifeless eyes followed me. I settled down, crossed my legs, and took another deep breath. "It's me, Maggie. I am your daughter."

He blinked twice before looking back out the window. "I thought I told my daughter I never wanted to see her anymore."

"Yes, but then you asked Mom for me to come."

He laughed, "Why would I want my daughter, who disappointed me, to come and see me?"

"Maybe because you missed her?"

My father cracked a smile. "I do miss her." He looked at me and said, "You look a lot like her."

Shaking my head, "I do?" My voice was shaky with his eyes on me.

My father looked back out the window. "Yeah, she looked just like my wife. She had my stubbornness, but she was also the smart one. I always thought she would be the one to run the hospital, " he said in a daze.

My heart was beating fast. "What happened to her?" I barely managed out.

"Aw," my father looked over to me. "My Maggie became a teacher." He laughed as if this were some joke. "I never could understand it." I looked away from him and down at my hands, which were trembling. "I think I used to be a doctor."

"You were sort of." I shrugged.

My father blinked, and there was a flicker of life suddenly. "Maggie?" he asked, then became confused. "Why the hell are you here?"

"Dad, you asked me to come. I work here in Bemidji now. You asked me to move home."

"Why the fuck would I want my laughingstock of a child back here?" He growled at me. "You make me sick looking at you, all that wasted potential." He looked up and down at me. "You were always so ungrateful and too good for this family. Now, look at you; you are just a pathetic teacher."

My eyes narrowed, "You know what, Dad? Fuck this. Fuck you." I snapped back at him. "Go to hell."

I started to stand up, and then my father's hand gently clasped my wrist. I looked back down at him. Life had vanished from his eyes, and now they were back to being lifeless. He now looked up at me like a lost child.

"What happened?" He whispered. "What is wrong with me? Who are you?"

It took almost everything I had left to say, "My name is Maggie, and you're sick, but you are safe."

His eyes were darting around, "But, but who am I?"

"Your name is Mitch." My voice was on the cusp of breaking. "Mitch Kensinger."

My father's eyes locked on mine. "Did I ever hurt anyone? Did I hurt you?" Before I could answer, he continued. "I never meant it; I never meant to. Please, please, Maggie, help me."

I kneeled beside him. "No, no, hey," my father began to cry. "You never hurt anyone, not even me." He looked at me, tears falling down his face. "You were a great doctor, husband, and fantastic father."

He shook his head, "That can't be true. I couldn't have been a good father. I haven't seen my daughter Maggie in years." He looked back out at the window. "She was a smart kid; she looks like you." My father looked over to me, "What do you think I did to scare my daughter away?"

Biting down on the inside of my cheek, "I don't know, but I am sure she will find her way to you." I squeezed his hand. "I bet you she still loves you."

My father was staring down at our hands. "I hope so because I never stopped loving her, even after what I did. I don't know what I did or said, but I know I love her."

Tears rolled down my face, "I bet you she knows you love her. Maybe one day, she will come and see you here."

Suddenly, he had the look of a happy kid, but still lifeless eyes. "I hope so; we could return to the lake and take walks." He started to talk fast. "I bet you my wife and other kids miss her like me. Maybe she can talk to me about her job when she comes, and maybe I will understand!" He looked at me and smiled a lifeless smile. "Do you truly think she still loves me?" I nodded my head. "I hope she comes." He whispered.

I stood up and closed my eyes, trying to shut away all the tears that wanted to come out. "I love you," I whispered so softly that I could barely hear it.

Looking back down at my father, he looked confused. "Who are you?" he demanded. "What are you doing here?"

Finally, I couldn't anymore. I grabbed my purse and rushed out the door. Jogging down the stairs, letting the tears roll down my face, telling the lady at the front to fuck off, and then slamming my fists into the steering wheel of my car.

"FUCK!" I screamed. "GOD DAMN IT." I started to sob hard. "Fuck," I barely got out as I sobbed into my steering wheel.

I couldn't do this. I can't do this. Why did I decide to put myself through this? When I was told about the diagnosis, I did my fair share of research. I even joined Facebook pages for support and to get an idea of what I would face. But none of that could prepare me for what I just endured.

Sobbing hard, I let myself cry and scream. My tears fell onto my jeans, mascara everywhere, and my nose began running. I set my head back and closed my eyes. I needed to do something. I couldn't just sit here and cry; no good would come of that. If anything, it was making me feel weak and pathetic.

Putting my car in drive, I found myself five minutes later in a dark pub downtown. It was a newer place, and only a few people were there in the late afternoon. The bartender was an older gentleman who looked like he would rather be doing anything than what he was doing. He greeted me with a forceful smile and asked me what I wanted to drink.

Knowing that I hadn't eaten all day, I should have one of the many greasy foods they seemed to provide. "Shot of tequila and keep them coming."

Without asking, sure enough, seven shots later, I flipped the glass over and focused on whatever sports news was on the TV. I was drunk, and it felt amazing. I felt like the outside world did not matter in this dark hole.

I didn't have to deal with the fact that my father still hated me when he was lucid. I didn't have to worry about my father going in and out of a lucid state. I didn't have to even think about how truly alone I was. For once, I could just sit here and let everything go. I could be free from all the burdens waiting for me beyond those doors.

I don't know how long I sat there, enjoying being alone and on a high. Then the door opened, and the bell chimed.

Chapter Six

As It Would Happen

Jackson

I had just gotten done working for twenty-four hours straight. I was starving and ready to go to bed. I had been in three surgeries and had numerous consultations. Calvin didn't talk much to me, which was fine because I didn't know what to say. How could someone hate someone so much? It just didn't make sense to me. My sisters had done some pretty messed-up stuff, but at the end of the day, they were my sisters, and I loved them.

Maggie had crossed my mind a few times. I found myself checking my phone more often than I usually did. Skyla ignored me like usual, which indicated that Maggie had not even brought me up in conversation with her best friend. I was beginning to think she had no interest, and she was just another girl I had met, and that she would fade away in my memories.

But a part of me didn't want her to fade away; she made everything seem different. I wanted to know more about her, the secrets and pain hidden behind those beautiful blue eyes.

Before heading back to my hotel room, I needed to eat. I was tired of having hospital food. Luckily, I found a house outside the city for a steal. I would not be moving in for a few more weeks. I wasn't keen on buying a home, but it was time for me to grow the fuck up. Plus, I would be out of the hotel for good.

Calvin told me about a bar or pub downtown that opened a few months ago. He said it had some of the best food in town. I decided to go and get some food to return to the room. I could also stop by the hotel's liquor store to snag a whiskey bottle. I didn't have to work for a few days, but then I worked six days in a row.

Getting out of my car, it was just a quarter past seven. The pub was decently full for Tuesday evening. As I entered, my eyes immediately fell on a woman sitting at the bar rail alone. She turned around, and my heart stopped for a minute. There she was, Maggie Kensinger. Her mascara was smeared in different spots on her face. Her cheeks were flushed, and she was bleeding from her thumb, which she was picking at.

She laughed and shook her head before turning away and gesturing for another shot. The bartender frowned and said, "I am sorry, but you're done."

Maggie narrowed her eyes, "Fuck you." She spat, reached down to her purse, and threw her card onto the rail.

"Maggie?" I asked as I settled into the bar stool beside her. "Hey, Maggie, look at me, what's wrong?"

She looked at me, "Why would you care?" Her words slurred together; she was drunk. "It's not like you're my boyfriend, so why bother asking?"

The bartender came back and looked at me. "Are you her ride home?"

Maggie was busy fumbling and putting her card away. "Um, yeah, I was also wondering if I could order food and two glasses of water?" He grunted in return and went to pour some water. Maggie took a deep breath and began to stand up. "Whoa," I said and helped her back into her seat. "Where are you going?"

She was now afraid to look me in the eyes, "Home."

I laughed, "You're not driving."

"Obviously not dipshit." She snarled. "I was going to call for a car or walk."

I shook my head, "Just let me give you a ride."

This caught her attention, and her eyes met mine. "Why? So, you can take advantage of me?"

"Is that what you think I am doing?" I was offended by this. "You think I am just trying to fuck you?"

She tilted her head. "I am surprised you remembered me." She laughed as she took the water from the bartender. "I am even more surprised you have cared enough to come talk to me."

"Why?"

Maggie looked at me and shook her head. "I am assuming by now you know who I am? Why would you want to be around your best friend's disappointing sister? I mean, I don't exist to him, so shouldn't that mean I don't exist to you?"

Wow, she really thought I was like Calvin, but who could blame her? He was my best friend, and anytime we would go out, he treated everyone else around him like dogshit. Calvin was an asshole, and he pretty much got what he wanted, but he was still my best friend, and he wasn't always such a dick.

"I like to form my own opinions of people," I said coolly and looked at the bartender. "Can I have two bacon cheeseburgers with a large side of fries? Please throw in some mozzarella sticks, too, please?"

Maggie rolled her eyes. "Expecting someone at home? Or are you secretly a fatass and going to eat all that to yourself?"

I smirked and took a drink from my water, "I was hoping you would share so my fatass doesn't eat it all."

She leaned back in her chair, "Is Jackson Calsen asking me on a date?"

"So, what if I am?"

Maggie closed her eyes and then smiled, "I suppose I would have to say yes." My heart began to beat faster. "Only because I wouldn't want you to become a fatass."

I shook my head and smiled at her, "Very funny."

She smiled, fuck was that a beautiful smile, "One of the many things I am good at."

"Oh really?" My eyes finally took the rest of her in. She was in tight skinny jeans and a tight-fitting top. Her hair was pulled into this half-assed bun. Her eyes seemed to be swollen, like she had been crying hard. She was still picking at her thumb, which I now assumed was a nervous or comforting habit.

"If I may request," she took a drink from her water, "can we stop at my place so I can at least change and wash my face?"

I smiled, "How about we just stay at your place?"

"You are a bold man, Calsen." She shook her head and smirked at me. "Hoping to score?"

"I think that would be a bonus, but not the main idea."

Maggie furrowed her brow, "So you're telling me I don't have to put out on a first date?"

"The ball is in your court, Kensinger."

She smirked, "We shall see."

The food smelled delicious. I could not even remember the last time I had a burger; maybe it was at med school. I was not a big cook, and after spending so much time in the hospital, I just settled for the crappy salad bar or chicken strips.

Maggie held the food in her lap as she directed me to where to go to get to her house. She looked comfortable in the front seat of my car and didn't comment on my music or the vehicle's temperature. She just stared out the window and gave me directions when needed.

The townhome we pulled into looked brand new. There were no cars in the driveway. It was a slate gray home with white finishings all around. The other townhomes looked as if no one lived there. In fact, most of them on the street looked sterile and unoccupied.

Maggie opened the garage door, and to my relief, no car was in there. I had forgotten about Skyla and had no idea how she would react to seeing me here. Maggie must've sensed my relief at Skyla being gone.

"She works the overnight shift, so you don't have to worry."

I smiled as she let me into the house. The inside matched the outside in color tones. The place had high ceilings and looked very clean. The kitchen was large and open to the living room: a fireplace and a beautiful mantle with a large TV mounted above it. A sliding door led to the back porch, which offered a glimpse of the lake through the bushes and tall grass.

Maggie set the food down on the island and carefully removed each container. I kept looking around. Some pictures of Skyla and her were on the coffee table, and some were on the walls. The fridge had pictures of Skyla and Maggie and a whiteboard calendar. Maggie was due to go back to work on Thursday.

"Are you nervous to go back?" I asked out loud as I settled into a barstool across from her. "I mean, are you nervous to be in a new school?"

She shrugged as she grabbed ketchup from the fridge and threw away the brown paper bag in which the food came. "I went to school in this building, so it isn't really all that new to me. But I am nervous about who my students are going to be." Maggie slid the plastic container of one burger to me and placed the fries in the middle. "Right now, they're just a list of names; by May, they are a list of lives."

"How many kids do you have in your class?" I took a bite from my burger; oh, good lord, it was good.

"I've got nineteen more boys than girls." She smiled and took a bite from her burger. "This shit is good."

I laughed, "I guess your brother wasn't kidding."

She rolled her eyes, "Calvin doesn't fuck around when it comes to food. Easily one of the pickiest eaters I have met."

When I mentioned Calvin, I was prepared to be shut out or given a look. I was not expecting her to keep the conversation flowing and chime in. We ate in silence for another minute. Maggie picked off the pickles and began eating them separately.

"That's disgusting," I said as she dipped her fries in the mayo.

She shot me a look, "Mind your business."

Maggie ate very delicately. She made sure she had nothing on her face and used six or seven napkins to keep her hands clean.

"May I ask why you were alone in a bar on a Tuesday evening?" I studied her body reaction; it tensed up. "You don't strike me as someone who hangs out at bars during the week."

She kept her eyes away and focused on the burger before her. "I just had to deal with some family shit, and I don't always have the best coping mechanisms."

"Better than me," I mumbled.

This caught her attention right away. "What do you mean, better than you?"

"I just mean, if I had to deal with something difficult, alcohol is not going to be my first choice."

She cocked her head to the side, studying me. "So, the great Jackson Calsen has a story?"

"Why do you keep referring to me as some popular asshole?" I said, irritated.

She shrugged, closed her plastic box, and threw it into the garbage. "You've got to be some popular asshole to be my brother's bitch."

Maggie turned and headed up her stairs, leaving me pissed. Did she just say that? For whatever reason, her pointing out something I already knew made me angry. I didn't understand why I felt angry, probably because I was embarrassed that what she said was true, and I knew people always referred to me as that. It never made me feel anything until now. Until Maggie Kensinger, the girl on the plane, said it. I felt anger and embarrassment, something I had not dealt with in a long time.

I wiped my hands with a napkin and followed her up the stairs. When I got to the top of the stairs, I was hit by the smell of vanilla and lavender. It smelled just like Maggie, who was in the bathroom getting to wash her face.

"You can't just say shit like that and walk away." I snapped at her.

She turned to me, stoic, "Well, I just did, didn't I?"

Maggie bent down and began to scrub her face. I then took in what she was now wearing: black biker shorts with a baggy T-shirt. Her hair was pulled into a high ponytail. I noticed her tattoos for the first time. She had birds that were wrapped around her arm;

they all looked like they were flying away. She had a few small ones on her other arm. All of them were in black ink, and they stood out on her pale skin.

"What do they mean?" I blurted out.

Her beautiful eyes looked over at me, "For all these demons I have, I am letting them go, and they're flying away." She cracked a smile as she turned off the bathroom light. "They wrap around my opposite hip. I've got a lot of demons." She brushed past me and headed back down the stairs. "It sounds like you've got demons, too," she yelled out, "I can see it in your eyes." Maggie glanced back up at me from the bottom of the stairs. "I never said it was a bad thing, Calsen."

Fuck me.

Chapter Seven

Night of Secrets

Maggie

Never was I one to share secrets. I always thought of secrets as something sort of special, something that should be left unsaid. I think of the whole thing with my father. Skyla only knew it was something terrible, but she knew not to push it out of me. I had other big secrets that did not belong to me. The secret about Calvin having drug problems, Skyla's alcohol problem, and my uncle's whore problem.

Everyone has secrets, but there is no point in telling others. It will only hurt more people. I have done my fair share of hurting people, so it is for the better that I remain quiet.

I settled onto the couch with a water bottle, even though I sincerely wanted to chug a bottle of wine. But I should be more alert and functioning since Jackson was here, who was practically a stranger.

Jackson carefully sat about a cushion away from me. He was dressed comfortably, which told me he had just finished working at the hospital.

"So, tell me, why are you so interested in me?"

He smiled, "Who said I was interested?"

I rolled my eyes, "Oh, come on, why wouldn't you be interested in me? I am the grand prize."

His eyes carefully took me in from head to toe before he spoke again, "I don't know why anyone would not be interested in you."

"Oh, come on," I said and took a drink from my water, "don't hit me with the cheesy shit."

Jackson settled back onto the couch, "Now I am starting to see how you and Skyla are best friends, you both are a couple of bitches."

Smiling, "Yes, we are also a bunch of pains in the ass, so tread lightly here."

"Have you seen any of your family since you have been back?" He asked uncomfortably.

I pulled my knees to my chest, reliving seeing my father. I bit my lip and let the stabbing pain inside me vanish before I spoke: "I saw my dad today. As you can probably tell, it didn't go great."

Jackson was studying me. "So, let me get this right: Your family doesn't speak to you because you choose to be a teacher rather than a doctor?" I nodded, and hearing it out loud made it sound worse. "But why does it bother your dad so much?"

"I don't know, probably because I embarrassed him. His best friend," All of a sudden, my heart rate shot up. "You know what? Enough about me. You tell me a deep, dark secret."

There was a ringing in my ears as I closed my eyes and focused on my breathing. Inhale, then exhale. Inhale, then exhale. I hadn't thought about Daniel in a while, and I hadn't had any nightmares for almost a month. Now, all my mind could fixate on was those horrible nightmares. If only they had just been nightmares.

"Maggie," I blinked, and Jackson returned to focus, "Maggie?"

Taking a deep breath, I smiled, "Sorry, I'm just tired." I shook my head and took a drink from my water bottle. "You know, you don't have to stay. I am sure there are better things you can do on a night off."

Jackson furrowed his brow. "Do you want me to leave?"

"Do you want to stay?" I fired back.

"Hey, you said you were a prize, so I'm trying to find out what this is."

I rolled my eyes. "Whatever, just say you want to get into my pants; don't sugarcoat it."

"Maggie," his voice became serious, "you are not just going to be a one-night stand to me." I bit my lip, afraid to take my eyes off him. "I want to know who you are, not just because of who your family is, not because you strike me as someone good in bed, and not because I want to get my dick wet. I want to know you because when I first saw you on the plane, I wanted to know everything there was."

I scrunched up my nose. "Now, that makes you sound creepy."

Jackson kept his face serious, "I am not fucking around. I am serious; I want to know you, Maggie."

"Well, it is going to take a lot more than a few sweet words and a greasy burger to tell you everything," I pointed out. "I am not that easy."

He smiled, "I never said you were going to be easy. If anything, you are going to be a pain in my ass."

"You said it, not me."

Jackson shook his head, "Well, let's start with easy shit, tell me your favorite color."

I shook my head. "Too deep. Start with something else," I teased. He did not look amused. "Okay, fine. I like green, you?"

He smiled, "Blue."

We spent the next two hours talking on the couch. I learned he was born and raised in California, where his mother worked as a waitress to support him and his sisters. His sisters were both stay-at-home moms. He hated California—there were too many people, it was too hot, and crowded.

Growing up, he was always forced to do what his sisters wanted to do. He had to dress up and have tea parties with them. He had to learn to love watching Barbie movies and other girly shows. He was even forced to be their canvas for painting nails and doing hair.

"It was sort of hell, but hey, they were happy, and it was the only way I could hang around them."

Jackson met Calvin in medical school. Calvin got in because of who he was, and Jackson put a lot of work into getting in. Calvin was his roommate, and Jackson talked about the amount of partying and shit they would do. That is not a shock to me; he was already like that in high school. Calvin felt as if he was invincible and nothing could hurt or touch him. There was an appealing side to Calvin; it was just hard to reach.

Growing up, Jackson always wanted to be a pilot, but then he discovered his fear of heights, and that was not going to pan out. The only way he could fly on planes was if he took Dramamine. It would help with motion sickness and make him drowsy enough.

His seventh-grade science teacher suggested he look into the medical field. Even if Jackson could succeed and get into a medical school, let alone a decent college, he would not be able to afford it. Lucky for him, a scholarship paid for his tuition, and he lived at home while he went to UCLA. It was at medical school that he found himself in horrible debt.

He didn't think he would be able to get the fellowship here at Bemidji, but Calvin got him in. My uncle wasn't very fond of him, but I assured him my uncle didn't like anyone. He was nervous about the winter here, as he had never seen snow or driven in it. He had recently found a house on the outskirts of town. He said it needed a lot of remodeling, but it would keep him distracted and busy.

Of course, we went through the basics of knowing someone, with favorites being blue, *Field of Dreams,* the movie, Meatloaf, basketball, Italian food, science, country music, *Friends,* the TV show, Russell Crowe, Jennifer Aniston as his celebrity crushes, liked cats better than dogs, and November 4th being his birthday. He hated sushi and pop. He had never been out of the country and had only really traveled through California most of his life. The drive to Bemidji was very eye-opening for him the first time.

Jackson had a high school girlfriend who ended up cheating on him when they got to college. I guess she was now married and had a shit load of kids from the guy she cheated on Jackson with, so happy ending there. Otherwise, he really didn't have any other relationship and never really had a lot of time. He did admit to having a few fuck buddies during medical school because every guy needs to get his dick wet. I frowned and rolled my eyes at this, which made him laugh.

With me, he learned that Calvin and I used to be attached at the hip. Anika and I had never gotten along; I was always annoyed with her, and she was always a bitch to me. I was a very competitive person and was always out to beat everyone at everything. I played basketball, volleyball, and ran track in high school. I graduated at the top of my class in high school, college, and when I got my master's. My favorites are green, *Pretty in Pink,* peanut butter, basketball, Italian food, social studies, rap music, *Big Bang Theory*, Rihanna, and Orlando Bloom for celebrity crushes, cats are better than dogs, and May 22 being my birthday. I could not stand sushi, fish, and pop. I had been all over the United States and out of the country many times.

I had grown up with every intention of being a doctor, and once I was in college, I was determined to be a psychiatrist. Of course, I changed my mind and fell in love with teaching, and I would not change it for the world. Jackson didn't push me on why I had a sudden change of heart, but reading his face, he knew there was more to that story.

Skyla and I met in the eighth-grade homeroom, and she was new to the area. I was the only one who went to talk to her because she had her resting bitch face. It was a simple hi, I am blah blah, and then hey, I am blah blah. From that point on, we were best friends. We ate lunch together and even switched our classes around to have the same ones.

"You want to know something about Calvin that he thinks no one knows?" I asked.

Jackson laughed, "Oh, good god, what?"

I smiled, "He had a crush on Skyla and still does."

"No way."

I nodded, "Yes, why do you think Skyla is extra bitchy to him? It is not because of me. It is because of him. She gets sick to her stomach, knowing he jerks off to her."

Jackson cringed, "Woah, Woah, I didn't need to know all of that." He made a face. "God, now I will never get it out of my head, Kensinger, that's fucked."

I laughed, "Fine, since I made you so grossed out, ask me any question, and I will answer honestly."

This silenced him. He waited to see if I was joking, but I wasn't. I was more curious about what he would ask. I was prepared for him to ask about my prior relationships and even my freak-out moment from earlier, but what he asked was not what I thought.

"How long ago?" He asked.

I gave him a confused look, "Excuse me?"

He scooted over closer to me, "How long since you self-harmed?"

Jackson grabbed my left arm and brushed his thumb over my faded scars. I focused on how soft his hands were and how my arm perked up with goosebumps. His hand grasped my arm very gently, and I watched his thumb pause at the most predominant scar.

I looked up at him, my hands beginning to shake. He looked up at me, grabbed my hands, and held them. "About a year ago," my voice sounded hoarse. "Um, it wasn't long before I attempted for the third time." I bit down hard on my lip. "No one but Skyla knows about the third time, so I would appreciate it if you didn't mention that."

"Why would I tell someone that?" He sounded hurt. "Maggie, that isn't my experience to share. Please stop biting down on your lip; you're bleeding."

I took a deep breath. "Sorry for killing the mood."

Jackson released my hands. "Why did you tell me?"

"Because," I shrugged, "I told you I would answer truthfully to anything you asked."

His expression was unreadable. "You amaze me, Kensinger." He cracked a smile. "Now we are sharing secrets, and I feel like I owe you one."

I shook my head, "Not tonight. I think enough has been said for one night."

He raised his eyebrows, "So there's going to be another night?"

"Yes, you dumbass, don't make me change my mind." I stood up and walked towards the kitchen to grab another water bottle.

When I turned around, Jackson was right behind me. He gave me a small smile as I looked up at him. He leaned down; his lips pressed against mine. I felt a warm rush through my body. He lifted me and set me on the counter, lips brushing against my cheek. I felt his hands trace down the sides of my torso as he kissed my forehead and then my lips one more time. My skin was tingling, and chills ran through my body.

He smiled, "I think that's enough for one night." I frowned at him as he walked away and paused before he opened the door. "I told you I was better than a bottle of wine."

Jackson turned and gave me a smirk before he closed the door. I was left sitting on my counter, cheeks flushed, and my head spinning. For a moment, I let myself smile, but then I felt a wave of fear.

Chapter Eight

Waves of Hell

Jackson

The weather was already changing; there was a new crispness in the air. I moved into my house over Labor Day weekend with Calvin's help. The nice thing was, there really wasn't a whole lot to move since I sold everything before I moved here. We spent the rest of the day at a bar downtown, drinking and watching ESPN constantly. We avoided any conversation about Maggie and got stuck discussing sports and how much we hated college kids.

It had been a few weeks since I had seen Maggie. We briefly texted, but I didn't want to push or rush it. She had to have been busy with the start of school, and I had been busy moving and getting my ass handed to me at work. Maggie was on my mind more frequently. I thought about how natural and chilling that kiss was. There were even times I had dreams of us going farther. Then, there were times I thought about her attempts at suicide and how shitty her family was to her.

Speaking of family, my mother called at least a dozen times because she was so proud of me for buying my house. She had never experienced that before, and my sisters basically moved into their husbands' homes. My mom missed me, I could tell, not just by the frequent calls but also by the conversations we had. She was curious about what it was like here: the weather, the hospital, the Minnesota accent, and how Calvin was.

At the hospital, I was starting to get the hang of where everything was. I was also beginning to build a better relationship with my direct boss, who had Skyla's attitude. The more shifts I started to work, the more I began to see Skyla everywhere. From what I gathered in the lounge, no one could stand her. She ate alone, and no one dared to wake her up when she was in an on-call room. Maggie was not kidding; she was intense.

The only person who seemed to pick fights with her was Calvin. In the last weeks, they went out of each other's way to fight. I had not yet witnessed the screaming matches that would happen. I just heard about them from Calvin and Greg, the other general surgeon fellow. There had even been a time when Skyla pinned him to the wall. I knew what they were fighting about; nothing else would set this off but Maggie.

Sitting in the third-floor lounge, where most fellows gathered, I was joined by Skyla. There was no one else in the room, just her and me, and this was a first for me. Her dark hair with the undertones of red was pulled back into a high ponytail. She was wearing scrubs that exposed the tattoos on her arm, one being a half sleeve that was not finished. She had pale skin like Maggie, but Skyla had way more curves and definition in her body, more built and stronger than Maggie. However, Skyla was shorter than Maggie.

Sensing I was watching her, Skyla turned around. "What are you looking at, Calsen?"

"Um," I was not prepared for her to talk to me. "I was just admiring your tattoos." At these words, my body cringed.

Skyla smirked at me. "No, you were looking at me because you know about Maggie." She grabbed a coffee cup and began to fill it. "I don't like you," she added.

"Excuse me?"

"You're Calvin's bitch, and Calvin considers her dead, so I can only assume you're out to hurt her or humiliate her. Either one, you will find yourself hurt."

I narrowed my eyes at her, "Is that a threat?"

"Nope, it is a warning."

Skyla threw me a look before putting the to-go lid on her cup and walking out of the room. She was a bitch, but I guessed I had been warned. But the thing that got me was the fact that Skyla knew about me because Maggie had talked about me.

"Hey," Calvin came in and plopped down on the couch, "guess who just resected a brain tumor in the frontal lobe of an eleven-year-old." He smiled at me.

"Dr. Jensen," I said dryly.

He rolled his eyes, "Fuck you." I smiled, rolled my eyes, and went back to my phone. "What did the wicked witch of the north want from you?"

I looked up at him, "Huh?"

Calvin frowned, "Skyla James? She is a cunt and a piece of work, but what did she want from you?"

"She came to get coffee, that's all."

"No, she only gets coffee from the cart on the first floor."

I frowned at him, "That's fucking creepy that you know that."

"That is beside the point. What did she want from you?"

I shrugged, "She just threw me a warning if I tried to pick a fight with her." My toes curled inside my shoe, indicating I was uncomfortable. "Considering you and she seem to have screaming matches every other day."

Calvin laughed and took off his scrub cap. He put his legs up on the couch and put his hands behind his head. In a way, he reminded me of Maggie, the way they both were confident in their comebacks. However, there was really nothing else that indicated to me that the two of them could be siblings.

"Alright," he sighed, "Skyla is Maggie's best friend. Maggie is my embarrassment of a sister, as you discovered at the wonderful dinner party my mother had." He chuckled and shook his head. "I have a younger sister who is a kindergarten teacher, and apparently, she has moved back from Colorado."

I shifted in my chair, not liking where this was going. "So, you've never mentioned her before…because she's a teacher?"

"Yes, but that isn't the only reason."

I shot him a confused look, "Is this where I am supposed to ask why?" I asked sarcastically.

Calvin rolled his eyes. "Maggie was always the one who won everything: awards, competitions, and even our parents' attention. I sort of resented her because she was better than I was. Then, when she dropped the ball on what her major was going to be, it was the perfect chance for me to outshine her. In the end, she ended up being the biggest disappointment, so I won."

"This is all about competition?" I asked.

"In a way, yes, but what I think embarrasses me more is the fact of her trying to kill herself." I squeezed my fist tightly. "I mean, she's no longer the shiny toy. She's the damaged one."

"You know how much of a jackass that makes you sound, right?"

Calvin looked surprised by my response. "You don't get it. Your mother loved you for whatever you did. I could never get them to look my way once."

"No, I'm talking about the part where it embarrasses you that your sister struggles with mental health."

He narrowed his eyes. "Why are you defending her?"

I shook my head, "I am just saying, Calvin, she is still a person and is struggling from an illness."

"Illness for attention." He muttered. "You still don't get it. Maggie always wants to take the easy way out of everything."

"How do you know that?" I finally fired back at him. "I mean, you haven't spoken to her or about her in our nearly ten-year friendship. So, how are you supposed to know the reason behind it?"

Calvin stood up, "Here is what I don't understand: Maggie had everything you could ever want, and then she is willing to throw it away for what? The attention? Because that is what it seems to be in my eyes, an attention-seeking act because, finally, she wasn't the favorite."

Before I could answer, the door shut behind me, and a flash of red streaked in front of me. Skyla had tackled Calvin to the floor and pinned him.

"Well, isn't this nice? You on top of me," Calvin said smugly.

Skyla punched him hard in the face. "And you think you're the favorite in your family? If anything, you're the embarrassment. Being arrested all the times you were, the number of STDs you've spread, and let's not forget your drug habits."

"Why are you always fighting her battles?" Calvin spat in her face. "If she had any fucking balls, she would've already come to face me." Then he started to laugh at himself. "Oh, wait, she's probably too busy planning the next craft her class will do."

Skyla sacked him in the face again. "If you only knew half of what happened to her, you would be defending her like I am."

"Like what? Oh no, Daddy isn't going to pay for my college. Oh no, I can't stand working for Daniel-"

Skyla sacked him hard again, and her knuckles had blood on them. She looked back up at me. "You, of all people, are going to let him talk like this?"

She stood up, and Calvin laughed, "Oh, baby, come back, the foreplay had just started."

Skyla kicked him hard to his side and then glared at me. "Fuck you, Calsen."

Before anyone could say another word, Dr. Frank Kensinger, our boss, busted through the door. He was fuming as he glared at Skyla, who was now washing Calvin's blood off her knuckles at the sink, casually.

"Both of you," he gritted between his teeth, "in my office now." He then looked over at me. "You too, Calsen."

I went and helped Calvin up, who was already forming a black eye. There were droplets of blood coming from his nose; Skyla got him good. Calvin avoided my looks and walked with his head down, while I could feel the daggers of Skyla's eyes shooting into my back.

For the first ten minutes, Skyla and Calvin sat looking away from each other. I awkwardly stood behind them, pissed at Calvin for starting this whole thing.

"I don't even-" Chief Kensinger started.

"It all comes back to Maggie." Skyla cut him off.

Calvin glared at her, "You're the one who started this."

Skyla mocked him, "You're the one who started this."

"ENOUGH, both of you." Chief Kensinger yelled. "For Christ's sake, Calvin, get over yourself. Maggie is your damn sister, whether you like it or not." He then turned and looked at Skyla. "You need to stop taking his bait to start fighting."

Calvin scoffed, "I don't understand; you hate Maggie just like everyone else does."

Chief Kensinger stood up, "Not that it is any of your business; your father and I agreed she needed to come back. Especially with-"

Calvin stood up, "Whatever, I am done here."

"Whatever, I am done here." Skyla mocked as she stood. "Pussy," she mumbled with a smirk.

Calvin got close to her face, fire in his eyes. "Wanna say that to my face?"

Skyla smirked, "Fucking pussy."

Before he could lay a hand on her, I pushed him back against the wall, and the Chief shoved Skyla the opposite way. You could feel the heat radiating from Calvin as Skyla smirked in the corner. He pushed past me and slammed the door behind him, leaving the Chief shaking his head.

"Stop picking fights and letting him bait you into one," he turned to Skyla, "or I will suspend you both."

He gestured for her to leave, and she left without saying another word or looking at either of us. It was now just me standing there in front of my boss, who was already not a fan of me.

"You're due for another test," he said, his expression unreadable. "Hailey can take care of that for you tomorrow." He paused and sighed heavily, and my throat dried. "I don't know how you fit into this mess, but stay out."

I nodded, "Yes, sir."

He gestured for me to leave. "Tomorrow at nine a.m., Hailey's office, " he called out as I left the room.

Ignoring the crowd that had surrounded the chief's office, I made my way down to my locker on the third floor. I changed into a t-shirt and shorts and slammed my locker hard.

Every month, I had to be drug tested. It was the only deal I could work out to continue working in the medical field. If I were caught, I was done, and my medical license would be suspended indefinitely. Chief Kensinger had decided he didn't trust me, so I had to be tested every two weeks to keep my job. It wasn't very pleasant, but I understood why it had to be done.

Back when I was at the bottom of my addiction, I was in the worst situation possible. I would be at every well-known strip club there was. I would pay women to have sex with me. I found myself snorting the pills because taking them wasn't enough. I wouldn't sleep. I didn't eat. I didn't care who I hurt. If I was getting high and getting my dick sucked, I was okay.

When I was at work, I would pop a few, and then I would find myself in an on-call room with a nurse. Outside of the hospital, I found myself at a house party, bar, or club. Most of the time, I really don't remember what happened. I would just wake up, and there I would be. It wasn't until I met Ginger that my addiction went from pills to cocaine and alcohol.

I had met Ginger at some bar, and she convinced me that coke was going to be ten times better than pills. She and I would get high with each other, fuck each other, get high, and then go to work. She was some actress wannabe. She loved the idea of me being a doctor: the drugs and the money. Ginger was like a whole different addiction. She loved fucking and sucking me off, and I just liked that I didn't have to do the work. She didn't care what I did if I showed up with the money to buy our next fix.

Most nights, I would find myself in Ginger's flat, which she shared with another girl named Melody. The best part about that whole situation was that Melody would suck me off and let me fuck the shit out of her when Ginger was gone. There were also times when we would all be so high that I found myself with one of them sitting on my face and the other sucking me off.

It's crazy to think I was able to have that whole other life. I would show up to work, functioning without a problem. No one suspected a thing. I did my best to hide my disgusting truth. Calvin and I would work on such different schedules that when we did get to hang out, we would be at a club or bar. I never let Calvin meet Ginger.

The only thing that got me out of that situation was my heart attack and the treatment. I never heard or saw Ginger again. I had been years sober from any kind of drug. I learned how to be human again. I learned how to sleep, eat, and take care of myself. It was not easy, and there were plenty of times when I found myself contemplating taking my own life. I was disgusted at what I had let myself become, but more than anything, I was ashamed.

I could understand why someone would feel the need to kill themself. I had been there at one point, and there were times when thoughts would pass through my mind, but I had never felt the urge to act on them. It took a while to dig myself out of that pit; it was not easy, and there were times I fell. Struggling was part of my nature, and Maggie understood that.

Nowadays, work keeps me busy more than ever. I was able to keep my mind from going dark. I tried my best to keep myself healthy: to run three or four miles a day and watch what I eat and how much water I drink. For the most part, my addiction wasn't what I thought about anymore. Maggie filled my thoughts.

I hesitated before I got out of my car. There were lights on in the house, so I was crossing my fingers that Maggie was home. I had driven to my house and sat in the driveway for a solid thirty minutes before deciding to go to Maggie's. I had to see her. I had to talk to her. If anything, I just wanted to hear her voice. The whole drive to her house, I felt like a psycho because of the choke hold she had on me.

Knocking on her front door, I was hoping this white Nissan in the driveway was hers and not Skyla's. Lord knows what that bitch would do to me if she answered the door. I heard footsteps coming to the door and the lock unclicking. Sure enough, before my eyes, Maggie Kensinger stood.

Her hair was down and wet as if she had just gotten out of the shower. There was no makeup on her face, not even a trace of it. Her eyes were as bright and beautiful as the first time I saw them on the plane. She was dressed in a baggy t-shirt that went to her mid-thigh. From what I could tell, there was nothing underneath them.

She looked concerned. "Hey, everything ok?"

I smiled, "Yeah, I'm good. I just wanted to see if you wanted another greasy burger."

Maggie saw through that bullshit answer, "No, you're here because Skyla and Calvin fought, and you witnessed it."

"That is part of it, but I am hungry, so technically, I am also here to see if you want to go with me."

She raised her eyebrow, "Yeah, dressed like this? No way, I am not leaving."

"Then can I come in?"

She narrowed her eyes. "Did you bring wine?"

Taken aback by her answer, "Uh, no?"

Maggie smiled, "That's good. I already opened a bottle anyway." She gestured for me to come in.

I closed the door behind me. "Is Skyla-"

"Yeah, I'm here fucker." She cried out from the kitchen and then came into view. "Don't worry. I am going back to the hospital, so I won't ruin the mood."

Maggie smirked behind her. "Um," I started, "why are you heading back up there?"

"Trauma attending went down with the flu, so I am taking over the pit tonight." She turned and hugged Maggie. "Let me know if he tries anything."

Maggie smiled, "I always do. Let me know if you need me to bring you anything."

Skyla nodded and glanced at me before heading out the garage door. Maggie looked back at me and said, "Let me go, change. I will be right back."

"Oh, come on, don't change." I pleaded playfully.

She glared at me, "Well, I am changing anyway. You're hungry, so I can't necessarily go out in just a T-shirt."

I watched her go up the stairs, my mind filling up with all the ways I could grab her and take her into her room. She must have sensed I was watching because, without even turning around, she flipped me off.

My phone buzzed, and Calvin asked me what I was doing tonight. Truth be told, I didn't want to see him, not just because of Maggie, but because of what he had said and done earlier. I would rather hang out with Skyla before I see Calvin. Either way, all he would want to do is go downtown to the club and bitch to me about his uncle and Skyla, and now add Maggie in there as well.

The light flicked off above, and there she was, coming down the stairs. She was in jeans and a tight-fitting shirt that had a plunging neckline. The shoes she had chosen were sandals that showed her toes were painted deep blue to match her eyes. She had even thrown on some mascara and ruffled her hair a bit.

"Look more presentable?" She questioned as she twirled.

I shook my head, and there was no hiding the smile on my face. "I truthfully didn't know what was wrong with the first outfit."

Maggie rolled her eyes. "Fuck off."

Looking back down at my phone, it was not even a debate. I wanted to be with Maggie. I clicked my phone shut and followed her out the garage door. I took note of the nearly empty wine glass with some kind of white wine. She was not kidding when it came to wine.

She closed the garage door and followed me to my car. Thank God I was a doctor, and I liked things clean. My vehicle looked practically brand new on the inside, and it even had that new car smell. I watched her settle into the passenger seat and smile over at me.

"So, Calsen, where will we get you food?"

Not much later, we found ourselves at a restaurant overlooking the lake. I noticed that her body language had changed since we entered the restaurant. She walked with her arms crossed in front of her and her head down. We were seated at an outside table with a candle in the middle of our table.

She looked over at me as the fire lit her eyes. "Surprised you didn't have anything better to do on a Friday night."

"I could say the same to you."

"Well, my only friend just left for work, and you saw what I was going to do."

"Have fun with a bottle of wine?" She smirked and opened the menu. "How's the first week of school coming along?"

"You don't have to ask if you're not interested." I shot her a look. "Well, on my first day, I had three kids pee themselves, and about every single one of them cried their eyes out."

I smiled, "Did you cry on your first day in Kindergarten?"

Maggie frowned, "If I answer truthfully, am I getting laughed at yet?" I shook my head. "I bawled my eyes out in music class on the first day." She admitted. "Let me take a wild guess: you didn't cry?"

"Sorry, Kensinger, you're wrong, I did cry."

She smirked as the waiter came and asked for our drink orders. I ordered Dr. Pepper, a guilty pleasure, and Maggie ordered water, surprising me. I did notice the lingering looks the waiter gave Maggie.

"Would you mind if I ordered a side of fries?" she asked, not looking up from her menu.

I made a face, "As long as you don't dip them in mayo."

Maggie rolled her eyes, and when the waiter came back, I watched his eyes focus on Maggie's chest. Jealousy flared up inside me, an emotion I had not really felt. Oblivious to it, she ordered a side of fries with a side of mayo. The waiter smiled at her and then frowned when he saw my face. I ordered a burger, but I was not really in the mood to talk to him.

"Why so grumpy?" Maggie asked in a playful voice.

I shrugged, not wanting to: A. bring attention to the fact that this man was staring at her rack, and B. I didn't want to admit I was jealous. "Just hungry."

She made a face and said, "So, I heard it got ugly today. Skyla told me you all had to go to the chief's office. Is there anything that you want to talk about?"

Her blue eyes shone from the moonlight, and her skin looked smooth like porcelain. "Later," I said, "let's take this time to hear how and why you cried your eyes out in music class, of all places."

For the rest of dinner, the conversation stayed mainly on Maggie, which I could tell was making her annoyed. I learned more about some of the places she had traveled to. When she was younger, her father was big on traveling and exploring the country. She had been to almost every national park, something her mom and she did alone. As a family, she had been to Paris, Thailand, Australia, and even Iceland. With Skyla, they went to Italy for their graduation present from high school, and they went to Brazil, London, and Japan. Maggie expressed how she always wanted to see new places, but she wanted to revisit the other places she had already seen.

She talked about how, throughout elementary and middle school, all the teachers were prepared for Maggie to be hell on wheels, but they were always surprised. Calvin had been hell, so they were just prepared for Maggie to be the same.

We talked about her new school and new coworkers. She seemed to like them; there were a lot of teachers there from when she went to school. Her class was good. They had gone through the basics of learning how to be in school and how they should act. There were two other teachers at her grade level. Both had gone to high school with Maggie. From what I gathered, they did not like her, leaving her out of many things. Maggie didn't seem to care. She would instead do stuff on her own.

I was hyperaware anytime our waiter came by. His eyes avoided me but were glued to Maggie. If she noticed, she did not indicate it. She ate her fries while dipping them in mayo in a dramatic way to gross me out.

Finally, we left and went down by the lake to sit on one of the boating docks. Because it had gotten cool enough, there were hardly any bugs. Maggie informed me that during the summer, it was bad with the bugs down on the boating docks. She sat there with her eyes looking up at the stars, whereas I watched the stars twinkle in her eyes.

"So," she looked at me, "do you want to talk about what you heard and saw today?"

I looked out at the water as it reflected the sky off it. "I really don't want to make you uncomfortable."

She laughed, "Listen, I have heard it all. I know Calvin has issues with me, but it is what it is. Skyla warned me that you would ask me about something else."

I looked at her. Maggie's eyes were focused on her hands on her lap. She was picking at the side of her thumb, and her entire body was tense. I didn't like how she had suddenly changed or how guarded she looked.

"I don't really need to know if it bothers you."

"It's okay. I will share my secrets if you share your secrets with me, Calsen." She nudged my shoulder, trying to brush off how tense she was.

I leaned back, "So that is the deal here?"

She grinned back, "That is the deal."

"Who is Daniel?"

Fear filled her eyes, and I watched her bite down hard on her lip. As she spoke and told me, waves of literal hell hit me.

Chapter Nine

The Broken Pieces

Maggie

When I went to college, I was destined to be a doctor. There was no question about my major. Luckily, Dr. Daniel Dobson, an old friend of my father's, wanted to take me under his wing. He specialized in psychology, the field of medicine I wanted to pursue.

I had known Daniel since I was a kid and was eager to learn from him. He worked for the police department's special victims unit in Denver. Before that, he worked with my uncle at Kensinger Memorial. When I was in high school, Daniel left to go work out in Colorado.

Now, as a freshman, I saw Daniel a few times a month when I would have time to shadow him. Then, by Thanksgiving time, he was making trips to see me and help me study through some of my classes. I would meet him at diners and soak up everything I could learn. I got to understand why he went into the field of psychology because he was a product of rape and suffered from depression, so he always figured that was his way of giving back.

Everyone loved him, and all the police and detectives wanted him to help with their cases. I was his shadow, and I got to see more than any freshman in college would see. I couldn't even begin to understand how these men, children, and women had been assaulted, raped, or sexually abused. Hearing their stories had an impact on me that sometimes I would even have nightmares myself. Of course, I had signed so many papers and documents that I could never share anything with anyone.

Instead of going home for Thanksgiving, I was given the chance to spend some extra time shadowing. My dad was adamant that I stay there, but Mom was not so much. Skyla ended up going home, hesitant to leave me, but I assured her that if anything happened, Daniel would be there. And a big surprise, Skyla was not a fan of Daniel and was always wary of him.

Thanksgiving night, Daniel and I went to eat and drink at a bar after working with a slew of cases. I had a few drinks, and the bartender didn't hesitate to ask me for my ID. Daniel began asking me questions about what areas I wanted to study. Eventually, he took me back to his house, saying I was safer there than in my dorm room. I didn't really question it, simply because I had known him since I was little, and I had been working with him.

Once I washed my face and slipped into sweats and a T-shirt, it changed. I wasn't even all the way out of the bathroom when he slammed me up against the wall. I was too stunned to speak. His lips traced down to mine, and I tried to shrug off.

He got frustrated and banged my head hard against the wall, making me dizzy. I was told what to do, and I wouldn't get hurt. My vision was fuzzy as he threw me down onto the bed in his room and pulled down my pants. I tried backing away, but I was hit one more time.

What I remember is moaning to make it stop, hot tears down my cheeks, and the pain. I remember the stings from the bite marks he left on my skin. I was dizzy and buzzed from the alcohol I had earlier. A small part of me was begging that this be some sort of dream, but it wasn't. It kept going, the thrusts, the choking, the biting, and him saying my name and telling me good job.

That night was the first of many to come. Over the next three weeks, I was always covered in makeup or long sleeves. I barely stayed in my dorm as Daniel forced me back to his place. I was drugged a few times; others, I was just flat-out scared. Several times, we were in his office, and he would force me onto his desk and plow me.

I wanted to tell someone, anyone, but I couldn't. The first thing was that no one would believe me. He worked for the police and specialized in special victims. Next thing, he would ruin my career, as I was later threatened with pictures and videos he kept from the times I was drugged. You could clearly see I wasn't struggling, and I was moaning and saying his name. I knew that if I tried to speak, he would do everything in his power to shut me down. At Christmas time, I changed my major to undecided without telling anyone. I then informed my father that I was changing my field of medicine and wouldn't need to study under Daniel.

Suddenly, Daniel disappeared. I was left alone with permanent scarring and untreated wounds. It wasn't long until the nightmares were too much, and the constant numbness was too much; it was the first time I attempted. Skyla found me in our dorm room. I passed out from the amount of blood I had lost.

It wasn't long after all of that that I changed my major, and my family never spoke to me again. My mother did her best to be supportive from a distance. She knew there was something more to the story, other than that I was just depressed. Skyla knew there was more, but I didn't feel like talking.

That spring, after I had confirmed with my mother that Daniel was working overseas in Europe, I told Skyla it all. It was hard watching her try to hold herself together. She was shaking and did her best to stay calm. She asked me what she wanted me to do; I simply told her, nothing, it will all pass. I knew she wanted to go and kill him or at least go beat the living crap out of him. But she knew with all the evidence he had against me and the fact that he wasn't even in the country, it wasn't an issue to press.

People never really understood our relationship before; they didn't know. Skyla was overly protective of me that first year, and then she said I had to get my shit together if I wanted it to be in the past. We did everything we could together; I even spent a lot of time with her and Bentley. We were hardly ever seen apart, and when we were, no one tried to fuck with either of us. I began seeing a psychiatrist who got me on some antidepressants for my depression.

Then Bentley killed himself, and I made sure Skyla was protected and cared for the same way she had done for me. In those weeks when I was enduring the abuse, I dropped about fifteen pounds and barely scraped by with Cs in all my classes. When Skyla was dealing with Bentley's death, I was the one who got her back on her feet, the same way she had brought me back on mine.

My depression got worse, and of course, I attempted two more times. I still had nightmares where I was put back in the situation, that room or office, and I could feel the pain. I had faint bite scars on my inner thigh, always there to remind me of what had happened.

Sitting on the boating dock and telling Jackson this out loud was strange. I had only shared what had happened to me with Skyla and no one else. He had kept quiet the entire time and was focused on me. In his eyes, there was a fire, a deep anger. I was proud of myself for not crying, but I spoke in a dull and unemotional voice.

"So, um, yeah, that is who Daniel is. And that is also some background on why Calvin commented on it being too hard to work for him."

Jackson was quiet for a minute, thinking his answer through before he spoke. "Thank you for telling me." I looked at him, not expecting that answer. "I can't lie to you; I would've probably killed him. I don't think anyone would have stopped me."

"Why? Why would you risk spending the rest of your life in jail? I know what he did was fucked, but I don't think I could live with myself knowing you wasted your life defending me."

"It wouldn't be wasting my life." He took a deep breath and reached and tilted my chin up to look at him. "Knowing that I did everything to protect you isn't wasting my life."

I frowned, "You're getting too cheesy here."

He shook his head, "I am serious, Maggie."

We sat there frozen like this for about another minute until I dropped my gaze away from him. "I would appreciate it if you-"

"You seriously think I would go behind your back and tell Calvin? Seriously, Maggie?"

"I don't know, Jackson. I am just trying to make sure I don't get hurt. I have been through enough of that."

He shook his head, "Your story isn't mine to tell. Neither is my story for you to tell."

I turned my whole body to face him. "Your turn," I said softly, "a secret for a secret."

"Please don't let it change what you think of me." He turned away from me, his eyes focused on the water. "I don't want to lose you."

I leaned closer to him and had him turn and face me. "Broken people will always love more."

"What?"

"One student of mine, years ago, told me that his mother said broken people like her will love more." I gave a sad smile.

"His mother died from blunt force trauma to the head from her abusive husband." I bit the inside of my cheek. "I am a very broken person; sometimes I think I am beyond fixable, but at the end of the day, I am always going to care and love more than most. So, what I am trying to say, in a really cheesy way, is I will care for and love you no matter what. That's what broken people like us do for others: give them the love and care we never got."

Jackson smiled sadly, "You're telling me you love me?" He teased.

I rolled my eyes. "Not the point there."

He looked away from me, "I get why broken people love more. It makes sense because Maggie, I am just as broken as you, just broken differently."

"Tell me," I whispered so softly I barely heard myself.

Jackson Calsen told me his story. He told me how the addiction started. He explained what spiraled and where he seemed to go wrong. Jackson told me about Ginger and explained why he hid his life from Calvin. He informed me about the drug testing he had to do for my uncle. Jackson told me how he felt as if there was nothing left for him to do but save lives.

"I believed for a long time, Maggie, that I didn't deserve a second chance." He then turned and looked at me. "Then you came out of nowhere, and now I have a second chance at something."

I bit my lip, "Addiction doesn't mean you can't have a life separate from it." I said slowly. "That's why you came here, isn't it?" Jackson nodded, looking away from me. "Are you glad you're here?"

Jackson turned to me and grabbed my face gently, his hands warm against my skin. His lips pressed into mine, and I felt the chills go down my spine. I moved my hands to his neck, and one of his hands cradled the base of my spine. When he pulled away, he looked down into my eyes.

"I am glad you're here, Kensinger." He whispered.

I smiled, "Call me Maggie."

"As long as you call me Jackson, we have a deal."

Jackson took me home that night. I lay on the couch and eventually drifted to sleep, my head resting in his lap. The following day, he left early to run while I got up and lay in bed. Skyla came into my room shortly after and fell asleep as I went in and out of sleep.

Hearing my story out loud last night made me feel weak. I had spent all these years building myself to be strong. To be a person who has conquered everything. I was strong but broken. I built myself back up, but once something is broken, it will never return to being fixed. When you break your foot, it is never entirely going to be the same as it was before. When a glass bowl shatters, you can spend the time gluing it back together, but it will never be the same sturdy bowl it was before. When someone breaks your heart, you'll never love or care the same way because it was broken. Once something is damaged, it will never be the same.

Sometimes, you need to get broken or damaged in life because it might make you a better person. Being broken doesn't have to be negative; it's a reality. I like to try and believe that with all my broken pieces, I am a better version of myself. I may have wounds and scars, but they built me into the person I am. I am trying my damnedest to like this version; sometimes, that takes more breaking to achieve.

Around midday, I convinced Skyla to hike in Itasca State Park. I needed to leave the house and be somewhere other than the city. Skyla and I had done numerous hikes in the Rockies and other parks. Skyla loved to work out because, in the end, it would be easier to fight someone if she was strong.

Itasca was not far from the city, and since it was September, the summer crowd had died off. Skyla drove as we listened to a shared playlist we had created; it contained everything from rap to pop to country. It was comforting when we started singing at the top of our lungs. This was something both of us knew we needed. We needed each other to heal. When one falls, the other picks them up. When we both fall, we are going to get ourselves up together.

I adjusted my ponytail and grabbed my backpack when we parked the car and got out. Skyla was stretching and tossed her backpack on the ground. The air was crisp, and with all the trees around us, the sunlight wasn't blazing on us. I started putting on sunscreen—yes, we pale people burn easily—and then threw the bottle to Skyla, who made a face.

I rolled my eyes, "You know you need to put that shit on. I am not going to be putting aloe on you and peeling your skin off these next weeks."

She stuck her tongue out at me, "Whatever."

We started hiking once we needed everything: water, flashlights, bear spray, protein bars, cordless chargers, and sweatshirts. Although there weren't many bears in Minnesota, there was still a risk, so we carried bear spray. Despite all our hiking, we were lucky not to have ever encountered a bear or other dangerous wildlife.

"Are you going to tell me how your little date was?" Skyla smirked at me as she started to pick up the pace. "Someone was tired when I got home."

I shot her a glare, "It wasn't a date, and we certainly didn't fuck, sorry to disappoint."

"I was just making sure I wasn't sleeping in the sheets where you two made love."

"Can you just say fuck?"

She turned around and shook her head. "No, because I know saying making love makes your skin crawl."

"Oh, how nice of you."

Skyla laughed, "So if you didn't make love," she exaggerated the love part, "what did happen?"

"You can't freak out," she stopped walking and turned to face me, "I told him about Daniel."

Her jaw dropped, "What the fuck? Why?"

I shrugged and walked by her, "Because he asked, and in return, I got his secret."

She caught up to me, "So you're telling me Jackson Calsen has secrets?"

"Everyone has secrets."

"Yeah, but people like Calvin and Jackson do a good job at hiding them and pretending they're perfect."

I sighed, "Yes, but you and I know there is way more to people than what they show."

"I am assuming you're not going to spill the great secrets he shared with you?"

I looked at her and smirked, "Not my story to tell."

She laughed and jogged ahead of me, "You're way too loyal, Maggie Kensinger. Way too fucking loyal."

For the rest of the hike, we talked about the hospital and the new drama. Calvin had slept with one of the new nurses, and it pissed off a bunch of other nurses. There was also a rumor that the head of Ortho was getting it on with an intern. Skyla may not like to be involved with drama, but what person doesn't want to sit back and watch others handle their drama?

"Skyla," she turned and looked back at me. "Am I opening myself up to getting hurt?"

She tilted her head to her side and considered my question. She took her time before responding, "I don't think it is bad, but yes, you are."

"What do you mean, not a bad thing?" I fired back.

"Maggie, I haven't seen you in years. Open yourself up and even let someone get to know you. All you've done at least these last three years is one-night stands, and then you vanish. I swear you're worse than most guys." I frowned as I stepped over a large rock. "I think it is going to be a better thing if you try."

"Is Jackson Calsen the right person to try this little experiment?"

She threw me a glare before she spoke. "First, I would not refer to this as an experiment. Second, there is not going to be the perfect person to do this with."

We walked in silence for a few minutes. She wasn't wrong; there wasn't just going to be the perfect partner to open myself up to. After last night, I had already taken a giant leap and shared one secret that haunted me. If Jackson hadn't run away at that, I would have been in the clear.

I looked over at her, "So if I am opening myself up to get hurt, then I think it's about damn time you do the same."

Skyla rolled her eyes. "Maybe, but I think I am more worried about you."

"Listen, it's been over six years." I watched her body tense up as I spoke. "I know you know this is not how he wanted you to continue to live your life. I know that, and you know that."

"Look, Maggie, it is not the same." She muttered.

I shook my head, "You're right, it is not the same. But you must try, for fuck sake. Whether that means you have a hook-up or you join one of those stupid dating apps, I don't care. I don't want to watch you be alone, and you know damn well Bentley would rather see you happy than alone."

Skyla was quiet for a minute and then sat down on a large rock. She curled her lip as I watched a tear fall down her face. I sat down beside her, my ass barely on the rock. I put my arm around her and squeezed. She covered her face with her hands and let out a sob before wiping her face and standing up.

"What if I never get something like that again? What if I end up with some fucking loser like my mom did with Bill? What if I find someone and they die? What happens when I am left broken again? I know I can't go through that shit again." She took a deep breath and looked up at the sky. "I am so fucking tired of people dying, leaving, and being fucked up. I am tired of trying in general. I am tired of waking up and feeling nothing. I am tired of being so pissed off everywhere I go." She shouted. "Why is life such a goddamn bitch?"

I stood up and stretched, "Because life is a bitch, and people are fucked up." I cracked a smile at her. "Because we are fucked up people."

Skyla shook her head, "No, we are broken people. There is a difference."

Smiling, I wrapped my arm around her. "Let's be broken people together."

She shook her head and put her arm around me. We were two broken people, doing the best we could to love the mended version we'd become.

Chapter Ten

The Difference Between

Jackson

During my entire three-mile run, I kept picturing Maggie helpless and being raped. I would begin to run faster, but that did no good. I kept hearing her cry out for help. Her blue eyes pleaded for help. My head was spinning, and I gave up around the three-mile mark. The way she was able to keep her composure while telling me the most horrible thing that had ever happened to her. I was amazed at her reaction and calmness when I told her some of the worst things I had ever done. Broken people will always love and care more. That kept echoing in my ears.

I had no furniture in the living room inside my house, just a TV on the floor. In the main bedroom, I had my mattress on the floor and another TV. My kitchen was bare, just one barstool. There was just milk in the fridge and nothing in the pantry, either. The backyard was large and backed up to state-owned land, meaning there would never be any houses built behind mine. The deck needed to be repaired, and the garden around the house required love.

The house was a four-bedroom and three-and-a-half-bath house. It was built originally in the '90s and has yet to be updated. The only thing the previous owners did was nearly finish the basement, which needed paint, fixtures, and the finishing touches. I could not explain to Calvin why I bought this house. He gave me shit that I should have gotten a bachelor pad on the water like him. I wanted to be somewhere where I had space. Growing up in California, I was used to everyone and everything being on top of each other. I was tired of it.

While I was in the shower, Calvin texted me that we were going downtown tonight, and there was no room for negotiation; there never was with him. I let the warm water fall on my back, steam swirling around me. It felt comforting, and it made me think of Maggie, her smile popping into my mind. I couldn't help but wish she was here with me. It might've been cramped, but the closer I was to her, the better.

Once I got myself out of the shower, I found myself lying on my mattress. I thought about some of the worst nights in my addiction that I could remember. I thought about how powerful I felt and how everything around me felt like it revolved around me. The outside world didn't matter; all that mattered was how I felt and what I wanted.

The risks that I took and the people's lives that I put in danger, I was lucky not to have lasting effects. The only health condition that I had to live with was my heart murmur, which was a minor one. Otherwise, I had not done any other damage to my body and never killed anyone.

I wondered if Maggie would have even talked to me or given me a look if she had met me then. I still looked the same, and I probably had more muscle now than I did then. Would she have given someone like me a chance? Would I have even looked in her direction? Would I have ever talked to her if I knew she was Calvin's sister? I closed my eyes and counted to ten, slowing the racing thoughts in my head.

I knew I was getting anxious because Calvin wanted to go out tonight. I was afraid to be triggered by something, but I couldn't let Calvin know about my fucked up past. I was already ashamed enough as it was, and now that Maggie knew, I felt like a fucking piece of shit walking the earth. Sometimes, I liked to think it would've been better if my heart never began beating again. I didn't have to live with the constant fear that I would relapse or that I would never be able to live again. I struggled more than I let on. The psychiatrist I saw at the hospital could see through my bullshit. I did everything I needed to do to prevent relapsing, but there was always that fear it would happen.

The rest of the afternoon, I began to walk around my house and figure out what the fuck I was going to do first. Every room in the home needed something. Whether a required wall was to be knocked down or painted, there was always something. The two bedrooms on the opposite side of the first floor once belonged to the kids who must've lived here. One room was purple with white flowers on the wall, and the other was baby blue.

Looking into both of those rooms, I tried to imagine growing up in a house like this. How different would my life be? Would my father not have gotten into the car drunk and died?

Would my sisters be different? Would I have still become a doctor? What if I had the childhood that these children had in this house?

Shaking my head, I decided to get dressed and head over to Calvin's place. I knew he had to be home by now, and I couldn't stay in the house much longer before the thoughts got to me. I threw on a T-shirt and some jeans and ruffled my hair around. It was as good as it was going to be.

The drive to Calvin's bachelor pad was not long. He lived on the fourth floor of an end unit with the best view of the lake. I pounded on the door; there was silence. Annoyed, I pounded harder, and that is when I finally heard footsteps. To my surprise, it wasn't Calvin who answered the door.

A beautiful blonde girl opened the door and smiled as she let me in. She was nude, with lovely breasts and a thick ass. She smirked at me as she walked back into the bedroom. Calvin came out a minute later in just shorts. He grinned as he came and sat down on the couch.

"You're here early."

"You seemed to have already started the party."

Calvin laughed, "Yeah, well, a long day at the hospital requires some of that."

I rolled my eyes. "You're such a jackass."

"And you love it."

Then the door pounded again. Groaning, Calvin got up and headed towards the door. I looked out the windows. The sky was clear, and the lake seemed to glisten in the sunlight. The whole living room and kitchen were completely surrounded by windows. Calvin's entire place was dark and light gray, looking more sterile than anything.

"What the fuck?" Calvin grumbled.

Sure enough, to my horror, Skyla James pushed by him. She clearly had just gotten done hiking. Then, to my second horror, Maggie Kensinger was right behind her.

"Oh good," Skyla said, "your bitch is here too."

Maggie remained with her head down. "Why are you both here?" Calvin moaned as he slammed the door.

"I got a call from Mom," Maggie said in a hushed voice.

I watched the blood drain from his face. "Why would she call you?" He snarled.

"Because you were too busy to answer her phone call," she snapped, her eyes puffy from crying.

Skyla had her eyes narrowed at me, clearly disapproving that I was there. "Let me guess," she said, "Carly, I think it is time for you to leave."

Calvin moaned, "Skyla,"

Before anything else happened, she went into the bedroom and grabbed who I assumed was Carly by the hair. She was still naked and crying out to let her go. Skyla wore a look of disgust and pleasure as she threw her out the door and slammed it shut.

"How did you know it was Carly?" Calvin said as he went into the kitchen and grabbed himself a bottle of water.

Skyla scoffed. "Please, you always run to Carly, the bartender, when you have the afternoon off."

Maggie leaned over to Skyla, "Little fucked that you know that." She whispered, and Skyla shot daggers at her.

"Why did she call you?" Calvin grumbled.

Maggie bit down on her lip. "I would rather discuss this without an audience." Finally, those blue eyes glanced over at me.

"Why don't you introduce Maggie to your friend?" Skyla said in a sweet voice.

Clearly, this was going to be a test. Maggie looked at me, unaware of how I was going to answer. I knew if I introduced myself like a stranger, there would be hurt in those eyes, and there would be no chance of ever seeing her again. On the other hand, Calvin would be hurt and pissed off.

The choice was easy, "I don't need an introduction," I narrowed my eyes at Skyla.

Calvin looked at me, stunned. "What do you mean you don't need an introduction?"

"Because I have already met Maggie," her face was unreadable, "more than a few times."

Skyla looked smug, and Calvin was now glaring at me, great. "How-"

"Calvin, we need to have this discussion. Anika is waiting for us to call her." Maggie's voice was sharp, cutting through the anger in Calvin's voice.

They both glared at each other, but eventually, Calvin led her out to the balcony and closed the door behind him. Maggie's body language was tense, and Calvin's was relaxed. She still glared at him as he spoke. I felt guilty watching them because there was sudden finger-pointing and yelling.

"Do you-" I started.

Skyla shook her head. "Don't bother; you won't get an answer from either of them."

"Should we be?"

"No," Skyla cut me off again, "and smooth, didn't think you would admit to it."

I glared at her, "Fuck you."

She smiled, and my eyes drifted back to Maggie and Calvin. We sat in silence for another ten minutes before they came back inside. Skyla had made herself comfortable on the couch while I stood tensely watching them on the balcony. What were they talking about? As they came in, Calvin clearly was shaken up, and Maggie once again was unreadable. Skyla stood up and asked Maggie if she was ready to leave, but Maggie paused and turned back around to her brother.

"You know what," she hissed, "just because I am not a doctor doesn't mean I can't have a say or input."

Calvin laughed, "I'm sure your knowledge of how to use scissors and glue will be beneficial here."

"He is still my father." She got close to his face. "I get to have an equal say."

Calvin spat in her face, "We don't want you here, he doesn't want you here, nobody wants you here." Maggie was wiping the spit from her face. "In fact, why don't you just take some pills and be gone?" He growled. "Not like anyone is going to miss you."

Skyla started towards him, and Maggie put her hand out to stop her. "You're right, Calvin," she began to laugh. "You're right, and you've won." She shook her head and looked up at him. "I'm done playing; you won. I will make sure that when I do take some pills, I will get the job done. Happy?"

Before anyone could do anything, Maggie walked away and out the door. Skyla hesitated before turning around and following Maggie out the door. Calvin turned to look at me, and I knew what decision I had to make.

I found myself walking away from my best friend to follow his sister out the door.

Chapter Eleven

The Repercussions

Maggie

While we were driving back from our hike, my mother called me. My father had a heart attack and was being treated in the VIP wing of the hospital. He was stable, but my uncle discovered a tumor in his heart. We were left with the choice to do surgery or to leave it because his dementia was deteriorating faster than we expected. My mother wanted us kids to decide what to do. Of course, that meant Anika and Calvin were going to choose.

Skyla drove me to Calvin's, and there was no way in hell she was going to let me go by myself. I was surprised at Calvin's initial reaction to my showing up on his doorstep. However, the thing I was most surprised by was the fact that Jackson admitted to knowing me. I was sure he was going to side with Calvin, but he didn't, and I had no idea how to feel about that.

I was almost all the way back to Skyla's car when I heard him call out my name. Once again, taking me by surprise, he chose me. I turned around, and sure enough, there was Jackson in the flesh. I glanced at Skyla, who seemed not to be phased by him. She kept walking to her car and sat on its hood, ready to watch how this was going to play out.

"What do you want?" I said a little harsher than I intended.

My tone didn't seem to bother him. "Please tell me that you didn't mean that." A confused look flashed on my face. "That you aren't going to get the job done."

I closed my eyes and glanced back at Skyla, "No, I don't mean that it's just what he wants to hear."

Jackson sighed, "Did you two go hiking?"

Skyla laughed, "Smooth way to change the subject."

I frowned at her, "Yeah, we're heading back home." I looked up and down at Jackson. "Going out?"

"I am assuming not anymore."

"Don't make this a choice between me and your best friend. It isn't fair, and I am not going to stand in the way of you two."

Jackson laughed and shook his head, "There isn't a choice, and quite frankly, if it were a choice, I would still choose you."

"Why?" I fired back. "I am just someone you met weeks ago, and he's been your best friend for God knows how long."

"Is that what you think I think of you as?"

I shook my head, "I am just saying, don't let me be the reason your friendship collapses."

Before I let him answer, I turned around, got into Skyla's car, and slammed the door. I pulled my knees to my chest and took some deep breaths before I watched us pull away from him.

Weeks went by, and the weather got cooler and cooler. The leaves were beginning to change color, and my students were getting excited for Halloween. Skyla was working longer hours at the hospital, and when she got home, she went right to sleep. I guess someone quit, so they were trying to find someone to replace them, but not fast enough.

Jackson hadn't called or attempted to come over. I spent my nights alone in my room, sleeping most of the time. Calvin and Anika had decided to have surgery to remove the tumor from my father's heart. He was now back at the private facility, responding well.

It was about a week before Halloween, one of my least favorite holidays. I just never got excited about it. My earliest memory is when I was three and got in trouble for putting Calvin in a chokehold. I had to stay home and hand out candy to everyone, and I was even forced to take my costume off. Another memory is when I got the stomach flu on Halloween when I was about seven and had to stay in my room while Calvin took care of me.

There were good memories, too, like the year I went as Sleeping Beauty, and my mom did my hair, and my dad spun me around like a princess. Calvin and I would sort out our candy and make trades with each other, but he would always gun for Hershey's while I gunned for Reese's.

When I got older, Halloween was more of a drinking and partying holiday. In high school, Skyla and I always had costumes, and we always went to the main party. Freshman year, it was Wonder Woman and Cat Woman; sophomore year, it was

Firefighters; junior year, it was Hermione Granger and Ginny Weasley from *Harry Potter*; and senior year, it was Jazzercise Girls.

Skyla was a fan of Halloween because one of her all-time favorite movies was *The Nightmare Before Christmas*. She was also into scary shit, so we would watch scary movies with dozens of candles burning. This was also the time of year when we did a massive Harry Potter marathon. In college, for the whole month of October, there was a party, and we did so many costumes, and we drank so much. As we age, there are no costumes or partying, just movies, bonfires, wine, and food. It was just part of growing up. Plus, this holiday was busy for the emergency departments everywhere.

A few days before Halloween, I found myself lying in my dark room. It had been a draining day at school, but the peace and quiet comforted me. I loved my job, but there were days like this when you felt like you had nothing left. These were the days that scared me the most because I was waiting to have a complete breakdown. So, on days like today, I did the one thing that comforted me: silence, especially since Skyla was working.

There was a knock on the front door, but I ignored it. Whoever it was, they would come back or just leave. I heard the knocking get harder, and finally, the use of the doorbell began. I put my pillow over my ears and closed my eyes, hoping it would go away. Sure enough, five minutes later, I came down the stairs and whipped open the front door to find my brother standing there.

I stared at him in disbelief. He clearly looked uncomfortable. "What do you want?"

"Can I come in?"

"Not before telling me what you want."

He rolled his eyes, "I came to talk to you," I raised my eyebrow, "about what happened."

I hesitated before I let him in and took him to the living room. He looked around, noting the pictures on the walls. He sat down on the far edge of the couch, and I sat at the other end, as far away from him as possible.

"Well?"

He took a deep breath. "First, I want to apologize for what I said. And no, Mom did not send me over here to do it. Second, I am sorry that I have criticized your career and who you are, and yes, Mom told me to say that."

I sat back, "But you still think what I do is a joke and that I am a crappy person?"

Calvin closed his eyes, "No, I don't think you're a crappy person, and no, your job is not a total joke."

"Thank you."

"However, I want you to tell me the truth."

I shot him a confused look, "Truth about what?"

He hesitated, "Skyla has always said if I knew even just a little bit of what has happened to you, I would understand."

"Why do you want to understand?"

Calvin shook his head, "Because Maggie, you're my little sister, and at the end of the day, whether I like it or not, I love you."

I placed my hand on my heart. "I am so touched," I said sarcastically.

He cracked a smile, "Fuck off," I smiled, "but I want to know what happened to you. I want to know why you felt the need to kill yourself or why you chose to stop studying medicine so quickly. I just assumed it was because you wanted to take the easy way out, but now something tells me there is more to the story."

"Okay," I said, pulling my knees to my chest. "If I agree to tell you, you can't freak out or tell anyone."

He rolled his eyes. "If you seriously want to do a pinky swear or an unbreakable vow from *Harry Potter*, be my guest."

I shook my head. "I'm not joking." Calvin sighed and nodded. " What answer do you want first?"

"Why did you stop studying medicine so quickly?"

Closing my eyes, "Because being raped and abused takes a toll on you, especially from someone you thought you could trust. That answer kind of fits the other question you had."

When I opened my eyes, the blood from his face had drained, and he looked sick to his stomach. I looked away, reminding myself to breathe and not relive moments. My fingertips brushed the inside of my thigh where the bite scars were. I kept counting to ten and back down, a technique that was given to me by my father when I was little and felt out of control.

"Stop doing the counting thing," Calvin mumbled, and I opened my eyes. "Why," he swallowed, "why didn't you say anything to anyone?"

"Who would've believed me?"

"I would've."

I scoffed, "No, the fuck you wouldn't. You worshiped Daniel and thought he was a God."

Calvin was clearly now uncomfortable. "Was it just a few times?"

I began to pick at my thumb, "Twice a day, on a good day, three or four on a bad."

"Maggie," he paused and closed his eyes, "why haven't you said anything to anyone?"

Biting down on the inside of my cheek, "Because he has photos and videos of when I was drugged, not fighting him off, and saying his name as if I liked it."

"So? That isn't enough to prove that it was consensual." He snapped back. "There has got to be another reason behind it."

"Because it would destroy Dad. It wouldn't do anyone any good. It is my problem to deal with, and it's been years now, so it doesn't matter. Plus, he's overseas anyway. He is not a threat to me."

Calvin shook his head. "Maggie,"

"Don't," I said. "I don't really need the apologies or the sad sappy shit."

He gave me a smile, "God, you're stubborn."

"I also have been told I am a great pain in the ass as well."

He rolled his eyes. "So, that is kind of what triggered everything else that followed?"

I shrugged, "That had to play a role. Then the whole family disowning me didn't help."

"That I can say I am sorry." He said and shook his head. "I hate to admit it, but if I had known, maybe I would've reacted differently."

"I'd rather know how you truly feel."

"That's the thing, I don't think your job is a joke. It is something that is so different from what anyone in our family has done. I think I was more jealous that you had the courage to defy the expectations."

"Thanks, it didn't come without its repercussions."

He smiled, "Now, on a more serious note, what's the deal with you and Calsen?"

I scrunch my face up, "Um, I would rather not discuss this kind of thing with my brother. And there isn't anything there; I haven't seen or heard from him in weeks."

"That's because he thinks you need space, dumbass."

"So, I take it you've talked to him."

"Not before I beat his ass."

"Calvin," I rolled my eyes, "not funny."

He smirked, "Either way, he's giving you space because he thinks it is what you want."

I shook my head, "I don't know what I want."

"Well, I would figure it out because I am getting sick of him looking like a lost puppy."

"How nice."

Calvin smiled and reached over and hugged me, something I hadn't experienced in a long time. "I understand." He whispered in my ear. "I'm sorry."

It took me less than ten minutes to find the house. It was barely on the outskirts of town, surrounded by tall evergreen trees. I knew that pulling up to someone's house at three in the morning wasn't the smartest thing, but I couldn't sleep.

Three days have passed since Calvin came to the house. Skyla didn't seem alarmed or suspicious about it. Something told me she had a part in making him come over and listen to me. She confirmed that Jackson had been miserable, not talking to anyone, and working at every chance he could. Skyla said he looked like shit, and she claimed it had to be because I vanished.

"I didn't vanish." I snapped, and she just shook her head and took a bite of cheesecake. "I didn't vanish," I mumbled.

Running on a few hours of sleep and drinking a fuck load of Red Bull to keep me functioning every day was not healthy. Staying in my room as much as I could every day was not healthy. Quite frankly, ignoring everyone, even Skyla at times, was not going to send me down the right path.

I had yet to determine if Jackson was going to be home or not. It took some pleading, but Calvin gave in and gave me his address. Skyla was fast asleep; if there were one person you did not want to wake up, that would be Skyla. I would rather face a bear in the fucking woods than her. She didn't get as much sleep, and she struggled to sleep, so when she was asleep, she wanted to stay asleep. So instead of poking the bear, I slipped out of the house and made my way to the outskirts of Bemidji.

It wasn't more than three miles from downtown, but far enough removed. The house looked dark as it should at three in the morning. The driveway was long, reminding me of my parents' home. I turned my headlights off so they wouldn't shine through the windows and stared at the house.

It was a faded white color, ranch style, with what seemed to be a lot of land. It was more private than I was expecting. It was all I could see in the pale moonlight, and the stars were shining brighter than the moon. There was no light pollution out here, and the sky was vast and clear. That was something I missed living in a big city; I never got to see billions of stars. Looking at the sky, it didn't seem real, like something from a painting or photograph.

I got out of my car, quietly closed my door, and walked up to the front deck, which was small and needed to be replaced. I hesitated; who knows how Jackson would react to a stranger in the night pounding on the door? He grew up in the ghetto of Los Angeles. I started to knock softly; there was no doorbell, and then I began to pound on the door.

Footsteps came, and the door swung open, and sure enough, Jackson was there. He was shirtless and in shorts, fuck did he have a nice body. His skin was smooth and had a faded tan. Jackson rubbed his eyes like a little kid. When it finally hit him that it was me standing there in baggy shorts and a zip-up hoodie, an unreadable expression crossed his face.

"Maggie? It is like three in the morning." He blinked a few times. "Is everything okay?"

"Yes and no. Can I come in, or do you have a girl over?"

He frowned, "Come in."

To my surprise, there was nothing in the living room. Nothing looked to be in the kitchen except a barstool. I could see the open door to the master bedroom, just a mattress on the floor, along with a TV. The house looked as if it had not been lived in at all. However, despite it not having anything in there, it felt cozy and warm.

"It's not much," he mumbled, clearly embarrassed. "I am supposed to start remodeling."

I turned and looked at him, "Look at you: a doctor and a handyman."

He rolled his eyes. "Hardly, I am considering paying someone to do it all."

"You shouldn't."

"Why? Are you some handywoman I don't know about?"

I laughed, "There are many things you don't know about me, Jackson Calsen."

"Why are you here, Maggie?"

I turned to look at him and said, "I wanted to see you, but I can gladly leave."

He shook his head, "I don't understand, I haven't seen you in weeks and-"

I pressed my lips against him while standing on my tippy toes. I pulled away and smiled at him. "I didn't think you wanted to see me, especially how bitchy I was."

Jackson's warm hand brushed my face. "God, Maggie Kensinger, you are so hard to figure out."

I chuckled, "I never said it was going to be easy."

He kissed my forehead, "Tell me what you want because if it is sleep, I will gladly go back to sleep."

I rolled my eyes. "Sleep is boring. I think I got something that is more entertaining."

Jackson picked me up, and I wrapped my legs around him. He carried me into the bedroom and laid me down gently. He pressed his lips against mine and sent chills down my spine as he slowly unzipped my jacket. He smiled as he could clearly feel I wasn't wearing a bra. His lips brushed along my neck, and he slowly took off my coat. The cold air from the room hit my chest, and I felt myself shivering. He smiled as his lips brushed against my breast, and I let out a tiny gasp.

Slowly, he pulled down my shorts, smirking at me when he realized I also had no underwear on. Kissing me slowly on the lips, his finger brushed my clit. In slow circles, he rubbed it, making my legs shake, and the more my legs shook, the faster he went. I cried out his name as he bit down on my lip.

I rolled on top of him, kissing his neck as he cradled me in his arms. I gently pushed him down as I brushed my fingers over his hardness. Taking off his shorts and boxers, I looked up at him, and I smirked before I took him in. He moaned my name as my tongue glided down his shaft. His fingers raked through my hair as I went deeper. My eyes locked on him while he was down my throat.

Gently, he pulled my face to his as he kissed me hard, as he rolled on top of me. His hands ran down my body, cupping what little ass I had. Jackson lowered himself between my legs, carefully kissing the scars on my inner thighs. His tongue felt incredible as I gasped. I bit down hard on my lip as he could tell how close I was; that only made him go faster. I cried out his name as I finished, his eyes locked on me.

Carefully, he pressed his lips against mine so I could taste myself. That is when he slowly guided himself inside me; he buried his face into my neck and groaned. He started to go slow and then started picking up the pace. I dug my nails into his back, crying for him to go faster. Gently nibbling at my ear, he thrust hard into me.

I slowly rolled to be on top, and he smiled at me. Leaning down to kiss him, he held me there as he pounded into me. I begged him to go harder, and he went slower. I whimpered as he cupped my face. He then carefully rolled me over and kissed the base of my neck as his movements began out slowly again. Then, without warning, he went faster and finished.

Jackson looked down at me, and his thumb brushed my bottom lip. I smiled as he carefully pulled me close to him, his body on fire. He kissed the top of my head while he traced circles along my arm.

"Better than a bottle of wine?" He whispered in my ear.

I smiled, "Mmmm."

It wasn't long before that I eventually drifted off into sleep, wrapped in the warmth of Jackson and some blankets.

Chapter Twelve

More to What Meets the Eye

Jackson

My mind was racing as I woke up to Maggie, who was fast asleep and curled up away from me. Her beautiful hair was a wild mess against the pillow, and her lips were parted just a little. Even fast asleep, she looked stunning, the morning sunlight reflecting off her pale skin. I brushed some hair from her face, and her eyes flashed open. Those eyes looked up at me as they shone in that sunlight.

She rolled over and stretched. I noticed the birds from her arm wrapped around her opposite hip. I pulled her close as she squeezed her eyes shut, moaning It's too early. I smiled and kissed the top of her head, not wanting to let go. She still smelled like lavender and vanilla, even in my house.

"What time is it?" She groaned into my chest.

"Six, for a teacher, I figured you would be a morning person."

She shot a glare at me. "There is something called Red Bull."

I smiled, "Well, you can stay sleeping. I've got to be at work."

Maggie rolled away to look up at me. "How long is your shift today?"

"I have a few surgeries today, and then I am on call tonight. So, basically, the next twenty-four hours."

She sat up, stretched, and reached to grab her shorts. Before she could get them, I pulled her back to me. "Hey," she gave me a playful glare, "you're the one who has to go to work."

"Yeah, not for another forty minutes." I kissed her lips, and I felt her hands slowly grip my hardness.

I rolled on top of her as she laughed. I began to kiss her down her neck, to her collarbone, and finally to her breasts. She quivered, body ready to go again. Everything about her was intoxicating, including her eyes, that smile, the sound of her laugh, and even the way she said my name. However, the way she tasted and her warmth were entirely different forms of intoxication. Every movement seemed natural, perfect.

My fingers brushed her clit, which was already wet. Her cheeks flushed as I slowly made my way down between her legs. She gasped as my tongue tasted her sweetness. Looking up at her fucking finishing in my mouth almost made me fucking cum.

The sun made her skin shine as I carefully kissed her, tasting her. Her bright blue eyes looked into mine as I slowly entered her. God damn, she was soaking wet, but she was so tight. I had to control myself because the minute I entered her last night, I swear I could've finished right there. At that moment, I didn't know if I was going to be able to control myself. Looking into her eyes as I thrust into her, there was no way I was going to last long. As she whimpered and moaned my name, I closed my eyes as I felt myself finishing so quickly.

Maggie smiled at me, and I felt my cheeks flush, embarrassed that I couldn't last any longer. "Sorry," I mumbled and rolled off her.

She sat up, a confused look on her face. "For what?"

I looked up at her, and she smiled down at me. The embarrassment faded away as she kissed me gently on the lips before rolling back over.

Although I barely made it to work on time, no one seemed to notice. I noted that Skyla was already in surgery, and Calvin only had one surgery on the surgery board. I was scheduled for two surgeries this morning and one this afternoon.

As I turned to start heading towards OR 1, Calvin was standing right there. He was in his scrubs and had a smug look on his face. He ran his hands through his perfectly messed-up hair and smiled at a nurse who was walking by.

I knew that Maggie and he had talked, but he didn't discuss what they had talked about. However, I knew damn well he was a lot more protective. Once Calvin realized that I had an interest in Maggie, he tried to give me the big brother's speech. It took everything in me not to laugh, knowing how she meant nothing to him.

"Someone looks happy." He said in a playful voice.

I rolled my eyes. "Let me remind you of this: your sister."

Calvin groaned, "Really? You had to put that image in my head."

"Yes!" I yelled out as I headed down to the OR.

"Fuck you!" Calvin fired back as he headed the opposite way.

My first surgery went by fast, and I had a decent break before my next one. I went down to the cafeteria and grabbed a coffee, which was the only thing I had at this point. While I was in line, I caught a few nurses watching me. I recognized a few of them as being some of Calvin's regular hook-ups. I wouldn't be shocked if there was a nurse who'd slept with him.

While I was heading into an on-call room to get a good power nap, I caught Skyla leaving an on-call room. Her cheeks were flushed, and scrubs seemed to be rushed on. There was this tiny smirk on her face as she cracked her neck and headed towards the stairwell, not even looking towards me. As soon as she had vanished down the stairs, Calvin fucking Kensinger came out.

I raised my eyebrow at him as he saw me standing there awkwardly. Panic rose in his eyes like he had just been caught doing something illegal. I was still too stunned to say anything at this point. From the moment I met Calvin, he referred to Skyla as the wicked witch of the north or bitch. They fought like cats and dogs and hated each other more than any two people could.

Calvin moaned, "It is not what you think."

I smirked, "Oh sure, it's not."

"Don't tell Maggie. Skyla still doesn't know how to feel about this."

"What do you mean by this?" I used air quotes.

Calvin's face flushed, "At this moment, you could say we're sleeping together, but we're not together."

"Since when?"

He sighed. "Not long after Maggie and she came in. She was part of the main reason I talked to Maggie. I decided to listen to Skyla and then look at what I was getting out of it."

I rolled my eyes. "You're disgusting. I don't even know why she would want to; you're a walking STD."

Calvin laughed and began heading down the stairs, "Who wouldn't want to fuck me?"

"Count me as one of them."

"Fuck you!" He yelled as I made my way into an empty on-call room.

It was hard trying to power nap, knowing that Skyla and Calvin were sleeping together. Knowing how close Skyla was to Maggie, it wouldn't be long until Maggie would pick up on it. All that I knew about Skyla was that she was not to be fucked with, and there wasn't a single person in the hospital who she liked or who wasn't scared of her. I am sure Chief Kensinger was intimidated by her; I know I was.

Maggie seemed to be the only person who was not ready to shit themselves when they saw Skyla, but Maggie was the only person Skyla seemed to like and care for. As much as she was a cold bitch, she was easily the best at what she did. I knew it, and so did everyone else.

After my pathetic power nap, my second surgery took a bit longer than I expected, but I was still done and out by one. I decided to check my phone; Maggie hadn't called or texted. I had no idea if she was still dead asleep in my sheets or if she had left to go back to her house. It was a Saturday, so I knew she didn't have to work. The image of her still wrapped in my sheets at home sent chills down my spine.

Halloween was only a couple of days away, and from that first night at Maggie's, I remembered her saying how much she hated this coming holiday. She was not a fan of the horror and shit that came with it. Skyla and she would go to haunted houses and get the shit scared out of them every time. The worst one was when Skyla pushed Maggie, and her shin banged onto the concrete stairs. They were running from a guy with a chainsaw. I guess another time, Maggie passed out from the smell of the gas and got a concussion.

By the time my third surgery was up, I met Calvin in the third-floor lounge again. He had finished his surgery and had done a few consults this afternoon. He had the night off, and he was pissed that I was on call. He was hoping we could go downtown. Even if I had the night off, going downtown with Calvin would not be my first choice. If I did have the night off, I would rather stay in and watch something; Maggie being with me would be a bonus. I was tired and just wanted to sleep more than anything.

As soon as I made it clear to Calvin that I was not going to trade shifts with someone just so we could go out, Calvin's pager went off. His face went pale, and he looked up at me. My pager hadn't gone off, but Calvin grabbed my arm and had me follow him. I didn't ask any questions as we rode the elevator to the chief's office. He looked just as pale and disturbed as Calvin. Clearly, something was going on, and I was not in the loop.

"How bad?" Calvin asked as we followed the Chief down the hall. "Any way we can stop them from coming through the pit?"

"No, they are almost here, and we can't risk it." Chief Kensinger said as we hopped onto another elevator. "You're going to have to be prepared."

As we headed to the pit, I was confused about what was happening. Calvin looked at me and mumbled, "I am sorry."

I hated the pit. There was always screaming and yelling, people on the phone, and doctors calling out orders. It was complete madness and chaos. It was always hard to hear anyone. I never could understand why people like Skyla loved it. But at that moment, everyone was frozen as the trauma doors opened and a girl on a gurney was restraining a man. She was bleeding from some shards of glass in her back.

"YOU UNGRATEFUL LITTLE SHIT!" The man screamed as the paramedics were trying to get him sedated.

The girl turned around, and my heart dropped. Maggie. Her one eye was already swollen, and she clearly had been hit. The man I now realized on the gurney was her father. She was holding her father down as he screamed and thrashed around. I was surprised at her strength in being able to hold him down. The paramedic was struggling to get the sedation in.

"Dad, stop, please." She whimpered as Calvin and the chief headed for them.

At the exact moment that they headed towards them, Maggie's father rammed his head into her, and she flew off the gurney, hitting the ground.

"68-year-old male, dementia patient at—"

"Yeah, we know, what happened?" Calvin grumbled as he helped his father get into restraints.

The female paramedic was flustered, "Apparently, he attacked his daughter; she refused to be treated and held her father down as he went in and out of consciousness, and his daughter performed chest compressions."

I raced down to Maggie, who was on the verge of passing out. She was barely holding herself up as her eyes followed her to where her father was. Her eye was now turning a dark shade of purple, and her hands were shaking uncontrollably.

It was then that her father went into cardiac arrest. Maggie let out this weak cry as the Chief began compressions, and Calvin called for a code blue. My fingertips brushed over her swollen eye as tears came down her face. They shocked Maggie's father, and Skyla slid down next to me. Maggie immediately clung to her for dear life as she watched her father get shocked again.

Calvin turned to look at me, and he finally got a good look at Maggie. For a second, you could see the flicker of pain, but then fear returned as he looked back at his father. There was a sudden pulse back, and orders shot out about going up to the OR. Calvin called out my name, but I looked back at Maggie, who was still bleeding.

"I've got her; she'll be okay." Maggie was fading in and out now, resting her head on Skyla's shoulder. "Go help her dad," Skyla whispered, "please."

Why was it so hard for me to walk away from Maggie? Jogging to catch up with Calvin and the Chief, I glanced back in agony as nurses placed Maggie on a gurney and Skyla began checking her pulse. I watched the elevator doors close, Maggie's eyes watching me. My focus went to Calvin, who was clutching his father's hand, while the Chief looked pained. What the hell happened? Dementia patient? Was this the reason Maggie had come back?

Before my mind could keep racing, we rushed onto the OR floor. The Chief was yelling at a surgical team to get scrubbed as scrub nurses took Maggie and Calvin's father into OR 3. That was when Calvin began hyperventilating. He sank to his knees, covering his face. That was when the extreme sobs started as the Chief stood outside the door, glaring inside.

They both knew better than to go in there. They couldn't do anything even if they wanted to—a huge rule: you never operate on your family and even friends. I was surprised that the Chief didn't try to push his way in, but from what I knew, he wasn't close with his brother. Either way, he still seemed bothered by everything he had just watched.

I scooted down next to Calvin, who wouldn't look at me, ashamed of crumbling to pieces. Sometimes, silence was the best medicine. The Chief's eyes didn't leave the door window, clearly focused. I don't know how long we sat there, Calvin sobbing into his hands, the Chief remaining frozen, and me staring at the opposite wall. We had to have been there a decent amount because I counted all the cinder blocks I could see on the wall.

The head of Cardio, Dr. Frazier, came out. "He's stable," she said, taken back to Calvin on the floor, "he's going up to the ICU; that's all I have for now."

The Chief grabbed Calvin, pulled him up, and told him to follow. Calvin's eyes were red, and you could clearly tell he was crying. I kept my head down and followed them both up to the Chief's office. The silence got my head thinking again. Dementia patient? That is what the paramedic said. Then I remembered Maggie saying something about having to return home after all these years, and it was because her dad was sick. Why didn't she tell me? Why didn't Calvin say anything? Skyla? Why had no one said anything about this?

When I entered the office, Skyla was sitting on the couch with Maggie, who was conscious. Maggie had an ice pack on her eye and looked eagerly at me, waiting for news or something.

"He's stable." I finally said, disappointed I didn't have more.

Maggie collapsed back into a lying position on the couch as she let out a huge sigh. Her hair had blood stains in it, and there was evident swelling where she had been hit in the head. I would like to say she looked okay, but she looked like hell. I glanced over to Skyla, who gave me a nod of encouragement that she was okay physically.

"What the hell happened?" Maggie and Calvin's mom came bursting through the door.

Julia Kensinger looked disheveled. Her shirt was on backward, her hair half-done, and her makeup was on one eye. Whenever she had received the news, she had been getting ready to go somewhere. As she scanned the room, her eyes zeroed in on Maggie.

"Maggie," her voice broke as she kneeled beside the couch. "What happened?" I watched her eyes go over to Skyla. "Is she okay?"

Skyla nodded, "Head CT was clear, and so was the MRI. I gave her a few stitches from where the glass got into her back, but she's fine."

Julia smiled at Skyla and squeezed Maggie's hand. "Honey, can you tell me what happened to you guys?"

"I went to see him as planned. He wasn't lucid until I was getting ready to leave." She squeezed her hand into a fist. "He saw me, freaked out, and shoved me into the wall where some pictures were hanging. He then collapsed, and I began chest compressions, and it wasn't long until paramedics came." Her eyes remained on her hands, and she avoided looking at anyone.

Julia closed her eyes as a few tears slid down her face. "Honey, your uncle said you refused to be treated by the paramedics."

"I wasn't going to let them fuck up taking care of dad." Maggie fired back. "They didn't know that he had a tumor on his heart. They didn't know his dementia status! All they see is a body, a John Doe." She finally narrowed her eyes on Calvin. "Contrary to everyone's beliefs, I know how to do CPR, or what to do with seizures, or even how to handle someone with dementia. Just because I chose to be a teacher doesn't mean I don't remember the things Mom, Dad, and even fucking Daniel taught me."

Ice went through my veins at the mention of Daniel's name. Skyla gripped Maggie's hand, and Calvin lost whatever color he had left in his face. Julia gave her daughter a sad look and pulled her into a hug. Calvin turned away and ran his hand through his hair. That was when Chief Kensinger came in, his face very pale.

"Julia," Chief Kensinger embraced her in a hug, "he's stable. However, there is a new tumor on his lungs." Everyone was silent as they processed the information. "His dementia has deteriorated much faster than we expected."

Calvin turned around, "We're not opening him back up. He can't handle that, and if it is already spreading this fast, why put him through the misery of chemo?"

I kneeled beside Maggie, whose head had to be spinning. She looked over at me, her eyes bruised and swollen, yet the blue was still stunning. Curling her lip, she looked back down at her hands and began to pick at the side of her thumb. Skyla was watching me closely; I could feel the glare.

Julia narrowed her eyes at Calvin, "You were the one who wanted to open him up in the first place!"

"Because I thought he had better chances of living!"

"What he is doing is not living," Maggie whispered so softly I could barely hear her. "This isn't living."

"Once he's stable, let him decide." Calvin spat at his mother.

"Once he's stable?" Maggie yelled and stood up. "He's never going to be stable! He doesn't know where he is! Doesn't know you or Mom! Jesus Christ, he doesn't even know who he is! He's not living, he isn't there anymore." Both her mother and Calvin looked over at her. "Skip the chemo and let him live out his life in that stupid facility; he's gone and has been gone. You two just must buck up and face reality."

I watched Julia break down into tears. Calvin left, slamming the door behind him. The Chief grabbed Julia, who was now uncontrollably sobbing. Skyla helped Maggie sit back down, holding her hand tightly.

Maggie sighed and rested her head on Skyla's shoulder and said, "I want to go home. I want to go."

After pleading with Greg, the other general surgeon fellow, I got my on-call shift switched for tomorrow. I showered and got dressed at the hospital, my mind still racing with everything that had happened. Why hadn't Maggie told me? Better yet, why did Calvin not say anything? Why did it seem to be some big ass secret? Mitch Kensinger was dying; it wasn't something to be ashamed of. Dementia was a very common illness, a cruel one, but common enough.

Thinking back on the exchange between the Kensingers, Maggie was right. With as rapid as dementia was taking over, there was no point in putting her dad through all that chemo. As she said, he's gone and has been gone. Everything made sense then: why she had to return home and why she and Calvin had to be on the phone with Anika. It all came back to the fact that their father was diminishing before their eyes, and no one knew what they could do. I then thought back to the night I met Maggie at the bar, she was clearly crying and drunk, was it because of her dad? Had that been one of the first times she saw him? Was he lucid then?

Skyla took Maggie home hours ago. There was no chance of separating those two, not with Maggie vulnerable. I wasn't going to push and insist I take her; I knew she needed to be with her best friend, but it made me wonder if Skyla knew about this. There was no way she didn't know; those two knew each other inside out.

When I got to their house, I took note that Calvin's car was in the driveway. I parked on the side of the road and knocked on the front door. Skyla answered the door. She was dressed in sweats and a sports bra; her hair was a mess. Her eyes had smeared makeup on them, and she had been crying. Without asking any questions, she gestured me into the house. I made my way towards the kitchen and living room, hoping to see Maggie, but Calvin was the only one there.

"She's been asleep for the last thirty minutes," Skyla said as she brushed by me and sat down on the kitchen counter. "I've been checking in on her every ten minutes, and she is so cranky that I keep waking her up."

Calvin was sitting on the couch, staring at the coffee table, ignoring the beer that was in his hand. "Did you know?" I looked at Skyla. "Did you know about any of it?"

She shook her head and took a drink from her water bottle beside her. "I figured something must've been up, but no, neither of them told me." For whatever reason, it made me feel better that she didn't know.

"We didn't have a choice," Calvin mumbled. "Dad made us sign shit, and we legally could not tell anyone." He shook his head and took a long drink from his beer. "Don't get mad at her; she didn't have a choice, and neither did I. None of us did. Fuck, mom didn't have a choice when it came to the divorce." Calvin downed the rest of the beer. "He's always been in control, and it keeps being that way."

Skyla shot me a sad look and said, "You can go up there. It would probably be better than her seeing me again." She tried to joke, but no one smiled or laughed, not even Skyla.

I hesitated before going up the stairs and turning right toward what I assumed was Maggie's room. The door was cracked, and I could smell the vanilla and lavender from the staircase. I slipped in, trying not to let the light from the hallway fill the room. I carefully closed the door and adjusted my eyes to the darkness around me.

There Maggie lay, curled up with a green blanket. She clearly had showered; her hair was wet. The room was lit only by candles, one being on the nightstand, two on her dresser, and one on her desk. They all smelled the same: lavender and vanilla. There was a TV mounted on the wall that faced the bed with two windows on either side, covered by see-through black curtains. There was a bookcase to the left of it, filled with books, some of which were piled over on the floor. Her desk had her computer, fake greenery, sticky notes, a bulletin board with cards and pictures, and a picture of Skyla framed to the side of the desk.

There were framed posters of her favorite TV shows or movies on the walls. On her nightstand was a lamp, a photo of her with her parents, and a small one of Calvin and Anika hugging Maggie. Her closet was open, and everything seemed to be put away neatly. Above her bed was a blue and gray tapestry that seemed to tie the whole room together.

I sat down on her bed, and her eyes fluttered open. She was in a daze, clearly unaware of what was going on. It took her a minute to get up, and she gave me a sad look as she carefully sat up. She was wearing a sports bra and spandex.

"If you're here to yell or be upset that I didn't tell you, there's the door, and leave."

"That is not why I am here." Offended that everyone seemed to think I was going to get pissed off. "Calvin explained, and I understand it also wasn't your story to tell."

She rested her head back, "How is it that everything in this world is just a fucking mess?"

"I wouldn't say everything is a mess, Maggie."

"Really?" She turned and looked at me, candlelight exposing the bruising around her eye. "Jackson, my life is a mess, and it has been since day one. I've seen and done shit that I am not proud of, and it haunts me. I have destroyed everything around me, so I won't get hurt. My father is dying, whether anyone wants to admit it or not. My best friend is screwing my brother. The world is just a fucked place. And you," she threw her hands up in the air, "I don't know."

I watched as her eyes avoided mine, and she looked down at her shaking hands. Without thinking, I grabbed her hands, which were freezing. She looked over at me, clearly trying her best to hold back any tears or emotion.

"Maggie," she took a deep breath, "I love you. You are easily the strongest person I know. You have dealt with shit, and instead of letting it hold you back, you have driven yourself forward. We have all done fucked up shit, and everyone has demons." Her expression was unreadable. "You have held others up when you could barely hold yourself up. You may think you're a mess, but I think it is a beautiful, broken mess.

You may be broken, but you are unbelievably strong. Don't let one word take away everything; don't let it have that power." The corners of her mouth twitched, her hands still shaking in mine. "You can be strong and broken all together; just remember there is more to you than just words." I squeezed her hand, gently. "I'm going to let you rest. I'll come by later to see how you're feeling."

Without waiting for a response, I let go of her hands and walked away and out the door. I didn't want to hear what she had to say; I was scared shitless.

That was the most honest and purest thing I had ever said, and I was too much of a coward to hear the response.

Chapter Thirteen

That Isn't How It Goes

Maggie

It wasn't hard to guess that Skyla and Calvin were fucking, I knew she had a role in his coming to talk to me. Plus, it was a matter of time before he realized he had a thing for her. I knew she was never keen on him, but she was the only one who could handle his shit and put him in his place. Did I like the idea? No. Did I know it was going to happen? Yes. Did I think Skyla was happy? I did. It was the first time she had been with someone other than Bentley, and I knew she wasn't just going and diving in with my brother if it wasn't for a reason. The reason was that he drove her crazy, and she liked that.

On the car ride back from the hospital, I gave her a brief rundown of everything with my father. Then I asked her about Calvin, and she admitted it. I wasn't mad. Instead, I asked her how it happened, and for a rare time, she got all flustered and giggly. One thing to know: Skyla was never one to start giggling over a boy, let alone get all red in the face. It made me happy to see that rare side.

When Jackson got up and left, I just stared at the door, still processing everything. First, you can't say something like that, so just walk away. Second, his words hit harder than I expected. He was right—don't let one word control everything. But my mind kept going back to: *I love you.* And once again, he left without giving me a chance to say anything.

Pissed off, I threw on a t-shirt and headed downstairs. Calvin was sitting on our couch, sulking. Skyla was in the kitchen making herself something to eat.

"I am going out."

She turned and looked at me, "No, the fuck you aren't."

"He can't just say the shit he said and leave!" I yelled at her. "That is not how it works."

Confusion crossed her face. "What shit did he say?"

I huffed, "Shit, about being broken and not letting it define you. Oh, and that he loves me."

Calvin gagged on his beer; Skyla dropped the fork that was in her hand. They both turned to look at me: "What?" They said in unison.

I rolled my eyes. "If you aren't going to drive me, then I am walking."

"Maggie, don't be a dumbass," Calvin grumbled from the couch. "Skyla will take you."

She shot him a dirty look before nodding and sliding on her boots. I followed behind her in my boots while Calvin casually waved us goodbye.

Once we got into the car, she looked at me. "He really said he loved you?"

"Drive," I instructed, "and yes, it took me a minute, but that is exactly what he said. Along with some poetic shit as well."

She threw a smirk at me as we moved around Calvin's car and out onto the road. "I can't say that I didn't see it coming."

"Could say the same about you and Calvin."

She laughed, "The difference there is he doesn't love me." She exaggerated the word love.

I rolled my eyes and smiled at her, "Yeah, just because he said he loved me doesn't mean everything is perfect. I mean, he left without giving me a chance to even respond."

"Jackass," Skyla mumbled.

I turned and smiled at her, "All boys are jackasses."

Once Skyla drove off, I made my way up to the door. It was cold out, easily in the low forties. It was a clear sky, and you could see more stars outside the city. For a minute, I let myself watch them, remembering the times Mom would use her telescope to show us the stars. She always said that in another life, she would've been an astronomer. Man, she loved that telescope. I swear she would be out on the back deck in every kind of weather there was, even in the brutal cold.

I hurried up the porch and banged on the door. I was pissed and cold, a combination that was not pretty. Nor was it a combination I wanted to be, especially with my head ringing. I kept banging and yelling Jackson's name before he whipped open the door.

"Maggie, how the hell did you get here?"

"I walked." I said sarcastically, and his eyes narrowed, "Skyla drove me, you dumbass. That is beside the point. You don't just get to say that shit and leave." I yelled. "You just don't tell someone you love them and not give them a chance to respond."

He could clearly see that I was shivering. "Maggie, come inside."

"No," I snapped. "This isn't how this is going to work. You don't get to run away and not give me a chance to talk. I have every right to have a chance."

"Okay," he said slowly, "but come inside, it's fucking cold out."

"No," I snapped again, "even though I am pissed off and cold, I love you too." I probably could have toned down the anger in my voice. "I love you, even though you walk away and don't give me a chance to speak."

I watched a smile spread across his face. "Now, will you come inside?"

"Yes," I huffed and brushed past him.

He laughed, "You drive me insane, you know that?"

"That's part of the charm of getting me."

Jackson pulled me into a hug: "God, you're freezing."

"If someone hadn't left, I wouldn't be."

He chuckled, grabbed my hand, and led me to his bedroom. The TV was on, and there was an NBA basketball game on. I curled up on the bed and wrapped myself in one of the blankets. I felt Jackson's thumb brush below my bruised eye. I looked back up and gave him a weak smile, feeling light-headed from the extreme warmth.

"If you think I look bad, you should look at the other guy," I mumbled as I closed my eyes.

Jackson laughed, "Alright, I am grabbing you some water, and you need to sleep."

I made a pouty face: "I don't want to sleep."

He rolled his eyes, "As much as I would love to fuck the shit out of you, I am not going to. You have a concussion and stitches on your back."

"Why do you have to be such a doctor?" I teased and carefully watched the TV. "Do you even know who is playing?"

My eyes followed him as he got up and made his way to the kitchen. He was in his boxers and a sweatshirt. "No, honestly, put it on to fall asleep." Jackson came back into the room with a bottle of water. "Now, seriously, go to sleep." He said as he settled down next to me.

I sighed in defeat, "You're lost, Calsen."

"Goodnight, Maggie."

Glancing at him again, I laid my head down and drifted off into a much-needed sleep.

Over the next few weeks, my bruising was going away nicely, and my stitches got to come out. Skyla had made a few deals to be home with me more on the weekends, because she was still nervous about my concussion. She insisted that I had to be driven to work and picked up, just like all my students. My students thought it was so cool that I had a black eye. I simply told them I had fallen off a ladder while putting away Halloween decorations.

My mother had visited our house, checking up on me and getting more details about what was happening between Jackson and me. I didn't even bother to mention Calvin and Skyla being an item. She would freak out or be disgusted, and I would not know.

Jackson was busy working, finding all the time he could to be with me, who was homebound because of her best friend. The hospital was getting busier because the Thanksgiving holiday was coming up. Skyla worked all week to have Friday night and Saturday off. By the third week of being babied, I convinced her that I was fine and that she could go back to working regular hours.

Calvin seemed to be at the house more often now, probably because Skyla was always here. He hadn't gone to see Dad, who had been discharged a week ago from the hospital. I planned on going to see him before Thanksgiving, but any time I brought up the idea to anyone, they didn't want me to go alone. Once I got my driving privileges back, that was the first thing I was going to do.

What had happened that day was mostly a blur. My father had gotten upset because he realized who I was, and then became aggressive and shoved me into the wall of pictures he had. While on the ground, he kicked me perfectly in the eye. Then, as soon as he realized what he had done, he began crying and pleading to make everything stop. Then it wasn't long until he collapsed, and from there on out, I don't remember much.

From my understanding, my father had been placed on some sort of medication to help with the seizures and another medication to help with the pain in his chest. My mother pretty much went to see him every day, but I knew she wasn't ready to let go of him yet. I know it was hard for us kids to see our father diminish, but my mother was watching her partner and love of her life diminish, and there was nothing she could do except watch it happen.

Anika was going to be home for Thanksgiving, so my mom was making a big dinner for us. Skyla and Jackson had the day off, and Calvin was going to be on call. Of course, our uncle declined to come for dinner, probably was going to be at the hospital the whole day. My uncle loved my mother, but butted heads with my father, but also with Anika. Those two would find some way to pick a fight. I don't know why she hated our uncle; I never could get a clear answer to that.

Lucky for me, we had the whole week of Thanksgiving off from school. I had also convinced everyone around me that I was good and didn't need a babysitter. So, this gave me the perfect chance to go and see my dad. I wanted to see him because I knew he didn't have much time left. I also wanted to see if he would remember anything, which was a long shot. As I stated before, my dad was long gone; all that was left was a body that looked like him.

It felt amazing to finally drive; you never really know how much something could mean for you until it is taken away. I was no longer bound to have someone cart me around; I had the freedom to leave and arrive whenever I wanted.

As I pulled into the parking lot, I took note that they had already decorated for the holidays. My dad had always loved the holidays because it was one of the few times we all could be together, and neither he nor my mom had to be on-call. Of course, for all that I knew, that had changed. I had spoken three words to him since my freshman year in college, when he was diagnosed last year. Even then, there weren't a whole bunch of words exchanged there either.

My father had been moved to a different room, with fewer breakable things and fewer pictures. He was sitting in a chair, staring out at the lake. It had already gotten so cold that students from the university were parking on it. You could even see where some people had already begun to ice fish. My family had never been big into fishing, so we all never understood the hype for fishing in general. People around here loved it; you would see the huts for ice fishing on the lake.

There was a glazed overlook in my dad's eyes as I sat down next to him. He didn't even bother turning my way; he was too focused on the lake and everything going down there. There weren't very many tourists this time of year, too cold for a lot, or just not interesting enough.

"Hey, Dad," I said, my voice a little shaky. "It's me, Maggie." He turned and looked at me, but there was no recognition whatsoever. "I forgive you," I whispered. "I forgive you for everything."

"Did I hurt you?"

Biting down on my lip, I nodded my head. "It was an accident."

"Do, do you know that I was a doctor once? I used to be married and had kids."

I smiled, "Could you tell me about your family?"

His eyes lit up, and he sat up. "I had the most wonderful wife. She was very beautiful, and I don't know what happened to her." Confusion crossed his face, but he shook his head. "Then I had a wonderful son: Calvin! He wanted to be just like me, and he reminded me of me when I was his age. Oh, and then there were my daughters, Anika and Maggie! Anika was a surprise, a great one. Maggie was the one child I could not understand; she was so unlike the rest of us."

"They all sound very wonderful." I felt tears forming in my eyes. "I bet they come and visit you often."

He looked over at me, recognition flared in his eyes. "Maggie?" Bracing myself for the cruel words or violent actions was going to be. "Maggie, why am I here?"

"You're sick, Dad. You're sick and being taken care of."

"I don't, I don't know." He started to get upset, tears rolling down his cheeks. "I can't be here, I can't."

I reached over and grabbed his hands as they were shaking uncontrollably. "Dad," I whispered, and he looked into my eyes, "everything is going to be okay."

My dad reached out and brushed some hair out of my face. "You look just like your mother." He smiled down at me and cupped my face. "I am glad you're here with me, Maggie."

I started to sob, "Oh God, Dad, I am sorry."

With a sudden movement, his hand was gone, and his face was confused. "Who are you? Who am I?"

Tears were rolling down my face. "Your name is Mitch Kensinger. My name is Maggie."

He sat back with wonder, "Where am I?"

"You're in Bemidji, Dad."

My father looked down at me. "Dad?"

I nodded, "Yes, I am your daughter, Maggie Kensinger."

There was still confusion on his face, "Was I a good dad?"

I closed my eyes. "You were good until I decided to be different and not become a doctor."

"Why would I be upset that you didn't want to become a doctor?"

I shrugged, "Because that is what our family is: doctors."

He shook his head, "I must not have been a good dad." He sounded defeated. "I, I wasn't a good dad because Maggie has never come to see me."

I reached out and grabbed his hand. "It's me, Dad. I am Maggie. I am right here."

There was a flicker of recognition before he looked away and out at the water. "The world is a cruel place," he glanced at me, a gloss over his eyes, "are you the nurse?"

Shaking my head, I squeezed his hand one more time. "I love you, Dad, even if you can't hear me."

As I walked toward the door, I paused, looked at him, and left. I finally let out a huge breath, and the tears started falling. I sank against the wall and pressed my hands against my face, letting the tears pile onto my cold hands.

To keep my mind busy and off what had happened with my dad, I decided to focus on Thanksgiving. I was sitting at the kitchen table, staring down at some pie recipes to make. I promised my mother that I would bring at least a pie over, one that wasn't pumpkin. I had gotten back from seeing my dad an hour ago, and all I could feel was his hand on the side of my face.

My dad hadn't always been so cruel. For my sixth birthday, he got me a pair of ice skates. Then, after everyone had gone to sleep, he snuck me out of the house and went to pound in the backyard. It was so cold, and there was at least a foot of snow on the ground. That night, he taught me how to skate. I fell so many times, and I cried and complained that it was too hard. That didn't stop him, and I eventually was able to skate around without needing his support. Then came the problem of mom coming out and yelling to get back inside, and did we know what time it was?

When I was eleven, I was mad because out on the playground, Jimmy Keller did a sick crossover move in basketball and made me fall, looking like an idiot. I came over, threw my bag on the ground, and yelled at my dad about it. He grabbed a basketball and told me to get my ass out there. We were going to learn how to do that and how to one-up Jimmy Keller. I gladly did, and I embarrassed Jimmy for all the years to come.

Some memories like that burned as I thought of them. I wondered how many memories I missed because I was afraid to tell my dad the truth. I asked myself if he would've ever gotten sick and how much extra time we would've had together.

Skyla kicked open the garage door, interrupting my thoughts. Her hair was in two crazy braids, and her cheeks were flushed. She threw her backpack on the ground, groaned, and slid across the table from me. Then, she put her head down and banged her fist on the table.

"Order, order!" I cried out. "The court is now in session."

Her eyes locked on mine, pissed. "Shut the fuck up." And then she put her head down and began banging all over again.

I rolled my eyes. "What did he do?"

"Who said it was he?" Her voice was muffled.

"Because if it had been some bitch, you would've already taken care of it. Clearly, Calvin fucked up."

She glanced up and smirked, "You know me too well."

"Don't leave me hanging, what did he do?"

Skyla sat up and leaned over to me. "Men are dumb. Men are worthless. Men are scums."

"Girl, this was like lesson one from the great Skyla James's rules of life."

"Yes, and your brother is the biggest asshole there was."

I shrugged. "You already knew that before getting involved in whatever you two are doing."

She moaned, "Can you just say yes?"

"I'll do you one better." I grabbed my phone and connected it to the speaker. "I bet Arvil Lavigne will cheer you right up." I began to play *What the Hell* by her.

Skyla was glaring at me, but you could see the hint of a smile that was forming in the corners of her mouth.

"You say that I'm messing with your head," I sang and stood up and grabbed a ladle from beside the stove, "All cause I was making out with your friend," Skyla rolled her eyes at me, "love hurts whether it's right or wrong." I got up on the counter. "I can't stop cause I'm having too much fun," I had to easily be the worst singer in history, "you're on your knees begging, please stay with me, but honestly, I just need to be a little crazy,"

In unison, Skyla and I sang this song at the top of our lungs, dancing around in the kitchen. We must've looked like idiots, but who cared? We were having too much fun. In moments like this, you forget the outside world. You forget all the critics. You forget the problems that cling to you. In moments like this, you feel a surge of adrenaline rush. You don't want it to stop. The feeling of being on a natural high felt terrific, so free.

Over the next hour, Skyla and I went through our clothes and picked out outfits to go downtown. Skyla then did both our hair and makeup, because there was no way you should let me try to do my own. In that time, we listened to various pop and rap songs, laughing and singing along. We then called an Uber to take us downtown because we were in the mood to get fucked up. Our poor Uber driver had to hear Skyla go on about something stupid my brother did, and then she proceeded to tell him he was just as fucked up as my brother because he was a boy. I tipped him more than twenty percent.

It was a little strange going out downtown here in Bemidji for two reasons. One being that we grew up here, so it was weird to transition to this age. Two, back in Colorado, we lived in way bigger cities with way more variety. There was one row of bars that was usually packed, and it didn't matter if students were here for college or not.

We decided we were going straight to the main bar. A lot of college kids loved it. By the time we got up to the bar, different guys had bought three rounds of shots for us. We took them all at once and found ourselves nursing a beer while we went out onto the dance floor with a sea of people, but Skyla was holding onto my hand tightly so we wouldn't drift apart. Never leave your wing-woman, Mom used to tell me.

At that moment, everything felt fuzzy, and all the pain and shit that were happening in life didn't matter. For once, I could be a girl in a club, a girl dancing without a name, a girl who was with her best friend, coping with our fucked-up lives with alcohol.

Chapter Fourteen

Oh Fuck

Jackson

Maggie hadn't picked up her phone in the last couple of hours. I wanted to check and see how she was doing. Skyla had left hours ago, and Calvin was still at the hospital. I made my way to the attending lounge on the third floor. Sure enough, there he was, looking pissed at his phone.

He glanced and looked up at me. "Good, you're here." He shoved his phone in his pocket. "Have you been able to talk to Maggie?"

"Uh, no. I was coming to see if you had talked to Skyla." I said uncomfortably.

Calvin moaned, "Fuck," he ran his hand through his hair, "I pissed Skyla off, and Maggie went to see our dad."

My heart jolted for a second, images from the day Maggie came into the hospital, trying her best to hold her dad down, the glass in her back, and the black eye.

"How did you-"

Calvin grabbed my arm. "We've got to go."

"What did-"

"Shut up and follow me."

This is where you could easily say I was his bitch boy. I followed him down to the elevator, not asking questions. A few nurses hopped on and off as we rode down to the parking garage, and they all gave smug looks to Calvin. One gave me a smile and a wink. She was cute, and I'm pretty sure she was a scrub nurse. Once we were down in the parking garage and Calvin's Range Rover, that is when he started to ramble on.

"Mom called me, chewing my ass because Maggie has gone to see our dad more than I have. She went on to remind me about how we might not have much time with Dad, and I needed to make time to go and see him." He whipped out of the garage and sped off towards the main road. "Then after that phone call, I ignored Skyla's pages, thinking she just wanted to fuck in between a surgery, turns out, I was needed down in the pit." He groaned and slammed on his brakes at the stoplight. "Once I got down there, she had suspected that he was brain-dead. Now, instead of me coming and saving the dude, she needed me to confirm brain death.

"She then proceeded to scream and yell at me about how I needed to get my head out of my ass and accept the fact that my father was dying, but that didn't give me a pass to ignore and do what I wanted. She then got in my face and yelled at me some more about being some jackass, and it should have been me brain dead, not the twenty-one-year-old man on the table."

That was a lot to take in at once. I was more focused on the part where Maggie had gone to see her dad. We all told her that it wasn't the best idea to go there alone, but everything seemed to have gone fine, especially since Julia knew that Maggie had gone to see him. Now the real question was: was Calvin upset he had killed someone, or that he had pissed Skyla off?

"I take it, she's not responding to you."

Calvin groaned, "I can't even get a hold of Maggie either." He chuckled to himself. "I know exactly where they are, too."

"Where?"

Calvin turned towards downtown and up the road to where the bars and clubs were. "When Skyla gets pissed, she runs to Maggie. When Maggie gets pissed, she runs to Skyla. When they are both pissed, they drink their feelings away."

I threw him a skeptical look, "I mean, how do you know that is what they do for sure?"

"One, because that is what Skyla told me word for word. Two, because that is how our family functions, and I would not put it past Maggie to do the same shit I do."

Calvin went around the block and found a parking space. I looked down at what I was wearing: shorts and a T-shirt. It wasn't bad if it wasn't twenty degrees out. It had yet to snow, but it was coming, and everything around had sensed it was coming too.

"How do you know where they are even at?" I questioned him as Calvin locked the car. "You're telling me, we're going to have to go to each of these places?"

He rolled his eyes. "No, they are at the bar with the most activity, I think." I threw him a skeptical look. "Fine, Skyla had posted something about them being at this bar."

I rolled my eyes and followed him down the street and up the stairs into the club. It was very dim and warm as we got our IDs checked. It was crowded, but I figured the night before Thanksgiving was a big day to go drinking. Or at least that is what we doctors assumed from the injuries we would get these nights.

The music was loud, and there seemed to be more men than women. I followed Calvin as he made his way towards the bar. A few college girls passed by, smiling at us. One of them dropped something on purpose, bending down with her back to me, then glanced over her shoulder. I gave a tight smile as Calvin and I reached the bar.

"Fuck," Calvin grumbled, and I was amazed to have heard that.

Following his eyes, I saw her right away. There she was, a tight black skirt, strappy heels, and a silver strapless shirt that complemented her breasts being pushed up from her bra. Her hair was curled in perfect, bouncy curls. Holding hands with her, Skyla was dressed in a form-fitting strapless romper. Her long hair was pulled into a ponytail and curled.

Maggie looked over towards the bar; she was wearing red lipstick and heavy eye makeup. Her body swayed to the song *The Color Violet*. Her hand was tightly gripping Skyla's, while her other hand nursed a bottle of beer. She looked carefree, her body relaxed, and a small smile on her face.

It was then that I noticed two guys approaching them. They both wore smug looks on their faces. They exchanged a few words before the guys headed towards the bar. A shot of jealousy went through my spine. The idea of someone touching her, making her legs shake, and those eyes looking up at someone else bothers me. I took this as my chance, and I headed towards them on the dance floor.

Right before I reached her, Maggie turned in my direction. She smiled, oh fuck, and she let go of Skyla's hand and held it out for me. Ignoring her hand, I stepped forward, grabbed the back of her neck, and began to kiss her. In all the noise, I was able to hear her gasp as my lips carefully brushed the side of her neck and back to her lips.

Beside us, Skyla's eyes were narrowed on Calvin, who just shook his head at her. He leaned in and said something to her, and she shot him a dirty look before letting him kiss her. Skyla glanced over at us and gestured with her head towards the pool tables.

"How did you know where we were?" Maggie asked in my ear as I refused to let go of her hand.

I looked over at Calvin, "Intuition, I suppose."

Maggie looked at her brother and just shook her head. I squeezed her hand tightly as I walked in front of her, shielding her from bodies. As we walked, her head remained down, afraid to meet the eyes of others. Even with her head bowed, she was able to turn heads. Once we got over to the pool tables, she smiled and went over to help Skyla convince a pair of guys to let them play against them. Calvin and I settled into one of the tables nearby. My eyes followed Maggie, and I was aware of the looks they gave not only Maggie but Skyla as well.

"She's still pissed, isn't she?" I said it was easier to talk to him as the music wasn't quite as loud.

"Oh, yeah." Calvin laughed. "She's also trashed, so she's not nearly as bitchy."

Calvin either was not aware of the looks the girls were getting or he trusted that they could take care of themselves. He grabbed a couple of beers in the sea of people, as I watched Skyla rack up the balls. The two guys were clearly in college; one had dark hair and the other had lighter hair. One of them was dressed in jeans and a flannel, and the other was in sweats and a T-shirt. The one with dark hair was watching as Maggie grabbed her stick and headed towards Skyla, whose eyes were already narrowed on this guy. Maggie was telling her something that made Skyla smile and glance in my direction.

Calvin slid back beside me, "This shall be fun."

"That was fast," I remarked.

He smirked, "It's nice to have contacts." I rolled my eyes at him.

Leaning back in the stool, he chuckled, "You're going to be in for a show, Calsen."

"Why? Because they both suck? Or because they're good?"

"Skyla could play blind and win, Maggie, from what I have been told, is better when she's been drinking." I watched as Skyla lined up and started the game. "Rule one: don't let Skyla break, because you won't get a chance to even hit."

Maggie set down her beer and smiled at me. My eyes were watching the dark-haired guy, who was watching her. Skyla barely missed, and it was the light-haired boy's turn. Maggie then went; her eyes narrowed with her body in perfect form. She hit one in and botched the next one.

"What do you see in her?" Calvin's question caught me off guard as he was watching me watch his sister. "Out of every girl out there, why her?"

I smiled, "I could ask you the same thing about Skyla?"

He rolled his eyes, "I know I haven't been the greatest brother, but if you-"

"Yes, I know, Calvin. When I met her, I had no idea if I was ever going to see her again. I had no idea she was your sister; all I knew was she was a girl on a plane, a girl who made me leave first class to sit in the back of the plane."

As Skyla bent down to line up her shot, the boy with light hair grabbed her ass. In one movement, she had him pinned against the wall. Calvin and I both stood, but no one moved.

The kid was trying to laugh it off, "It was a joke, fucking chill. It was sticking out."

Skyla laughed, "Oh," she glanced down, "what do we have here?" In one fluid motion, Skyla grabbed his hard dick and squeezed it hard, sending him down. "Whoops, it was sticking out," she sarcastically said as the boy groaned in pain, "it was just a joke, chill."

The dark-haired guy stepped towards Skyla, and Maggie stepped in front of him, blocking him.

"You got a problem?" She snarled.

He narrowed his eyes, "I do, get out of my way." He tried to shove her aside, but she held her ground. "Do you have a problem?"

Her eyes were narrowed, "Lay another hand on me, and I will have a problem."

"Fucking bitch," he grabbed her face, and in one fluid movement, Maggie had him pinned against the wall. "Why isn't this a turn on?" he said smugly as she slammed his head against the wall.

"Lay another hand on me and you'll find yourself in a lot more pain than your friend."

I was already making my way towards them when Maggie turned around, and he reached out and tried to grab her. I slammed my fist hard into his face as I shoved Maggie behind me. He looked at me, with a clear bruising forming around his eye.

"Control your fucking bitch." He growled, grabbed his face, and walked away, leaving his friend on the ground.

Before anything else could happen and more of a crowd formed, Skyla yanked at Maggie's hand to follow her. Throwing one more glance at the dark-haired guy, I followed Maggie out the door and out towards Calvin's car.

The car ride home was dead silent; Skyla and Maggie sat in the back. Calvin kept throwing glances back at them as he drove with me in the passenger seat. I was more in shock at how physically strong Maggie was. She could hold her own in a fight, seemed to be something she had to do, but not anymore.

Once we got back to their house, I followed Maggie silently up to her room. I closed the door behind me as I watched her throw down her cell phone and wallet on her bed, which was unmade. She proceeded to take one heel off at a time, throwing them towards her closet. She then shimmied her skirt off, exposing her black lace thong, and threw the skirt into the closet. Then, she carefully undid her shirt and threw it with the rest of the pile of clothes in her closet. Lastly, she grabbed an oversized shirt and threw it on, and turned to look at me.

"You know I didn't need your help." She said coolly as she flopped down on her bed. "I had it taken care of."

I sat down at the edge of the bed. "I know you had it taken care of, but I couldn't just stand there."

She looked up towards me, "You should've."

"I am not going to stand by while you try and fight a grown ass man." She opened her mouth to protest, and I talked over her. "I know you can hold your ground and fuck is that sexy, but you have to accept that if you're going to fight someone, I am going to help you, not step in for you."

Maggie took in my words, frowned, and laid her head flat down. "I can hold my own. I just don't want you to think I can't."

I smiled down at her, "You could stand a fair chance at beating me."

She rolled her eyes, "Whatever you say, Calsen." Maggie flipped over. "The world is cruel, Jackson."

I frowned. "It can be cruel." She was staring off into space, clearly reliving something. "What happened with your dad?"

Maggie closed her eyes and took a deep breath. "He was never a bad dad. Did he handle my change in career well? No. I think at the end of the day, he just wanted to make sure I was taken care of and could hold my own. I don't think he thought I would be okay as a teacher, I think he was afraid."

"Yes, but Maggie, that didn't give him the right to treat you the way he did."

She shrugged, "You're right, but there are ways I could've gone at it better, and that is what keeps me up at night now. I think of all the time I could've gotten with him if I had just been honest or if I had let him explain his feelings. I could've had nine more years with him."

"I never knew what it was like to have a father," I said, "he died not long after I was born. He and my mom got into this fight, and he had been drinking. She must've said something to piss him off enough, because he was on the road and crashed his car, killing only himself." She was watching me closely as I gripped my hands together. "I like to think he was a good man. My sisters never talk about him, and my mother gets flustered when I ask. In my mind, he was just a man with demons, demons that eventually won."

Maggie reached out and squeezed my hand, "Everyone has demons or some sort of battle they're fighting. There are people like Calvin, who hide it well, there are people like me who bear physical scars, and then there are people like Skyla who bear mental scars." Her eyes darted down to her arm, which had faint scars from her self-harming.

I lay flat down on her bed and took in the words she just said. It made me wonder what Calvin hid or what Skyla had gone through. I wonder what she went through; that is the reason she is cold and protective of Maggie.

"You and Calvin are more alike than you think." I made a face, and she slapped my leg. "Not like that, you fuck perve, no, you two share similar stories."

"Not possible," I said defensively.

She grinned and rolled her eyes, "I am breaking my rule of sharing a story that's not mine." This got my attention, and I sat up a little more. "When Calvin was in high school, he had a bad drug problem; weed was just always the cover story that was told. He would skip school, go smoke some crack or meth, basically poison, with these people he had met while he dated this girl named Kara. I liked her for the most part, the thing was she was twelve years older than him, and he was only sixteen.

"By the time Calvin was a junior, he had been kicked out of high school and sent to the alternative school, and even then, he barely showed up. He was never home. Some days, Mom was determined that we were going to find him on the side of the street, strung out. It freaked Anika out; she would have nightmares. My dad was to the point where he felt like nothing could be done. Sure enough, Calvin went and got Kara knocked up."

"Excuse me, what?"

Maggie gave a sad smile, "I had a little niece, Heather, she died when she was six months old." I watched her fight back emotions that flooded her eyes. "One night, both were strung out on crack, they got into a fight, Calvin left and went to some guy's house. Next morning on the news: Kara had smothered Heather in her sleep and then OD."

I felt like I had been stabbed in the gut. How did I never know any of this about my best friend? How did he walk around like a cocky dick? Because he hides his demons, my thoughts echoed.

"Calvin went dark, and if it hadn't been for Mrs. Caldwell, he probably would've OD. Mrs. Caldwell had been his kindergarten teacher, and you probably guessed: Calvin had been like her all-time favorite student." Maggie smiled. "She was the one who held his hand to take him to rehab. She was there at every milestone and achievement he made. The day he walked across the stage and got his high school diploma had to be the happiest day for us all. It wasn't long into medical school that Mrs. Cadwell died from colon cancer; it took her two months before she lost."

Once again, I was lost at what I was supposed to say. I was still trying to wrap my mind around the fact that Calvin understood me, and some parts of me understood a part of him. I never thought we could have something in common, granted, this isn't the thing you want to have in common, but it was what life had dealt us.

"At the end of the day, Calvin has a past like all of us. He worked his ass off to get out of the places he had been; my dad had never been able to forgive him for some things. Anika has a hard time trusting anything he says, and Mom is just happy he is standing in one piece. If my brother had decided to be a cashier at Walmart, my mom would be just as happy."

The moonlight that was shining through her thin curtains hit her pale skin perfectly. Her eyes shone as they always did, and her smile filled me with warmth. She was fucking wise and a smartass because what she had said was true: everyone has something they're fighting or dealing with, some hide it better than others, and some bear the scars they have from their battles. My eyes glanced down at the faint scars on her arm.

"One of the wisest shit I have ever heard came from Skyla," she chuckled and looked away, "just because you lost a battle doesn't mean you've lost the war. Just because you won a battle doesn't mean you've won the war." She looked back at me, a perfect tear running down her face, "Wars last lifetimes, the question is, are you ready to be a fighter?"

I reached out and pulled Maggie close to me. As much as I found it hard to believe that Skyla could say that, there was a part of me that knew she had said it. I kissed the top of Maggie's head and thought about what it means to be a fighter, but a fighter of your own life.

"I might be pushing my luck here, but what happened with Skyla?"

Maggie scoffed, "Yes, Calsen, you're pushing your luck there." She looked up at me. "I guess you're just going to have to pack up the balls to ask her."

I rolled my eyes and pulled her to my chest, "Fuck you, Kensinger."

She looked at me, her makeup clearly messed up, and smiled at me. Looking at her, right there, all perfections and imperfections, I didn't want to lose her. I didn't want to lose the color my world had gained from her. Ever since that day on the plane, everything about my world seemed brighter. She seemed to have brought life back into this cruel world.

Maggie was not wrong: this was a cruel world. Life was a bitch. Everything was a double-edged sword. Then there were rare pieces like Maggie, who was broken glass, but the sun hit her, and life reflected off of her, giving it to the cruel world. She is strong by giving this world what little life there was left, but broken by everything she's had to carry and deal with.

As I tried to scramble my brain for a better analogy, Maggie was fast asleep on my chest, snoring. I laughed softly, pushed some of her hair out of her face, and kissed her forehead before I drifted off into my own sleep.

Chapter Fifteen

It Never Ends

Maggie

Once I had managed to vomit everything I could, I sat in the shower for thirty minutes. While sitting on the floor of the shower, cold water whipping my skin, I remembered that I had promised my mother I would bring dessert. Fuck. I struggled getting up; the motion made my stomach tie in knots. I wrapped myself in one of the towels sitting out, and I sluggishly made my way into Skyla's room.

Her room had blackout curtains, she couldn't sleep with light, and she had to have a fan going (just like me). Her walls were bare; she had more floating bookshelves and bookcases than anything. There was a picture of her and me on her nightstand and on her computer screen, which was open on her desk. Her bed was unmade as usual, and her closet had clothes coming out of it, just like mine at the moment.

Skyla was sitting at her desk with her head between her legs. She had been struggling to get moving all morning. I lost track after shot number four and beer number two. I flopped down on her bed, dark red sheets with a black comforter. She grunted, acknowledging my presence. Lucky for her, she had about a whole 24 hours before she was due for her next shift.

I vaguely remember Jackson kissing me good morning. I hadn't seen Calvin, assuming he left with Jackson. I looked at my phone and moaned, and we had to be at my mom's in less than two hours. Even though I had sat in the shower, it did not mean I showered.

"We have to be there soon," I said dully, looking up at the ceiling. "I didn't bake anything."

Skyla groaned, "I can't think about eating."

"Can't really cancel Thanksgiving."

She shot me a dirty look. "If she asks, I am blaming you."

I rolled my eyes. "Just blame it on Calvin."

"Yeah, that will go over well, especially since he is the one on call today."

I smiled, "You want to just not move for the next hour and look like trash for this Thanksgiving?"

She held out her hand, "Amen."

I pretended to air-five her before putting my head back down. This lying in silence was a common thing between us. Sometimes, when Skyla would have nightmares about Bentley, she would crawl into bed with me. Sometimes, if I couldn't sleep, I crawled into her bed, and we just lay in silence. There had been plenty of times when we were both drained that we didn't even want to speak, so we lay down on the bathroom or kitchen floor, wherever the closest place was.

The year or so we lived apart from each other was hard. I swear, sometimes we would just call each other to hear one another breathe or Facetime just lie on the floor and not speak. Of course, we texted and talked like sane people did, but most of the time, we just needed to feel each other's presence.

Oddly enough, Skyla and I had never fought. Of course, there were things we disagreed with, but in the end, we didn't fight. If anything, we joked around about who cared more or who would go to jail first and stuff like that. Between our two lives, we definitely didn't need any more drama. We already had enough of that.

Not long into drifting in and out of sleep, my phone buzzed on my chest. I looked at it, and the caller was my mother. I double-checked the time to make sure we weren't late, but we still had over an hour left.

"Mom?" I said sheepishly.

"Maggie," you could hear she was somewhere with people, "I know you planned on coming to the house for dinner, but your father is lucid."

I sat up, "Lucid meaning?"

"He is here. Your father is with us today. Anika and I went straight here from the airport." She sounded so excited. "The doctor told us to spend as much time as we can with him because we will probably never get another chance."

"What does that mean for me?"

My mother laughed, "He's been asking for you. Try and make some time to come down here."

I bit down on my lip, "Does he understand that I am still a teacher and embarrassed the whole family?"

She was silent for a moment before taking a deep breath. "Yes, however, he still wants to see you."

Skyla had tilted her head to look at me. "Mom," I sighed, "I don't know if it would be good for either of us."

"Maggie Grace, I am telling you to come by, even for five minutes." There was clear frustration in her voice. "We won't get another chance."

"I'll see what I can do." I then quickly hung up and lay back down. "Lucky for us, there's no Thanksgiving."

Skyla grunted in reply. I stared at the ceiling; he was lucid. He had to have been lucid for a while for everyone to be in such a frenzy about it. It made me happy for my mom that she was getting a chance to talk to my father. Lucky for Anika, she was getting to see this because I didn't know how she would handle seeing him the way he was.

It was probably selfish for me not to want to go, and probably more fucked up that I didn't want to face my father fully lucid. I don't entirely know how that would go. Would he be his usual frustrated, pissed, and cruel self? Or would he be in the mood to have an actual conversation that didn't require me to be called the biggest mistake of his life?

"Go," Skyla groaned, "I know you don't want to, but here is your chance. Truthfully, you won't get another, so go."

Closing my eyes, I let her words sink in. Everyone was right, but what if I didn't want this chance? I didn't want to have to reveal to my father the truth behind the sudden change in. I didn't want to have to answer questions. I didn't want the pity. All I wanted was for my father to just say I am sorry, without me giving the whole dark backstory. It wouldn't happen, he was stubborn and was one to never say the words sorry. Nothing was ever his fault; those were always his famous words.

Mom always used to say he was like this because of the way he grew up. Growing up, my uncle and father were always in the running for one-upping each other to get the attention of my grandpa. But also, to make my father look even better, he would always point the finger at someone else, mainly my uncle. Because my uncle was a pussy, he always admitted to it. Hence, feeding into this attitude that my father was never at fault.

Once again, I found myself in the parking lot of this fucking place. I took note of my mother's BMW, which is by far the nicest car in the lot. This would be the first time I would see not only my father fully lucid but also Anika. Growing up, Anika and I fought like cats and dogs. She would always try to steal my shit or push my buttons for me to try and fight her. We never really got along, constantly at odds with each other. Calvin and she fought, too, but that was because Anika thought that he was spoiled, and he thought she was a spoiled little shit.

Snow had begun to fall, but it wasn't sticking to the ground. However, before long, it would. It would then turn into feet of snow, and then would come the snow tunnels and snowmen all over town. It also meant that it was going to be busier at the hospital, just because people did stupid shit when it snowed, and it also signaled it was the end of the year, and everyone wanted to get last-minute appointments before the new year.

Growing up somewhere where it snowed every year, at least a foot or more, I knew how to drive in it. It ended up coming in handy when Skylar and I went into the mountains or traveled further north. I loved the snow as a kid; it usually meant we would get to bring our snow pants to school, and we would get extra time before recess to put all of our snow gear on. The snow also meant the holidays were here, or that it was a new year. It also meant at home that we got to make our tunnels and sled down the mountains of snow. I swear we spent more time outside in the snow than we did when it was summer.

Entering the building, it looked like Christmas had thrown up here. I was greeted by another overly happy nurse, who led me to the standard room on the first floor. There were more families and visitors than I expected for Thanksgiving. I spotted Anika's dark hair in the corner. I carefully made my way over. My father was sitting in a leather chair, and the light was in his eyes.

Before I had even reached them, my father glanced over at me. I stopped walking, waiting to be told to go away. His expression was blank as my mother and sister turned around. As usual, Anika wore a look of disgust on her face, and my mom was beaming at the fact that I was there.

Slowly, I walked the final steps over to them. My father's eyes were glued to me. "Can I have a minute with just Maggie?" His voice was clear and smooth.

My mom leaned in, "Please don't cause a scene."

Anika rolled her eyes and got up with my mom, leaving me to stand there alone with my father. He gestured for me to sit in Anika's chair. As I was sitting down, I double-checked to make sure my hair was in place and that there were no wrinkles in my jeans and sweater.

"Hi, Dad." I forced out as I began to pick at my thumb.

His stare was still unreadable. "Hello, Maggie."

I darted my eyes away from him, afraid that any moment he was going to vanish like all the other times I had been here. I was worried the moment he spoke my name, somehow the dementia would take back over. I was nervous that I was a trigger for him to just vanish because it was easier. It sounded ridiculous, as you can't control dementia like that, but fuck, it was on my mind.

"Your mother tells me that you and Skyla live together." I nodded my head, looking past him. "Still haven't found a boyfriend yet?"

That was not what I was expecting. "Uh, I mean I have a boyfriend." My words were jumbled together.

"Calvin's friend, Jackson, correct?" I felt my mouth drop slightly before closing it quickly. "He seems to be alright, the fact that he has put up with Calvin this long."

I did not want to have this discussion. "Why am I here, Dad?"

Finally, he cracked a smile. "Because I am going to die, Maggie." He said it so bluntly. "If I don't die from dementia, then my heart is going to give out. You're smart, you know this."

My thumb had already begun to bleed, "I know, but what am I doing here, right now?"

"Stop picking at your thumb." He said sharply, and I stopped without thinking. "I wanted to see that you proved me wrong."

I furrowed my brow, "What?"

He chuckled, "The day you told me about your change of heart and refused to take my money, the last thing you told me was that you were going to prove me wrong. You didn't need my money, my support, or my approval. You were going to prove to me that you didn't need me."

Digging through my memories, I remember vaguely yelling at him these things. It was the first time I had found my voice again after all the abuse. For the first time, I felt like I had power, like I could make a choice. I felt strong, and I realized I had something to prove; not just to him, but to myself as well.

"If you're seeking an apology, you're not getting one," I said coolly, crossing my legs.

My father chuckled, "You proved me wrong, Maggie. You showed me that you didn't need me, that you were capable of doing whatever you set your mind to."

I rolled my eyes. "Are you just telling me this because you know you're going to die, and you don't want to die feeling like shit for the way you've treated me these last years?"

"Is that what you think of me?"

I stared at him in disbelief, "How else am I supposed to think of you? You degraded me. You banished me. You pretended I never existed. What kind of parent does that?"

My father looked away from me, uncomfortable. "I wasn't a parent to you." He muttered. "I let my pride win."

I rolled my eyes, "You sure as hell weren't a parent to me, and you sure as fuck did let your pride take over." I snarled, sitting up a little straighter. "Not even when I was at the lowest point of my life, ready to die, you couldn't set your pride aside."

"How was I supposed to sit there, watching my child die, thinking it was my fault?"

I laughed, "Oh, don't play martyr here."

"Maggie," he said sharply, "what I am saying here is: I let my pride, and my own emotions, overpower my duty as a parent."

I narrowed my eyes, "Yeah, you did."

My father was now glaring at me. "I am sorry, Maggie. I am sorry for whatever role I played in causing you pain. I am sorry that I am a stubborn ass. I am most sorry for not being your father." He sighed. "I am not just saying that because I am dying either."

This is where he got me. I sat there, speechless. I had never heard my father apologize in my life. Not even when he clearly was in the wrong. I curled my lip and bit down hard on it. I wasn't sure what I was supposed to feel or even what I was feeling right now. I didn't know if I wanted to laugh, cry, or just walk away. I was frozen, unable to move, think, or feel.

"I don't expect you to forgive me. What I did was not fair." He sighed. "I just wanted to tell you that before I am gone again."

I looked down at my hands, which were clasped together. "Why do you think you're lucid?"

"I don't know," he whispered.

Closing my eyes, I let myself breathe. Never would I have guessed that he would apologize. A part of me makes me wonder if my mom had a part to do with it, but I don't think so because Anika would've thrown a hissy fit about it.

Standing up, I looked down at him. "Dad," he looked up at me, but life was still in his eyes. "I have forgiven you."

Before waiting to hear his reply, I walked away. I walked past my mother, who knew better than to stop me. I had done what she asked, I had come here.

"Maggie," I turned around to see Anika, "I always knew you were a coward."

I frowned, "You haven't seen him lifeless." I fired at her, taking a step forward. "You haven't seen him just being a corpse with nothing left. You haven't been around to say I am a coward. You have no fucking right." I was up in her face. "You don't get to call me a coward because I chose to be something different. You don't get to call me a coward for having depression. You don't get to pass judgment on me, Anika, because you have no fucking clue how I have fought to be here."

She laughed, "Whatever, Maggie. It turns out that I am the only child who hasn't fucked themselves in the head."

"You think I asked for it?" I yelled. "You think I asked to hate everything about myself? You think I asked to feel like the world is better without me? You think Calvin asked to have substance issues? You think Calvin asked to lose his child? You think people asked to be broken? You think people like us asked to be like this?" I laughed and looked around at everyone who was now watching us. "You think Dad asked to have dementia and end up here?" I yelled. "No, because we didn't. We hoped and begged not to be what we are. We feel ashamed of what we are, so we don't need people like you, calling us cowards or freaks. We already do that enough ourselves."

I turned away, kicked open the door, and left the whole room dead silent, and my little sister stunned.

Skyla was sleeping when I got home. I checked in on her, making sure she had water and a puke bowl. I squeezed her hand, and she lightly squeezed it back before I locked myself in my room. I threw my phone across the room, ignoring the nonstop calls from my mother. I rolled over and put my face into my pillow. I screamed and cried at the top of my lungs into the pillow, making it all sound muffled. The numbness that spread through my body scared me, warning me that I was shutting down. Warning me that there was a battle being prepared inside me. Knowing this, I cried into the pillow.

It wasn't long after my crying that I drifted off into sleep. It was the kind of sleep where I felt or thought of nothing. It was this kind of sleep that I craved to have. I didn't want to feel anything, I didn't want to have to get up and face myself anymore. I was so fucking tired, tired of having to get into battles, tired of having to pretend there was nothing wrong with me.

The truth was: there was so much shit wrong with me, but it was the kind of shit that had to be all hush-hush or people would view you differently. I was the kind of person that everyone feared talking to, because they didn't know what they could say without setting me off. I was the kind of person people whispered about. I was nothing more than a black mark on this earth because my brain was broken.

I woke up to Skyla banging on the door. I halfheartedly unlocked it and let her in. She immediately went to my phone and powered it off. I went right back into my bed, face first onto the pillow. Skyla then threw herself onto my bed.

"Why is everyone losing their shit because of you?"

I moaned and rolled over, "Because I lashed out at Anika in front of a room of people."

Skyla laughed, "About time the bitch was put in her place." Safe to say Skyla and Anika did not get along. "You want to talk about what happened?"

I closed my eyes, "It is the same shit. Just because our brain is broken, we get called freaks or cowards."

Skyla sighed, "I like to think that having our brains broken makes us superior to others."

"Quit trying to be positive."

She laughed, "People like you and me, broken and fucked up, will always be treated differently. There's going to be pity, name-calling, hushed whispers, and so much more shit. With that and having to deal with the battle inside, we become stronger."

"Mental fucking illness sucks dick."

Skyla rolled over to look at me, "I know," she whispered, "but hey, we've got each other."

I smiled at her, "True, we got each other, broken and fucked up and all."

"I like to think we're rare collectables, something no one else can get." I rolled my eyes. "Somehow saying that makes me feel okay."

"Are you okay?" I asked.

"I am okay, are you okay?"

"I am right now."

Skyla smiled and pulled me into a rare hug. We ended up spending the rest of Thanksgiving on the couch. We ordered Chinese food and were binge-watching the TV show *The Office*. Skyla's phone remained off, and my phone remained upstairs and off as I just let my mind focus on the TV. Focusing on the lives that were on the screen comforted me, and feeling their emotions was better than the emotions that I was feeling right now. Letting myself feel a part of this fake reality helped me feel something rather than numbness.

Our door to the garage opened, and I didn't even bother turning around. I had a few guesses about who it was, but I didn't care. I didn't want to break the spell of being in the world of Scranton on TV. Skyla had gotten up and was talking in a hushed voice to the person behind me. I still did not care to turn around.

Out of the corner of my eye, I saw Jackson come and sit down in Skyla's spot. I turned my head to see Skyla and Calvin walking out into the garage, leaving us alone. Jackson was watching me as I began to pick at my thumb, which was already covered in a band-aid.

"Are you okay?" Jackson asked as his eyes fell to my hands.

I shrugged, "Depends on how you define okay."

"I don't know what happened; all I know is you went to see your dad."

I looked at him; he had clearly just gotten out of the shower. I could smell the spearmint on him. He was dressed in sweats and a hoodie. I took note that I was dressed in the same jeans and sweater this afternoon.

"Why do people think we asked to be like this?"

Jackson was not prepared for that question. "What do you mean?"

"I mean, why do people assume that we asked to be freaks or fucking fucked up?"

He pulled me close to him, "Because people will never understand, and when someone doesn't understand, they judge or assume things."

"You sound like a wise old man."

Jackson rolled his eyes. "Yes, but you know that's true. It all comes down to them not understanding and not trying to."

I sighed, "People suck."

He smiled, "Yeah, the world sucks."

"For the record, you don't suck," I added.

"You don't suck either, Kensinger," Jackson said, kissing me on the top of my head.

Chapter Sixteen

Northern Lights

Jackson

The hospital had been quite busy since Thanksgiving. I honestly didn't have a full day off in at least a week. There were at least four surgeries a day that I had when I was there. Not to mention the incoming traumas from the pit. I hadn't seen Maggie in over two weeks; she had been busy wrapping up at school. Plus, the time I was off was late at night, and she was fast asleep.

At this point, I had seen Skyla more than Calvin and Maggie. She seemed to be the one who was living at the hospital. She had even made one whole on-call room, hers. Somehow, she found a way to lock it and be the only one with access, as well as Calvin. News had already spread across the hospital that those two were hooking up. I had watched a few poor nurses try to talk to Skyla, which turned into them getting told to fuck themselves. Calvin seemed not to be approached by anyone; if anything, the nurses were still giving him dirty looks.

The Chief, who was still not fond of me, was finding ways to be in the OR with me. Something told me that there was still distrust there. He seemed to be watching my every move even more closely, now that he knew there was something between

Maggie and me. Calvin told me I was being paranoid and that his uncle had nothing better to do.

I was getting ready to leave on a Sunday night, and strangely, I had Monday off entirely. Lucky for me, it was only seven, and I was finally going to see Maggie. She had been oddly distant. When I talked to her on the phone, she seemed off, and when she texted, it was simple words or phrases. I was concerned that she was either upset that we had been working opposite schedules or that there was something else that was bothering her entirely. I was really hoping for the first.

Skyla came into the lounge as I was about to head out. Her hair was a complete mess; she looked and smelled like she hadn't showered. There were bags under her eyes, and her body was screaming exhaustion. She lay down on the couch and covered her eyes, moaning.

"When's the last time you showered?"

She looked at me and narrowed her eyes, "Fuck you."

I rolled my eyes. "I do have a question for you."

"I am going to assume you're just going to tell me, even if I tell you to fuck off?"

"Yes," I said, "has Maggie been okay?"

This got her attention, and she sat up. "What do you mean?"

I shrugged, "I've just noticed that she's been distant."

"It doesn't help that we're always here, but I am going to assume because it marks ten years since she was abused. She usually goes dark around this time."

"So, I should be concerned?"

Skyla shrugged, "She's been okay when I've talked to her. I even made Calvin go check on her. He said she's just been spending a lot of time in her classroom."

"Once again, should I be concerned?"

"Jackson," she said, "it has been a long time since I have seen her open to someone besides me. It has been a long time since she has wanted to stay up and talk to someone. It has been a long time since I have seen Maggie Kensinger care and love for someone besides me. With that being said, you should always be concerned for her."

Skyla looked away. "Are you always concerned for her?"

"Yeah, when you've seen her at her lowest, you are always afraid it will happen again." She sighed and lay back down. "It is the same with me; she's always concerned for me."

I sat down across from her. "What was it for you?"

Skyla looked over at me, "I am not one to tell my story."

"I used to pop pills, and I have to be drug tested like every week here," I said dully. "I was so deep in addiction I didn't see the damage I had done to the world around me, but myself as well. I did the whole rehab and therapy shit. I've been clean for four years."

Skyla's face was unreadable. "I'm sorry," she mumbled, "I don't know what it is like to have an addiction, so all I can say is I am sorry."

I gave a sad smile, "I told you mine. Now, time for yours."

She rolled her eyes. "You and Maggie are so weird, trading secrets for secrets." She smiled and took a deep breath. "I will give you the short version: growing up, I was put in a lot of situations where I was left alone with my mom's boyfriend, who found it enticing to have sex with me. It went on from the time I was seven until I was about thirteen. No one knows that except Maggie.

"I also had a boyfriend, Bentley, the love of my life. He suffered from depression and didn't handle the change from high school to college very well. He reassured me that everything was okay. Next thing you know, he killed himself." She shook her head, eyes unable to meet mine. "Maggie was the only one who was able to pull me out of that dark place. I wanted to die, Jackson. I was mad and upset that I didn't know, and that I believed him when he said he was fine. I was upset that I lost the love of my life. It felt like the world had ended."

I reached out and squeezed her hand, "I'm sorry."

She was looking down at my hand, "I am, too; he would've been such a great husband and father." Her eyes met mine. "Ever since I lost him, I don't want that anymore. I don't want that with anyone because he was the one."

"Do you ever think he can see you?"

She smiled, "I like to think he sees only the good moments, same with my mom."

"I like to think that my dad was the one who saved me from going to the other side," I admitted out loud. "I never got to meet him, but I want to believe he was always there, making sure I didn't end up in the same place as him."

Skyla wiped the tear coming from her eye, "The world is a cruel and fucked up place."

I smiled, "Yeah, but not with Maggie."

She looked over at me, "You feel it too?" I didn't exactly know what she meant. "She brings out the life in me. I will never tell her that, but I swear to God, she is the sun giving me light."

"She brings out the color for me," I whispered.

Skyla shook her head, "Don't fuck it up with her."

We both smiled sadly before I got up and left without saying another word. I thought about how Maggie said that Skyla carried mental scars. It made sense now. It also explained to me why she was cold and defensive, not only of Maggie but of herself as well. She never let anyone sit with her, let alone talk to her. The only person who seemed to give her some good advice was Maggie.

It was refreshing to know that someone understood the way Maggie made me feel. It was even more refreshing that it was her best friend who understood it. I felt like it wasn't something I could have a conversation about with Calvin, knowing that he and his sister hadn't been on the best of terms these last years.

However, something told me that he would understand how Skyla and I both felt. There seemed to be something different with him when it came to Maggie. It was hard to explain.

I had not texted Maggie that I had gotten off, so I was hoping she was going to be at the house. There was a good four inches of snow on the ground, and it definitely had gotten colder. The lake had officially frozen, and the roads were icy. This had been a hurdle for me, driving in the snow. It honestly was the first time I had really been in snow, and really the only time I had driven in it. It was very eye-opening as I was late to work because I didn't realize I had to shovel. Then I realized I needed to invest in a snowblower because I was not fucking doing that again.

The streets were well-maintained, most likely because they were used to it. People seemed bundled up and prepared for this weather, whereas I had to do a lot of winter clothes shopping online. There appeared to be snowmen in every yard you drove past, and you could see kids still outside playing in the snow. If I had been a kid growing up here, I don't think I would've ever gotten out of the snow. I was never one to play in the ocean; my sisters had loved it, and I refused to go, pissing them off.

Once I got to Maggie's house, I noticed that her driveway had not been shoveled and that there were no lights on. I parked on the side of the street and got out of the car. I stepped through the snow and up to the front door. I pounded on the door first before ringing the doorbell twice. Just as I was about to turn away and call her on her phone, I heard footsteps.

Maggie opened the door, wrapped in a towel, her hair soaking wet. Clearly, I had gotten her out of the shower. I walked in, understanding she was probably freezing. She didn't say anything as she ran back up the stairs. You could see the steam coming from the bathroom. I took off my boots, headed up the stairs, and watched as Maggie turned off the shower.

"Sorry if I cut your shower short."

She looked at me and gave a small smile, "I was about to get out anyway. What's up, anyways?"

I watched as Maggie dropped her towel and wrapped it around her hair instead. "I, uh," I was left speechless for a moment as I took in the sight of her. "I figured since I have the night off and tomorrow, I would come and see you."

She didn't care that I was staring, or she didn't know I was staring, because she went to walk by me and into her room. "I didn't realize you were going to be off."

"Why? You got a hot date?" I teased.

Maggie looked back at me and rolled her eyes. "I was planning on going to bed."

I looked at my phone, "It's seven-thirty."

She shrugged, "I have to be up early."

"Maggie," she looked at me, "are you okay?" Her eyes darted away from mine quickly. "It's okay if you aren't."

She curled her lip and focused on putting lotion on her body. Fuck, why did I find that sexy? I was getting hard watching her. She must've noticed because she threw a wicked smile at me.

"Somebody's lonely." She teased as she now began to rub lotion on her breasts.

I shook my head. "You're avoiding my question." I gritted my teeth as she turned to face me and then bent over and rubbed lotion along her leg. "Fuck, Maggie."

She paused and then straightened up. "Do you want me to stop?" Asking in such an innocent voice.

Fuck I didn't want her to stop, but I needed her to answer my question. "Answer my question, please?"

Maggie frowned, "I am okay. This time of year has mixed emotions. Some days are better than others, but today was better. I spent it mostly lying in my bed." She now smiled. "Can I go back to putting lotion on?"

I shook my head, walked over to her, and kissed her. She smelled heavy of vanilla, and her hair smelled like lavender, which was an intoxicating mixture. My hands ran down the side of her body as her hands tugged at the ends of my shirt. I grabbed her ass, and she wrapped her legs around me. My lips traced down her neck, taking note of the goosebumps on her skin. I smiled and sat her down on the bed. She sat up and began to undo my jeans, her eyes locked on mine. Fuck. Fuck. And fuck.

She took me in, making me groan. I observed the goosebumps forming on my skin. Her eyes never left me, making me want to cum right then and there. I gently grabbed the back of her neck and guided her in and out of my mouth. She then wrapped a leg around me, and I found myself on the bottom, and she was slowly putting me into her. That sight alone was close to making me cum. I gripped her hips, and she slowly rode me, once again her eyes on me, the slightest smirk on her face.

Then, she leaned down and kissed me, and I began to thrust hard into her. She cried out my name, and I could feel how wet she was. I needed to slow down, but then she started to beg me not to stop as she whimpered, she was going to cum. That alone meant I wasn't going to stop, and I could feel her whole body shake as she cried out. I knew I wasn't going to last long; she just felt too damn good, but I somehow managed to plow her for another ten minutes, making her cry my name out.

Once I had finished, she smiled and kissed me one more time before getting off me. Maggie went into her closet, pulled on a lace thong, and covered it up with leggings. She then threw on a lace bra that matched her thong. Lastly, she pulled a sweatshirt over her head. I sat up, and she came to stand between my legs.

"What do you want to do?" I asked her.

"I already did what I wanted to do." I looked up at her and smiled. "However, you're the one who came over here, so what did you want to do?"

"Would you be opposed to coming to my house?" She shook her head. "Would you say no to some food?"

Maggie shook her head and smiled. She grabbed her black puffy coat and slid on her boots. I followed her down the stairs, and at the bottom, she grabbed her wallet and keys that were on the table by the door. Once out in the snow, she trudged through it behind me to my car, which I had already automatically started when we were upstairs. She kicked off the excess snow from her boots before she got into the passenger seat.

After some debating, we settled for McDonald's. Once we got back to my house, she had already eaten all her fries, which was the only thing she got. I parked in the garage and opened the door to my house for her. She then took in the rest of my home, and now I realized I had not shown her the entire place.

"I would've loved to grow up in a house like this." She said in awe as she stepped into the purple room. "I bet this little girl loved it." She traced her hand around the flowers that were painted on.

"I lived in a two-room house that was less than nine hundred square feet. I slept out on the couch; that was my room."

She turned to look at me, frowning. "Your sisters wouldn't share with you?"

I scoffed, "No, I wasn't going to share a room with two girls, especially two girls who were already almost ten and eleven."

"Fair point." I followed her out of the room and walked into the baby blue room, and she turned to look at me. "Why did you buy such a big house?"

I shrugged, "Something to maybe grow into."

Maggie walked around the house in awe at this bare-bones house. She then started pointing out things I could do in the basement and how I should keep the carpet. She suggested making an office and movie den in the basement. I watched and followed in awe of her, pointing out what she liked, what I could keep, and what could be fixed up. She didn't want to paint the purple or blue room. She said it made it feel homier and more alive.

The kitchen, which I agreed with, was going to be the biggest project. Clearly, the appliances had to be the original ones in the house. She was astonished that there was absolutely nothing in the kitchen, not even any plates or glasses. Maggie loved everything about the house; she kept saying that it had good bones. Once she finally finished walking through the entire home, she sprawled out in the empty living room.

"Okay, so when are you going to start renovating? It makes me a little sad that you're sleeping on a mattress on the floor and that you have no food or plates."

I stood above her and smiled, "I don't know, mattress beats couch."

She shook her head, smiling. "You know, I can be pretty handy."

"Maggie," I said seriously.

She stood up rather ungracefully. "Jackson?" Her serious tone matched mine.

I brushed a piece of hair from her face. "I want marriage and kids." Her facial expression didn't change. "I want it to be with you."

Her expression was unreadable. I couldn't believe that I had said that. I didn't exactly know what made me say it. I had a feeling it had to do with how much she seemed to love the house. Either way, I must've sounded like a desperate fucker, already hating that I admitted that out loud.

"If this is a proposal, I have to say it's a pretty lousy one." She finally said, cracking a smile.

I laughed, "No, it is not a proposal."

"Good, because that would've had to go down as one of the worst ones in history."

I rolled my eyes. "Geez, you're a harsh critic, Kensinger."

She smiled and then frowned, "Why me? You haven't known me for that long. What makes you want all of that with me?" She challenged me. "Someone like you doesn't strike me as making rash statements."

She was correct; I was not someone to make rash statements. I was not someone who just believed in love at first sight. If anything, I didn't really think that there was such a thing as soulmates. I was as far as you could get from being a romantic.

After my stint in rehab, I was determined to just be alone. There was not going to be a chance for someone to understand and accept. There just wasn't going to be that person, and those things didn't happen in the world. It was only in stupid fairytales and movies that shit happened. I was nothing but a fucked-up person, someone who didn't deserve anything. I had done so many bad things and risked too many lives by being selfish. I deserved more than anyone to be alone.

That was all before that moment on the plane. I will reiterate this: I wanted to be alone. I didn't want anyone. I wanted nothing more than to just be alone. Then Maggie Kensinger boarded the plane. Then, suddenly, everything I had told myself vanished, and my world became colorful. Life was something worth fighting for. I didn't feel any of that, none of it, until her. I knew there wasn't such a thing as destiny or luck, but meeting Maggie made me question it all.

I had become a different person. I had started to feel once again. I cared. I wanted nothing more than to just live. The more I was around her, the more I realized she was my reason. Maggie was the reason for life. She gave Skyla life, pushing her past those demons. However, Maggie had demons, and she understood the impact it had. She knew battles would always be there. She was strong, so strong, but she was broken. For being broken, she cared and loved more.

I smiled, "I always assumed that I would be alone. Then, after my stint in rehab, I made it a point to be alone. Just as I was getting settled with that, there you came. The moment I saw you on the plane, I knew something was different. I gave up my seat in first class and took a risk." Her face remained stoic. "You give me a reason, Maggie. You give me life. You understand how complex everything can be. I don't want to lose you. Everything is brighter and worth it."

She curled her lip, "I may understand, but I am toxic. I am broken. The closer you get, the more hurt you will get."

I shook my head, "You are far from toxic, and you were the one to tell me broken people care and love more. You're not the only one broken here."

I watched as a tear escaped her eye. "Damn it, Calsen." She said, and she wiped her face.

I brushed her face, "I am here and will love you through the days you're okay and the days when you're not okay. I will be there for the highest moments and the lowest moments. All I ask in return is that you do the same."

Biting down hard on her lip, tears fell down her face. "I don't want to scare you away."

"Maggie," I wiped her face, "I understand, and I know it's not going to be easy, but is anything we do easy?"

She looked up at me: "Even on the days you're not okay and I am not okay, we will make it?"

I pulled her close to my chest, "I will do my damndest to make sure we make it."

She looked up at me, "I will too." She whispered.

There we stood, two broken people, two people who believed that love wasn't something they could have. We were broken in different ways, but broken was still broken. We both knew that life wasn't just going to be a walk in the park. We both knew that being with each other wasn't going to be easy. There were going to be days that would test us, but there will be days and moments that make up for that. Holding her right here, right now, was one of those moments.

Maggie pulled away, eyes focused on the back door. She then walked towards the sliding glass door and turned to look at me, her face in disbelief.

"Northern lights, in all my life, I have never seen them. Mom and Dad said one day, and now, here they are."

Before I had a minute to respond, Maggie opened the door and risked walking on the much-needed repaired deck. She then jogged out into the middle of the yard. I followed her out, my eyes immediately drawn to the lights. They were breathtaking and mesmerizing. The sky seemed to be painted. There was no way it could be real. Maggie stared up at them in shock and had a smile on her face. In her blue eyes, you could see the lights reflected.

I smiled over at her, "You've never seen them before?"

She shook her head, eyes unable to move. "No, I had kind of given up that I was ever going to see them."

"Well, people weren't kidding. They're breathtaking."

Maggie smiled and finally looked at me. I grabbed her face and kissed her. She then pulled me down to the snow, laughing. I shook my head as snow engulfed her hair, but the gold stood out against the white. It didn't matter how fucking cold it was to be in the snow; seeing her smiling and laughing was enough, but with the northern lights above, it was all too perfect.

Chapter Seventeen

Buffer

Maggie

Christmas was probably my favorite holiday, and Thanksgiving would be a close second. Even though my abuse occurred during this time, I tried to focus on thinking about all the better memories I had during this time. In all my years of growing up, there was never a Christmas when both of my parents were gone. They were very determined to be together on Christmas Eve or Christmas Day, and it usually was Christmas Eve. Either way, they always made that day feel so magical.

My mom always decorated our house, and she was determined to keep it as cozy as she could. Her decorations were rustic to match the rest of our home. We had four trees around the house, the biggest one being in the living room. Besides decorating, my mom baked as much as she could with her little free time. I loved her toffee squares. Calvin was always a fan of her sugar cookies. My dad liked the chocolate-covered pretzels, and Anika was a fan of whatever new shit my mom would try making.

In the last few years, I had a small tree, and I didn't bake anything at all. I usually spent my Christmas break sleeping, reading, and watching a few movies. I obviously was not invited back to my family during Christmas, so I got used to spending it either alone or with Skyla. A lot of the time, she would be working on the holiday. She was pretty mellow about the holiday, especially since she spent most of it at the hospital.

This year was different; everything about it was different, so it was no surprise this holiday fell into that category. I had invested in a normal-sized tree and stockings to go over the fireplace. I had tested out a few recipes online: white peppermint cookies, cranberry orange pie, and peanut butter fudge. They all had turned out okay, but there was nothing that reminded me of the holidays.

It had been a couple of days since the breathtaking northern lights were spotted. My mind was still swimming with everything that had happened, everything that had been said. I hadn't been able to talk to Skyla, who was home and had a day off. I hadn't seen Jackson since that night, and I was busy finishing off school.

There were only a few days until Christmas Eve. Skyla was on call that night and worked Christmas Day. Somehow, Calvin scored both days off, and Jackson worked all day on Christmas Eve but was on call Christmas Day. Mom had informed Calvin and me that she was going to be spending the days with our father. He hadn't had a fully lucid day since Thanksgiving, becoming nothing more than just a body. Because my mother was not going to be at the house that much over the holidays, I decided to spend Christmas there. Skyla was down for that, and Calvin was too. I hadn't really spoken to Jackson, but I had to assume he would be okay with it. The nice thing was that Anika wasn't going to be home; there was no way she could make it back.

"So, what important information do you have to tell me?" Skyla came down the stairs and flopped on the couch. "You're not pregnant, are you?"

I rolled my eyes. "No, but Jackson confessed to me about wanting marriage and kids." She sat up, looking at me. "He only wants it with me."

"Was that supposed to be a proposal?"

"No, he was just informing me of what his intentions were, I guess." I shrugged and sat down next to her. "I was a little taken aback."

Skyla crossed her legs. "I mean, it doesn't surprise me."

This is what surprised me, "It doesn't?"

She smiled, "I don't think you understand the depth of love he feels for you. I know you don't know how much you mean to me. I know it's scary to feel something for someone, but Maggie, when is the last time you ever felt anything for someone?"

"You know I know how much I mean to you, and you know how much I mean to you," I said, crossing my arms. "Don't you think it's just a little rushed?"

Skyla shrugged, "Time is a bitch, we can't control it. I think he is just as scared as you are. You both are so broken, but together, you seem to heal each other."

I shook my head, "No, you heal me."

"Maggie, you know I don't believe in true love or destiny, but I am positive Jackson Calsen didn't just pick you out and take an interest in you because you're hot." She gave me a small smile. "I know you're my soulmate, and I am yours, but there is such a thing as having a person who can love and care for you in ways that your soulmate can't.

"As much as I love you, I can't love you in the way he does, just like you can't love me as Bentley did. It is not a bad thing. It is just a thing."

I rolled my eyes. "I hate things."

Skyla smirked, "You hate everything."

"Not you."

She shook her head, "No, that is everyone else's job."

I laid my head on her shoulder. She wrapped her arm around me. We sat there for a minute in silence because sometimes that is all that we need.

The famous Kensinger house was what the house was known as in town. Sat on a twelve-acre lot surrounded by tall pine trees. It had a wrap-around porch, something my mother insisted that we have. The driveway was over 200 feet long, a bitch in the winter to shovel (yes, our parents refused to own a snowblower because they had us kids to do it). The house was over five thousand square feet with six bedrooms, seven bathrooms, a five-stall garage, a heated pool, and three floors. It had a rustic feel, cabin-like, with all the wood. There was only carpet in the bedrooms and the basement; otherwise, natural hardwood was present throughout the whole house.

Inside, there was a formal living room, dining room, half bath, den, and then a kitchen and family room combo on the main floor. In the basement were two bedrooms, a movie theater, a wet bar, and two bathrooms, plus a half bath. On the top floor were three bedrooms, three bathrooms, and an office.

My room was downstairs, while Calvin's was up, and Anika's room had always been upstairs. Each bedroom had a bathroom attached to it. The office upstairs belonged to my dad, and the den was my mom's office. Funny enough, all the rooms looked untouched. My bedroom looked the same as when I left it nine years ago. My bathroom still had all my body sprays laid out, and pictures of Skyla and me taped up. It felt as if I traveled back to my freshman year of college.

"So, this is where the great Maggie Kensinger slept?"

I turned around to see Jackson standing in the doorway. I gave a halfhearted smile and turned to look around my room some more. My dresser had a big mirror, and more photos and notes taped on it. All my jewelry was still in its place, and more body sprays. I took note that the pictures of my family were all still in place, and all my awards and medals hadn't been messed with either.

"They left it the way I left it," I mumbled and sat down on my bed, which smelled like clean sheets. "The only thing that's been messed with is the bed."

Jackson sat down next to me. "Obviously, your mother missed you."

I shook my head, "I would've thought my dad would have gotten rid of everything. If not him, Calvin, or Anika."

He stood up and walked over to the dresser: "You really were one for the body sprays," he laughed and shook his head, "no, you were a choker girl?"

"Hey," I said defensively, "that was the thing at the time, and there was a greater variety of smells with body sprays."

He pointed to one of the pictures in the mirror, "No way, Skyla had braces when you were seniors?"

Something she was mortified by. "Yes, but don't laugh. I had braces, too."

Jackson smiled, "God, you guys look so different in these pictures."

"Because none of the shit had happened yet," I mumbled and lay down. "Life was just a tad easier then."

His eyes were frozen on the picture of Skyla, Bentley, and me. "Is this Bentley?"

"How do you know?"

Jackson shrugged, "Believe it or not, Skyla and I had a conversation about the shit we've been through. Bentley was her one and only."

"Yeah," I said sadly, "he was a good person, just a lot of demons, and I think he just got tired of battling."

He came over and lay down next to me, "So, how many guys were you able to score within this room?"

I rolled my eyes and shoved him, "Get your mind out of the gutter, Calsen." He was laughing. "For the record, I never slept with anyone here."

Jackson smiled and kissed me on the forehead, "Weren't you just a little angel?"

"Fuck you," I mumbled and got up. "I am going to get stuff ready for dinner. Are you going to stay down here and fantasize about me being such an angel, or are you coming up with me?"

Jackson got up and laughed, "Now, whose mind is in the gutter?"

I flipped him off before heading back upstairs. It was the night before Christmas Eve, and Skyla, Jackson, and I had the night off. My mother was up seeing my dad, so the house was ours. Skyla was on the couch, eating popcorn, when I came upstairs. She was watching a Christmas movie, and Jackson sat down to join her while I went into the kitchen to grab a bottle of water.

Watching them both, I noticed the fact that Skyla had told him about something she held so dear to herself. The fact that Jackson had shared his story said to me that they trusted each other. I was prepared for this to take a lot longer, her and Jackson. It reassured me that it was all going to work out, I hoped.

While everyone was at work, Calvin and I decided to go see our father together. I knew that he had only seen Dad once or twice. Calvin didn't handle death very well, especially after seeing his little girl, whom he said was the love of his life, dead. There was no doubt in my mind that Calvin loved Kara, but a part of me always assumed that she didn't feel the same. She only met the family twice before she got pregnant, and then once before Heather was born. My mom hated her. My dad was just disappointed. Anika was going to do whatever made my dad happy. I just tried to be friendly, especially after I knew she was going to be the mother of my niece.

Calvin was a good father, well, as good as you could be to a baby. He loved Heather, and he was so proud that he had become a father. Kara and he always fought drug use, and I think the depression Calvin had was all a perfect mix for the storm that ended up happening.

While Calvin was in rehab, I was the one to go and see him the most. My dad would have cared less, but it was too hard on my mom and Anika. Calvin had been diagnosed with depression while in there, and he was dead set on not telling anyone. Too many people already knew he had drug abuse issues, a baby mama, and a dead child. The last thing he wanted to add to the mix was the fact that he had depression. I did my best to try to make him feel better, but at the time, there just wasn't really a lot. He began to self-harm in creative ways in rehab, and they eventually had to drug him with antidepressants and place him in one of those rooms where there was no chance of hurting yourself.

"Calvin," I said while he drove with his eyes on the road, "I have a fucked-up question."

He didn't take his eyes off the road. "Shoot."

"Why were you so ashamed to have depression? But also, why did you throw back my own struggles in my face? Why did you wish I finished the job?"

Calvin still did not take his eyes off the road. "Believe it or not, I really didn't want to think my sister struggled like me. It bothered me that you were able to get closer to death than I ever was. I envied that you were okay with it. Being told that I had depression was worse than being told I had substance issues. I figured drug addiction was going to be easier to manage than the constant thought of hating myself and life."

"What makes you think I was okay with it?"

He shook his head, "You're not afraid to admit you're broken. You are also not afraid to face challenges that come with it."

"Doesn't mean I am okay with it," I mumbled.

Calvin sighed, "I have never been able to admit to anyone I have depression, but I am not afraid to talk about my substance abuse. Something about admitting to depression has more negativity than drug abuse. There seems to be more of a cure for that than depression."

I sat back in my seat and thought about what he said. For substance issues, you just take away the drug or alcohol, and you learn to live without it. I'm not saying it is easy, but at least you can live without that drug or alcohol. When it came to depression, there was nothing you could just take away to help. You could take medication, but even then, you still are depressed. With drugs, you can say how many months or years sober; with depression, you are always going to stay depressed.

When we arrived at the facility, I stayed in the car. Calvin needed to see our dad alone. I just wanted to be alone. The whole drive back to our parents' house, I was silent. Calvin was silent. I didn't say anything, and I just curled up in my bed. I spent the rest of the day going in and out of sleep. I would slowly wake up to get a drink of water and go straight back to sleep. There was no sunlight coming into my room; I had blackout curtains up. In one of the moments I woke up, I lit a candle that was close to ten years old, but it still smelled good.

Today was just one of those days. It was one of those days when I just needed a break from fighting with myself. In the slew of dreams I had, most of them involved Calvin and me playing in the snow when we were younger, but there were also images of my mother and me dancing around in the living room. They were happy dreams. Then, I would slowly blink my eyes open, and then I would be reminded that those days were long gone.

It had been a while since I had one of these days. They sucked, but that was part of my depression. Here is the thing: depression, grief, addiction, abuse, and any other mental health issues are going to look different for each person. Calvin and Jackson both handle their addiction differently, and their stories are different. Skyla handled Bentley's death differently than his mother and even I. Skyla handles her depression and abuse by working all the time, keeping her mind distracted from it. For me, I honestly try to pretend I am not fucked up by denying it to myself.

The day I was officially diagnosed with depression, I remember it clearly. It was a Thursday morning, and I didn't have any classes until later that afternoon. Skyla was sitting next to me, and it looked as if we had rolled out of bed to be there. She was holding onto my hand tightly as the doctor explained and gave me options and ideas.

I remember just a tiny piece cracking inside me, like a sharp pain that radiated through my whole body. I could physically feel myself breaking. I didn't cry, I didn't speak, I just stared at a poster on the wall of a woman.

I could barely hear Skyla talking. All I was focused on was the word cure on that poster. There was no cure for depression. There was no cure for mental health. There was no cure for even fucking cancer. So why do I see the word cure in this office? That was all my mind was thinking about: there is no cure.

At that moment, lying in bed, I was haunted by the thought: there is no cure.

Chapter Eighteen

A Hidden Piece

Maggie

It was a few days after the New Year, and Jackson had been busy at the hospital. Calvin and Skyla had been spending more time at his place, and I had a few days before I had to go back to school. In the last few days, I have been able to catch up on all the reality TV I needed and cleaned up the house. I went through my closet and got rid of clothes that I no longer needed, more than I thought. I cleaned the pantry and scrubbed the floors. I rearranged the furniture and flipped my room around.

While I was in the downstairs powder room, I heard the door to the garage open. I stepped out to see Jackson dressed in sweats and a hoodie. He had just gotten off a forty-eight-hour shift, and you could clearly see the bags under his eyes. I set the towel and Windex on the kitchen counter. Jackson gave me a sheepish smile as he grabbed me in a hug.

"You smell like bleach and cleaner." Jackson laughed as he pulled away from the hug. "I don't mean that as a compliment."

I rolled my eyes and grabbed the Windex and towel. "Thanks."

"Hey," he said as he took off his shoes, "Calvin said something about snowmobiles tonight."

I froze, "What about it?"

"He said we could use the fun."

I turned around, "We as in?"

Jackson shrugged, "He said Skyla was in, and that automatically means you would be. I've never done it, but I guess there is no harm in trying."

"Where are we going to be driving?"

Jackson shrugged again, "I don't know, Maggie. I am just relaying the message." I turned around and went back to wiping down the mirror in the powder room. "You okay?"

"Yeah, just a little out of the blue for him to want to do that," I said, and sprayed more Windex on the window. "Has he been okay lately?"

He leaned against the doorframe. "I mean, he still is a jackass as always, but he seems fine." Jackson crossed his arms. "Why do you ask?"

I took a deep breath and set down Windex. "January 3rd is the day Heather was born. This has been the first time in a while since I have been around to see how he is."

Jackson sighed, "I still find it hard to believe all of this, the fact that he has never mentioned any of this to me. I just don't know why he wouldn't tell me."

"Calvin is ashamed, ashamed of the life he had. He misses the life he could've had. It isn't something he wants to have to relive, and talking about it, you are reliving it." I gave a sad smile.

"I wouldn't take that personally, but at the same time, you have never told him about your past."

Jackson closed his eyes. "You have a point."

"Go shower and sleep; you're just tired." I brushed past him and put the cleaning supplies away. "Go," I urged.

He gave me another sleepy smile before heading upstairs. I sat down on the couch and pulled my phone out. I opened my iCloud on my phone and scrolled back to the day Heather was born. I gave a sad smile as I examined the photo of Kara, Calvin, and Heather. They both were smiling as Heather looked fast asleep in her arms. Calvin had this goofy smile on his face as he looked at both Kara and Heather. My mother and father looked tense as they stood next to Kara.

In the other photos from that day, I was smiling down at Heather. I was wearing one of the choker necklaces, and my hair was curled perfectly. I had smoky eye makeup, which was trendy at that time. My mother held Heather, smiling just as goofy as Calvin was. My father wore a straight face in all the pictures, and Anika stood by his side the entire time.

Flipping through photos over the next six months, Heather was in quite a few of them. There were a few photos of Skyla holding her, which were the only photos I had of her holding any sort of baby. Ironically, Skyla was not a huge fan of kids. She always told me that she would love my kids, but she told me she wouldn't have kids of her own. I know the only person she would have even considered this with was Bentley. As I flipped through more photos, sure enough, Bentley was in a few photos holding Heather.

I kept scrolling, and finally, I got to the day when we got the phone call. I had a few photos of my mother holding Calvin as he cried, and a photo of the police taking out the bodies in bags. Then, the next thing you knew, there were all the funeral pictures. Calvin looked like shit, bags under his eyes. My mother's eyes were swollen, my father was stoic, and I stood beside him with the same stoic look.

Setting down my phone, I ran my hands through my hair. I felt tears forming. Taking a deep breath, I brushed my thumb across one of the birds on my arm. The grief of losing my niece was a minor pain in me, a small demon that was marked on me. I sometimes like to wonder what she would've been like. Would she have been a smartass? Would she have addiction problems? Would she have been happy? I wonder how different Calvin would've turned out if they had still been alive. Would he still be a user? Would Kara and him still be together? Would I have more nieces and nephews?

I shook my head; getting lost in what-ifs will drive you mad. I took one last look at the picture from the funeral, closed my phone, and sat my head back.

Apparently, Calvin was not lying about wanting to go on snowmobiles. It had been almost ten years since I had ridden one, and I am pretty sure the last time I rode one was during the winter of my senior year in high school. Mom and Dad had four snowmobiles in the work shed, something Dad liked to do with us kids, but Mom, not so much. There was enough snow on the ground, a good foot plus, and it wasn't below zero, so it seemed to be a good time.

When I arrived with Jackson at my parents' house, I was surprised to see all four of the snowmobiles. Calvin and Skyla were already bundled up and filling gas into each of their vehicles. Jackson had to go to Walmart to buy snow pants and heavy-duty boots. I could tell he was nervous. This was something he had never done.

"So," he started as we walked to the work shed, "what should I expect?"

I looked up at him, "You know you don't have to go. I am sure my mother would love to have you keep her company."

"I am not a pussy." He mumbled.

Smirking, I nudged him, "I will show you; I am positive you will catch on fast."

Jackson did not look convinced. Skyla was bundled in dark pink snow pants and a jacket with black boots. Her hair was pulled into a high ponytail, and her face lit up when she saw me. I was dressed in purple with the same boots. My hair was pulled into a tight bun. Calvin and Jackson were both black.

"Ever ridden Calsen?" Skyla said.

"Er, no."

She laughed, "This is going to be fun."

Calvin glanced over at him, "Never?"

"I am sure that is what no means." Jackson spat.

I rolled my eyes. "Anyways, you have a plan as to where we're riding?"

"Take the trail in the backyard that takes us out onto state-protected land and do the loop. I am hoping it will be clear enough to see stars and, if we're lucky, the Northern Lights." Calvin said as he finished filling up the last snowmobile. "I checked, and all the lights are working. The helmets should be good to go as well."

Skyla, eager to get going, grabbed a helmet, turned on the lights, and hopped onto the first snowmobile. She roared the engine to life, and the lights blinded us. She eased her way out and towards the back. Calvin followed her quickly, leaving Jackson looking very pale.

"No one is going to make fun of you if you pussy out," I said as I grabbed a helmet. "Trust me, it is not as hard as doing a bypass surgery. Just come here and let me show you the basics."

He hesitated before walking over. "How long is this loop and trail going to be?"

I handed him the last helmet, "It's like twenty-some miles in total, if I remember right. Now, I want you to focus on me and save your questions until the end."

Jackson laughed, "Spoken like a true teacher."

Rolling my eyes, I began to explain to Jackson how to turn on, speed up, and brake, and explained to him that it might seem like driving a car, but it's not. He was listening to me, eyes following my hands, and he did not interrupt me once.

"If you don't feel up to it, you can ride on the back of mine."

Jackson shook his head, "Yeah, no. Somehow, that is worse than pussying out."

"Whatever, I'll go slow and keep up with me. The helmets, thankfully, are connected through a wireless network, and we can talk through them." I said and smiled. "Here we go."

I got up onto mine, and the engine came to life. Jackson slowly turned his on. I slid my helmet on and double-checked to make sure all my extremities were covered up. Before going, I looked over at Jackson, who had his helmet on, and he gave me a thumbs up.

Going slow, I followed the path Skyla and Calvin had already formed. They were waiting up ahead as Jackson and I glided over slowly. Sure enough, we were off through the woods and through the trail that ran through the back. The good thing was that snowmobiles were loud, and if anyone was out, they would hear, but the trail that led to the loop was usually deserted in the winter anyway. Plus, thankfully, we would probably not run into black bears, but there was other wildlife. Coyotes and deer were just some of the few.

As we made headway, Jackson seemed to be getting the hang of it, and I was able to pick up our speed. Skyla and Calvin were ahead of us, racing each other and talking mad shit to each other through the headset. It didn't take long to reach the clearing of the loop. The sky loomed above, covered in thousands upon thousands of stars. The moon shone brightly as well. I glanced up and smiled. It was a beautiful sight.

It didn't take long for Jackson to start trash-talking, especially since Skyla was egging him on. It was a smooth ride, especially out on the loop. It was open, and we seemed to be the only ones in sight. We passed several deer and even a few coyotes, which I figured we would.

The snow was hard-packing snow, which helped with the riding. It felt amazing to be out here. I felt free. Out here, life seemed to be a dream. Out here, you felt like you were in a whole different world. Being out here, you could see more stars than you thought would fit in the sky.

Out here, I didn't have to worry about my father dying. I didn't have to think about my job and how to keep all my kids engaged. I didn't have to wonder what my future held. I didn't have to be on guard waiting for my mind to strike a battle. I got an escape from those things. At this moment, I wasn't reliving a memory; instead, I was making one. It sounded cheesy, but being out here brought back a hidden piece of happiness.

This was home, and this was always going to be home. By the time I was nine, Dad had taken Calvin and me on plenty of snowmobile rides, and eventually, I was allowed to go on my own with Skyla. I knew how to snowboard, thanks to my dad, and I had some experience with skiing, thanks to my mom. Skyla and I weren't fazed by the cold. Growing up, there were many days when it was below zero, so we were used to it.

I never realized how much I missed my home until that moment, out in the clearing. My home was a hidden piece of my happiness.

Chapter Nineteen

A New Look

Jackson

Things finally started to slow down at the hospital, and finally, the Chief was letting me go month to month for my drug testing. I had been staying at Maggie's for the last few weeks while I hired a construction crew to gut the bathrooms, kitchen, and some of the walls. I wasn't going to start renovations until she was ready, and I knew she wasn't. She had been swamped since she had gone back to work. She would get there early and stay late. By the time she was back at the house, she would be passed out on her bed in her work clothes.

Skyla had reassured me that this was normal. Getting back into the groove of things, Maggie is in panic mode. She said, truthfully, the second semester is more challenging than the first semester. I guess she was not wrong. I hadn't seen her awake in nearly two weeks. It was the end of January, and there was still a good foot of snow on the ground. The warmest it had gotten was maybe twenty degrees.

It had been a while since I had talked to my mother, and I felt guilty for not calling more. I hadn't really said anything to her about Maggie, but it didn't take her long to figure it out. She was just referred to as the girl, and mom didn't want to pry. My sisters seemed to be doing okay, and my mom visited them more and more. I never talked to my sisters. This had always been the way it had been with us. It was not because we hated each other; it was honestly the fact that we didn't have anything in common and that our childhood hadn't been great.

My mother had never been on a plane, so trying to convince her to come out here was hard. She had also grown up in California and was used to the weather there, and I am pretty sure it was going to be quite a shock when she visited here. It had been an eye-opening experience for me. I also didn't want to put any pressure on Maggie to move things quickly anyway.

On a rare Friday night that I had off, I was expecting to find Maggie passed out on her bed. Instead, I was left to find an empty house. I checked Maggie's location, and it said she was still at school. It was damn near seven-thirty at night. I decided to go and see her. I hadn't had a conversation with her, and it was killing me. It also was killing me that we hadn't had sex either, but that was just me thinking with my dick.

The school parking lot was empty except for Maggie's car, which had frosted over. I parked right next to her and called her cell phone. It rang a few times before she picked up, but there was no good reception.

"Hey," she said sluggishly.

I smiled, "Hey, can you let me in? I am at the front."

She was silent for a second. "You're here at school?"

"Yes, and I would appreciate it if you would hurry; it is only nine degrees out."

"Stop being a baby." And she hung up.

About two minutes later, Maggie appeared in the doorway and pushed the door open. Warm air greeted my skin, making me shiver just for a second. Maggie was dressed in jeans and a T-shirt that had the school's name on it. Her hair was a frizzled mess, and her mascara was smeared as well. She was in slippers, and her name badge was hanging off her hip awkwardly.

"You okay?" I asked as I followed her in. "You look like you've been sleeping."

She avoided my eyes. "What time is it?"

I looked down at my phone. "Almost eight."

"Yeah, I am pretty sure I fell asleep around six. That was the last time I got up to get something off the copier." She took a left turn down a brightly painted hallway.

There was a flag that hung above her door that said Ms. Kensinger in fun colors. And then there was a banner in the hall that said Hey, Kindergarten! The other teacher was across the hall, her lights off and the door shut. I followed Maggie into her classroom and was taken aback by it. It was not like the kindergarten classroom I had growing up.

The far wall was lined with windows that looked out to some pine trees. The whiteboard and projector were at the front of the room, and a bright carpet spread on the floor. There was a rocking chair painted white and a small table beside it that had a snowman book on it. There was an alphabet line and a number line above the board. In the front, in the far corner, were books galore, surprisingly, all neatly organized. Her desk was in the far back, and the back wall was lined with cubbies for students. There were tables throughout the room with various kids' names. The wall on the door side was filled with all the different kinds of work the kids had done. Snowflakes were hanging from the ceiling, giving the room a cozy, snowy effect. And along the wall by the door, a black couch sat with a blanket and pillow.

"This is the famous classroom?" I asked as Maggie settled in at her desk, which had stacks of papers.

She nodded, "I swear I spend more time here than I do at home."

I sat on one of the tables near her desk, "Can I ask what we are doing here so late all the time?"

Maggie paused and then avoided looking me in the eyes as she began to put stacks of papers away. "You wouldn't get it."

"Seriously, Maggie, come on."

She sighed and turned her chair to look at me. "Teacher guilt. That is why I am here. I feel like I haven't done enough and haven't taught them the stuff they need to know. There's so little time left, and I don't know how I am supposed to get it all done." She covered her face with her hands. "I haven't focused on these kids this year because of everything else going on, so I feel guilty. I am here late, trying to find ways to get everything crammed in and how to make it fun. Also, I am trying to make up for all the time I haven't made them my life focus."

She rubbed her eyes and bit down on her lip. I got up, stood over her, and pulled her up into a hug. Then, as she pressed her face into my coat, she began to sob. Her whole body shook as she cried. I rested my chin on the top of her head and smoothed her hair down as I let her cry.

"I am in year six of teaching, and yet every year, this feeling happens. Every year, I feel like the only thing I focus on is my job. It has become the only part of me." She looked up at me, mascara totally ruined. "Then, this year, I finally have an identity, and I have been able to have a life apart from work. And instead of feeling proud and happy, I feel so guilty for not devoting every minute I have to my job." She wiped her nose and shook her head. "I always knew burnout was a thing, and work balance was something I needed to control, but here I am with no work balance, and I feel so dead on the inside."

I brushed a strand of hair out of her face. "Have you considered taking a vacation or a break?"

She squeezed her eyes shut, "That is the thing, I get breaks at holidays. I don't work in the summer. So why should I take a vacation when I have all the breaks in the world?"

"No one is going to judge you," I said as she sat back down, looking defeated. "If anything, I would admire you for standing up for yourself."

Maggie was staring off, "The kids can't afford for me to be gone. When I am gone, the more we'll be behind, which will only cause me more stress and heartache."

I crouched down in front of her, "Maggie," her eyes were still focused out in space, "let's go home so you can shower and get some sleep."

Her blue eyes locked in on mine. "This is a day when I am not okay." She whispered.

I smiled, "I know."

"I'm a mess." She barely whispered.

"A chaotic mess." There were dark circles under her eyes. "Let me take you home."

Without speaking another word, Maggie grabbed her coat and slid it on. She grabbed her backpack and put her school keys inside, and her car keys in there as well. She put her water bottle in the side pocket and began to walk towards the door. I turned off the lights, closed the door, and followed her through the dark school.

I opened the car door for her, and she stared out the window as I pulled out of the parking lot. I wasn't even on the main road when Maggie passed out, clutching her bag in her lap. I smiled and drove her home.

When we got back, she was on autopilot because she didn't acknowledge Skyla, who was sitting in the living room. She went upstairs, took her clothes off, and stood in the shower. Maggie didn't say a word as she dried off and slid on sweats and a hoodie.

She curled up onto the bed, and she was out like a light. I picked up her clothes and threw them into the hamper. I closed the door softly and went back downstairs to Skyla.

"I am surprised she listened to you." She said as she closed the book she was reading. "Getting her out of the classroom is the only thing she won't listen to me about."

I plopped down on the other side of the couch. "She's killing herself. When I got there, I guess she had been sleeping."

Skyla gave a sad smile. "It was awful her first year of teaching, and I thought it had gotten better, but this year has been hard for her."

"I can't help but feel responsible for it."

Skyla scoffed, "Please, you are not the reason. Whether she admits it or not, watching her father waste away is impacting her. I know her depression is getting bad because she hasn't been on any medication since she moved here. I would say those are the things that are responsible for it."

"What do you mean she hasn't been on any medication?"

"Have you seen her take any?" Skyla had a point. "I know she has never been good about taking it, but this is the longest she's gone without it."

"Why? Why aren't you up her ass about it?"

Skyla gave a sad look, "You can't force someone to get better. They must get better for themselves. In all the years I have been her friend, forcing her to take care of herself led to more self-harm and turned into her trying to take her life." Skyla crossed her legs and set down her book.

"I am worried about her," I admitted.

Skyla smiled, "Calsen, I worry every damn second about her, even when she is at her best."

I looked away from her. "What can I do?"

"Just be there, whether it is just lying next to her or watching TV or something. I know for me, her presence is sometimes all that I need to get better." Skyla reached out and squeezed my hand. "I am telling you, she is worth it." My eyes were locked on Skyla's hand. "Take her for all the bad, but all the good."

"She's always going to be worth it. Fuck, just hearing her voice or seeing her smile brings me out of the darkness. She sees me in ways I never saw myself."

Skyla laughed and leaned back, "Yeah, it's annoying that she holds that power, but I wouldn't trade her for anything."

Standing up, I gave Skyla a nod before heading back upstairs and sliding next to Maggie in bed. I brushed a strand of hair out of her face before rolling over and closing my own eyes.

Maggie had gotten up before me, sitting in front of her mirror and staring at herself. I sat up and gave her a funny look.

"What the hell are you doing?"

Her eyes did not leave the mirror. "Skyla wants to color my eyebrows, and I am trying to debate whether that is a good idea or not."

"You can color your eyebrows?" She nodded silently, still not looking back at me. "And Skyla knows how to do that?"

Maggie got up; she was dressed in fleece pants and a tank top and sat down next to me. "Once upon a time, Skyla was going to go to cosmetology school. She does her own hair and cuts mine, but she also does nails. Lucky for me, I have never had to pay to get my haircut or nails done."

Skyla James, a hairdresser? My mind was struggling to try to come up with an image of her even holding a hair dryer. If anything, I would have thought Skyla would've considered being a lawyer or police officer or some shit. But going to cosmetology school?

Maggie was grinning at me, "Funny to picture, right?" I smiled at her. "I always thought she would be like Detective Benson on *SVU*."

"On what?"

"*Law and Order*, I always pictured Skyla being just like Olivia Benson." I still didn't know what she was talking about. "I am disappointed in you, Calsen. That is like one of the greatest shows ever."

I made a face, "Is it a girly show?"

She rolled her eyes, "No, anyways, I just always pictured her like that. Now she's like this bad bitch trauma surgeon, still the same concept, just a different field of work."

Maggie lay back on the bed and sighed, still looking exhausted. "Are you feeling okay?"

She nodded, "I'm alright," she looked over at me, "You don't work until tonight?"

"Yeah, for the next three days. Go me, whoo." I said sarcastically.

Maggie smiled, "Well, that just gives me the greatest excuse to stay in bed all day today."

I rolled on top of her, "Is that so?" She was grinning up at me. "Does staying in bed all day mean you've got to keep those clothes on?"

"Get your mind out of the gutter," she tried to say, but she broke into a smile.

I kissed her on the forehead. "I love you, Maggie."

Chapter Twenty

Kill or Die

Maggie

It was oddly warm out for the end of January, and it was about thirty degrees. It was sunny out. It was peeking through the curtains, falling on my skin. Jackson hadn't woken up yet, and the sun glossed over his bare back. It was one of those mornings when I woke up before my alarm had gone off, and there was no chance in hell that I was going to be able to go back to sleep.

I took my time in the shower, probably standing in the warm water for a good ten minutes doing nothing. I shampooed my hair twice and scrubbed my body clean three times. When I got dressed, in black dress pants and a dark blue sleeve, Jackson still wasn't awake. The alarm had about ten minutes left. I sat in front of the mirror in my room and carefully brushed my hair, put mascara on, and put on pale pink lip gloss.

By the time the alarm went off, I had successfully showered, gotten ready, and eaten breakfast. I was downstairs flipping through the book Skyla was reading that she left on the coffee table. Jackson came down in shorts and no shirt, and he was surprised to see me awake. He walked over to the coffee maker and poured himself a glass, black with no cream or sugar.

I made a face and sat back on the couch. "I don't know how you can drink that."

He chuckled and sat down next to me. "I don't understand how you don't like coffee, yet you'll drink Red Bull like it's water." A bad habit of mine. "What is your plan for the kiddos today?"

I smiled and looked at him, "Well, we are working on subtraction and focusing on the letter G this week. And if we have time, we will watch some science experiments on *Mystery Science*."

Jackson sighed, "The days when your biggest concern was if Sally, your best friend, would be at school."

"Did you have a best friend named Sally?"

"No, I just thought Sally was a generic name that everyone uses. Just like Joe or Bob."

"Ironically, I have students named Sally, Joe, and Bob," I said as I stood up.

"Liar."

Shrugging, I grabbed my coat. "Wanna bet?"

Jackson smiled, walked over, and kissed me. "What time are you coming home today?"

"I will be home before five-thirty. You and Skyla are off at seven."

"I love you," he kissed my head one more time, "I will see you later."

I gave a grin before grabbing my bag and keys. My car was turned on and ready to go. The drive to school was as regular as always, just bright out. Nothing indicated that there would be a problem.

Jackson

The hospital was oddly quiet; Calvin was asleep on the floor of the attending lounge. I had one surgery scheduled in the morning and two in the afternoon. Skyla was going to be in the pit, and Calvin was going to be working with some interns for the day, which was something he intensely hated.

The weather was warm, in the thirties. I saw people out walking and jogging in just sweats. Some of the snow had begun to melt into slush, which just meant that it would freeze and everything would be slick, causing the rate of crashes to go up, making the pit busy for the night shift.

I was sitting in the lounge on the third floor, flipping through the newspaper that had been left there. Calvin plopped on the couch after sleeping on the floor, groaning.

"You wanna trade places today?"

I laughed, "Yeah, no thanks."

"Interns piss me off."

"We used to be interns." I pointed out.

Calvin shot me a look, "We knew our shit. These guys can't tell their ass from their head."

I rolled my eyes. "Stop being such a dick."

"Someone is cranky," Calvin said. "Someone hasn't gotten laid." He taunted.

I made a face, "Dude, you realize if I get laid, it means I am fucking your sister."

"Don't remind me." He mumbled. "If you need a neuro consult, please page me."

"Ok, don't page you, got it."

"Jackass."

Calvin's pager buzzed, and sure enough, he vanished out the door. I got up and stretched, knowing I should make my way down to the OR floor. I knew today was going to be a long day, but tonight was going to be the night Maggie was going to see the house completely gutted. I was eager to see what her reaction was going to be. I, honestly, was just happy to spend time with her besides sleeping. Nothing could go wrong.

Maggie

My kids were mellow this morning. Most of them could barely keep their heads up during the morning meeting. I was thankful they had PE right away in the morning because that seemed to get them to wake up a bit.

We had snacks and were cleaning up when it all started. In my six years of teaching, I have gone through numerous drills and training. I always braced myself, having my mace and a baseball bat ready. After a while, I had gotten comfortable with the idea that it would never happen, especially when I moved back to Bemidji.

It all started with the intercom announcing that we had to lock our doors and that this was not a drill. I double-checked to make sure the door was locked, and I quickly turned off all the lights. My kids were all sitting on the carpet, looking at me with wide eyes. I tried to give them an encouraging smile, but that was when you could clearly hear the gunshots go off.

"Get over here, now!" I yelled as I started pulling them to the blind spot. "Come on, come on."

My kids were too stunned to speak. They were stiff and rigid. The tears that were coming down their faces fell into their shaking hands. I heard a few more gunshots before I quickly went behind my desk and grabbed my bat and mace. My kids were all watching me as I got close to the door to get a better sound of what was going on.

My mind was racing, and I could hear blood pumping in my head. My head was pounding hard, triggering a headache to come on. My stomach felt utterly empty, which made me also want to throw up. I could feel sweat dripping down my back, and I could feel heat rushing to my cheeks.

Thankfully, there was only a tiny window on my door that was covered by a curtain anyway. My problem was that I had a wall of windows, and I had no idea what I was facing. One shooter? Two shooters? As far as I could tell, there seemed to be one shooter as the gunshots were spread out.

My kids remained low, and I whispered, "Cover yourselves with the blankets in the corner."

My sweet Sally and Grace began to pass the blankets down. I had a good four or five blankets. I met Sally's eyes, and they were full of fear and confusion. Her eyes then went down to my hands, which were shaking badly. That is when her eyes filled with more tears at the sight of me being scared.

Another gunshot went off, and it seemed to be getting closer to my room. I didn't know what to do. There was no one over the intercom giving information, which did not sit well with me, knowing they were either injured or dead. I reached for my phone, but when I clicked it on, I had no service, which was common in my classroom; the service would go in and out.

I threw my phone to the side, irritated that it was not going to be any help. Crouching by the door, I looked back at my nineteen-six-year-old students. Some of them had their heads peeking out from the blankets, and others kept themselves covered as if the blanket was going to be a shield against gunshots. I felt completely helpless. Without having information on how many shooters or even where the shooter was, there was no way in hell I was going to open the door and risk my kids running towards the exit doors. I also knew the windows didn't break or open. They were bulletproof. I could try, but I didn't want to attract noise to the room or attention to the possible shooter outside.

My stomach sank as I heard a gunshot. The shooter was clearly in our hallway.

"RUN!" Someone yelled, and I could hear footsteps. A class was risking it, and that was when a few rounds were fired.

I covered my ears, and my kids covered their heads. There were screams and shouts from outside. I squeezed my eyes shut and let tears fall down my face. Then, there was knocking at my door, and then a trail of blood came through it.

"Ms. Kensinger," a kid cried, "please, please open up."

I covered my mouth, vomit coming up to the back of my throat. I could hear muffled sobs. My eyes watched the blood trail down the floor, and that was when a gunshot went off right outside my door.

Jackson

I was halfway through my bariatric surgery when the pagers began going off like crazy. Annoyed, I shot one of the scrub nurses a dirty look. My attending loomed by my side as he was judging every movement I was making. He clearly had nothing better to do this morning.

Looking up at the gallery, I noticed that it was empty, odd because I felt like just a minute ago, there were at least ten people up there. My pager buzzed three times in a row. One of the scrub nurses, whom I knew had fucked Calvin, picked up my pager.

"Dr. Calsen, it is from the Chief." I froze and looked up at her. "You need to close. Multiple traumas are going to be coming in, and they will need this OR and your hands down in the pit. It also says all your other surgeries have been postponed."

"I can't-" I started.

"Just go scrub out, get prepared, I'll close up." Dr. Jensen mumbled as he grabbed my forceps out of my hand. "GO!"

Without arguing, I slid off my gloves and gown. I snagged my pager and began to scrub out. What the fuck was happening that we needed to be prepared? When I stepped out of the OR, there was a madhouse, people grabbing blood, and people shouting and screaming. No one was even stopping. They were all shoving past each other and bumping into me.

I began to make my way down the less crowded stairs, and to the pit. This was going to be a first for me, whatever it was. I had never been told to shut down a surgery and prepare for a massive trauma intake. My mind was trying to wrap around the possibilities it could be.

"CALSEN!" I looked behind me, and Calvin was racing down the stairs with me. "What the fuck is going on?"

He was wearing a panicked look, "I don't know, I just got kicked out of surgery to prepare for this."

Calvin shook his head. "Whatever it is," we swung the door open to the pit, and everyone was frozen, looking at the TV. "It's not good." He whispered.

Skyla looked sick to her stomach as her eyes flashed to us. I looked up at the TV; it was the news, and the headline read Active Shooting.

"Reports of one shooter inside Perry Park Elementary School," my stomach sank, "we can confirm there are at least ten dead, multiple injured."

My eyes looked at Skyla, and now I knew why she was sick to her stomach. Calvin sank back on the wall, clearly putting two and two together. Maggie was inside that school. Maggie was there. Maggie could be one of the ten confirmed dead. Maggie could be injured. Maggie was there.

"Alright, people," the Chief boomed as he made his way across the pit, "we don't know what we are up against. I don't know what we are going to see, but you need to prepare yourselves. All the traumas are going to be routed here first, and non-emergency cases will be sent to Sanford." Everyone was pale, and the Chief himself looked pale as well. "Listen, I know that everyone in here has a connection to someone in there, but we are here to save their lives."

I closed my eyes and looked away. Maggie was there. Maggie is dead. Maggie is injured. My mind was racing, flashes of the horror of walking into her classroom and seeing kids dead, and her. I held back the vomit as I could see it clear as day in my head.

Skyla stepped over, "Okay, I need extra O negative on hand. All ORs are cleared, and make sure we are stocked up. We are going to need all the hands we've got." She yelled as she began to get herself up.

The Chief was watching Calvin and me. My hands were shaking at my sides, and Calvin looked stunned. My eyes went back to the TV, where they had an overview of the school, police, fire trucks, and ambulances. She was going to be okay. She was strong. I knew she would not let those kids get hurt, even if that meant she got hurt in the process. That is what scared me more, knowing she would take a bullet for them.

Maggie

There was no telling my kids not to scream and cry at this moment. They just heard the same thing as me, and I was barely able to keep it together. I didn't know what to do; whoever was out there clearly knew people were in here. The question is, how much was this person willing to work to get into our room?

In one of the training sessions, I was told that shooters usually look for the easiest target. They aren't typically going to work for their prey, hence why the phrase 'Lock doors save lives' is huge. Another reason why elementary schools get picked is that they are an easy target. I'm not saying this is the exact MO for a shooter; sometimes, it is a deranged parent who is fighting a custody battle, and they want to take their kid. Sometimes, it can be an old employee who is mad about something.

The person outside our door yanked hard. You could hear groaning and yells of frustration. Whoever it was knew their time was running out. In all the years since the Columbine Shooting and Sandy Hook Shooting happened, response time was fast, and typically, the shooting only lasted less than five minutes total. In the situation, though, it sure felt longer than five minutes. At this point, I feel like I've been trapped for hours.

Just as soon as I thought the person was turning away, I stood up, and bam! The person threw their body at the door. Fuck. I guess my room was the one.

My kids were all grabbing onto each other, bracing for what was going to come next. I turned away from them and grabbed my bat, gripping it tightly.

I always assumed that in the moments you knew you were facing death, everything flashed before your eyes. That is one big fucking lie and something the movies do to make a more dramatic effect. Instead, at this moment, I was overcome by all these different emotions: anger, sadness, jealousy, happiness, embarrassment, etc. I could feel every emotion there was for a human. A last feeling of life before it is taken away.

I gripped the bat and steadied my feet as if I were preparing to swing at a pitch in baseball. I could feel the cold sweat running down my spine. I could feel all my kids' eyes on me as the door was shot at this time.

Losing my balance briefly, I steadied myself as the door came open, a black rifle coming into view. With everything I had, I swung the bat, colliding right into the face of the shooter. This knocked him off his feet, and he started to fire his gun. My kids were screaming, but everything around me sounded like I was underwater. My vision was blurry on the outside, but super focused on what was directly in front of me.

Swinging the bat again, the gun went flying out of the hands of the shooter. This is when I got a look at his face for the first time. It was a high school-aged boy. There was a look of fear in his eyes as I stood over him and swung again, hitting him in the face. He reached out with his hands and grabbed part of my leg, which sent me screaming in pain.

Looking down, one of the bullets he had fired hit the inner side of my right thigh. The shooter was digging his finger into the bullet lodged in there. More blood rushed out onto his jacket. I could feel the tears coming down my face as I swung again. This time, I heard a crunch, and the searing pain in my leg stopped. I turned again, this time harder. I felt blood spray on my face as I continued to swing down onto this boy. I screamed as I finally took in what I was seeing in front of me.

There was no face anymore, just blood and swelling. The realization hit me: I had just murdered this boy. A horrified scream and sob escaped me as I stepped back and dropped the bat. My kids were all frozen, staring at the deformed boy's face. I looked down at my hands, covered in blood and a bit of flesh. I sank to my knees and cried out as my shaking hands tried to grip my heart. I had just murdered this boy. Sobs came out of me. I killed him.

My thigh was still bleeding, but I could not feel the pain. My eyes were focused on the young boy, who clearly was dead. Right outside my door was a little girl who was in the kindergarten class across the hall, dead with bullets in her back. I closed my eyes and continued to sob with my hands gripping my thigh, trying to stop the blood, trying to stop the screams coming from me.

My eyes scanned my classroom, and nothing was out of place in my room. Everything was still set and ready for whatever craft I had planned. Their backpacks and coats are still hanging up.

The room where learning and nurturing were supposed to take place had now become a murder scene. The place where I once found comfort and peace was now destroyed.

The next moments were hazy for me. I watched with my fading vision as police officers came in. They each made a sickening face at the dead boy before grabbing and getting my kids out of the room. I carefully stood up, only to be pushed back down again by a woman not much older than me.

I could not hear what she was asking me as my eyes remained glued to the dead shooter. She kept waving her hand in front of my face as she bandaged up my leg, as she waited for a gurney. I killed that boy. I had become a murderer. Not only was I a fucked up and broken already, but I was also a whole different set of fucked up and broken. The good that had been left in me was gone. Shattered to pieces. I had taken a life away from someone, a young boy. Any good or pure left was gone.

Jackson

It was hard to focus once the kids started coming in off the ambulances. Various gunshot wounds. Various ages. Two had died in route here. Another three had died in one of the trauma rooms, one of them being my patient, a seven-year-old boy with a gunshot wound to his stomach.

My mind was preparing to see Maggie. I wanted her to be safe, but if I had to choose, I would rather have her come here with a wound than be dead on the scene. If I could choose, she would be coming into the hospital on her own two feet. My heart could stop pounding, and the need to throw up would go away. But every kid I kept seeing come in made my fear of her being dead heightened.

As I was walking out of one of the trauma rooms, I found Skyla, Calvin, and pretty much everyone glued to the TV screen. It was silent, and you could hear the TV loud and clear:

"Perry Park Elementary's shooter was killed. Fifteen-year-old Maxwell Fath has been identified as the shooter. He was a ninth grader who had attended Perry Park." The woman took a deep breath and closed her eyes. The confirmed total found in the building is twelve. Out of the twelve, two were staff members. As of right now, there are over twenty injured, many of whom are in critical condition."

My eyes locked with Skyla, who closed her eyes. Calvin pulled her into a hug as she started to silently sob into his chest. This had to be the first time I've seen her cry. Calvin smoothed her ponytail as she shook in his arms.

The Chief brushed past me, "Calsen, Kensinger, James, outside now." He barked.

Keeping her head down, Skyla followed, making sure no one could see her tears. Calvin had a painful look as he stuck close behind her. I brought the rear up so I could feel everyone's eyes on us as we left the pit and went out to the bay.

"I have patients I need to go back and see," Skyla mumbled. "You guys can handle this."

The Chief took a deep breath. "You're going to want to be here for this."

An ambulance pulled into the bay, but its lights weren't on. This meant whoever was there was either dead or non-critical, and if it was the latter, they should be rerouted. It came to a halt, and the EMT from the front hopped out.

"Chief," she said, "I figured you would take an interest in this." She opened the doors, "This is who killed the shooter."

There was a loud sob, and it was her eyes that I saw first. Skyla shoved past one of the EMTs and brushed some of Maggie's hair from her face. My eyes went down to the bandages, and I noticed blood seeping through.

"Twenty-eight-year-old female, gunshot wound to the inner right thigh." The male EMT said. "Most of the blood you see is from the shooter, but she has lost a decent amount of blood herself."

Maggie cried out again, and Skyla looked at her in pain. I walked over and gently placed my hand over her shaking hands. They were ice cold. She looked up at me, tears trailing down her face. A wave of relief washed over me as I held her hands as we carted her into the pit. Her sobbing was painful to listen to and pierced my heart.

"We need to get that bullet out," Skyla said as she didn't look away from Maggie. "I will meet you in an OR?"

The Chief shook his head, "None of you are operating on her. Now, I need you all to go do your damn jobs. You know she is safe, and you know she is here." Maggie grasped my hands tightly as she shot Skyla a sad look. "GO!" He yelled.

Maggie

All I could see was that boy's eyes, how afraid they were. I kept picturing myself smashing his face in. These all came in flashes, like a strobe light. It was worse when they put me out, as the bullet was lodged deep. All I kept hearing was that little girl crying for me to open the door, the kids screaming, and the endless gunshots.

I don't remember the ambulance ride at all. However, I remembered seeing all the bodies covered up. That young boy killed them. I killed that young boy. That puts us both into the same category. That means if there is a heaven and hell, I am sure as fuck going to hell. I had murdered someone. I had taken someone's child and brother away. I murdered him just like he had murdered all those people.

Sitting in my hospital room, thankfully being moved out of the ICU quickly for more critical patients, I stared out the window. The perk of your name being in the hospital is that you got the best room and the best service, which made me sick. All I could do was relive the scenes through the strobe light flashes. The only thing I had said was to be left alone, and no one was to visit. Otherwise, I sat there, staring out at the cloudy sky hovering above the lake.

I was a murderer. Nothing more than a killer. Then, a haunting part of me wished I had died. That dying was better than having to keep seeing myself killing. Dying was going to be easier than having to live; it always had been the case, but now, more than ever, I just wished that bullet had hit me somewhere else.

With all this thinking, a wave of guilt washed over me. How could I even think that? Most of all, how could I live with myself, wishing that I had died instead of killing? How much of a piece of shit had I become?

Chapter Twenty-One

Silence

Maggie

Maxwell Fath was fifteen years old. His mother had passed away in a car crash, and his father was an alcoholic. He had been a smart, quiet kid and pretty much kept to himself. His family owned guns, and a lot of them were used for hunting. Looking through Maxwell's social media, there was nothing that indicated that he was considering this, nor that he was unhappy. There was no note, no explanation. Maxwell Fath was dead, and we would never know why he decided to shoot up his old elementary school. He was dead because of me.

There had been a total of twenty-one deaths, and no one else was in critical condition. Three of the twenty-one deaths were adults: a secretary and two teachers. Thirteen students were from the opposite kindergarten class, all six or seven years old. The other five were in second grade, and all had died at the hospital or en route.

It had been almost three days since the shooting, and I had refused to talk to anyone. Skyla lay with me when she was on break and refused to go home, so she slept on the hospital bed with me. She didn't try to force anything out of me. Instead, we just binge-watched all the Disney movies we could on TV.

Jackson tried to get me to talk, but I avoided all eye contact and focused on the window outside. He still came by to hold my hand and talk to me. Truthfully, I didn't listen to a single thing he had to say. My mind was focused on the flashing memories and the rising fear in my chest. My heart rate had been so unstable over the last three days due to the panic attacks and night terrors that had become frequent. Also, it didn't help that I refused to take any pain medicine.

My mother sat with me when Skyla couldn't. It was either she or Skyla who was always with me. My mother just kept to herself, holding my hand and reading her book. She would try to talk, but learned quickly that I was not in the mood to talk. So, instead, when she spoke, she would tell me about the latest drama with her sister down in Arizona. Calvin had come by a few times but didn't stay long. He would check my vitals and leave without saying a word to me.

For the last three days, I have kept the TV and the news off. I didn't know much more about what happened. The police came and talked to me twice, but I realized I was still in shock. What had happened in the doorway of my room was caught on camera. They had seen me beat this kid to death. They had witnessed me becoming a murderer. They had seen me change in a matter of seconds.

The weather had turned cold again, and there had been no sign of the sun. Today, it was finally snowing again, covering up the ugly, dead parts of winter. I had always hated it when the snow melted because everything would just be dead. It wouldn't be until close to April that things would be warm enough again to start blooming. From May to August were the only times it would get into the eighties and nineties.

After taking two bites of toast and a glare from Skyla, a new doctor entered the room with my uncle behind him.

"May I speak to Ms. Kensinger alone?" He addressed Skyla, who was glaring at him. "I just want to talk."

She scoffed, "You're one of the freaks from the psych floor; you want to evaluate her to see if she is fucked up enough to go to your floor." She then turned, stood up, and hugged me. "Please talk, please," Skyla whispered before leaving the room with my uncle.

"Ms. Kensinger, I am Dr. Loggin, from psychology. I believe I met you when you were younger." He did look familiar. "I met with you a few times regarding what happened with your brother and his issues."

I sighed, "Call me Maggie, and yes, my father made us go talk to you freaks."

Dr. Loggin smiled, "Ah, I see you are like your father, and I find the field of psychology to be a joke."

I shot back, "When people like me try to go to you for help, it's never helpful. You just remind us of what we are and drug us up so we can live with ourselves. All while ready to whisk us away into your loony bin so you can study us." I said harshly to him as I looked away. "To me, you're just another person ready to label me."

Dr. Loggin sighed and took a seat in the empty chair near the window where my mom usually sat. "Maggie, I am not here to label you. I am here to just ask what happened in the school."

I curled my lip. "All you have to do is ask to watch the footage, and that will provide you with all you need to know."

He set his clipboard down, "I am not going to pretend to understand what you are feeling or whatever shit you have been through. I am, however, going to figure out what is going through your head, that is all." He held his hands up. "I am not here to whisk you away or drug you up, and I can promise you that."

I rolled my eyes. "So you just want to hear what I saw and felt?" He nodded, relaxing back in the chair. I closed my eyes and squeezed them. "Where do you want to start?"

"When you knew you were in danger."

"I didn't think it was possible," I whispered, looking at him. "You get trained and talked to about this stuff all the time, so there is always this fear that it might happen. But there is also this other side of you that assumes there is no way it could happen to you. I pretty much had the mindset of the latter.

"Nothing can prepare you for how you react in that moment, no amount of training or drills. What I did," I paused and took a deep breath, "is something I feel like any person would do to protect others."

Dr. Loggin crossed his legs, "You seemed bothered by this. Why?"

"I killed the kid," I whispered. "I killed a young boy."

"In response to saving lives, including your own."

I shook my head and looked over at him. "That is what I try to tell myself, but all I can think is I have become a murderer."

He sighed, "Maggie, if you hadn't put up the fight, think of all the people he would have killed in your room alone. If you had not done everything you could, think of all the families who would not have their child returning to them."

"Think of all the trauma those kids are going through because they saw me murder someone." I fired back.

Dr. Loggin shook his head, "Maggie, they were going to have trauma even if he didn't come into your room. They still would've had trauma if they had watched you put up a fight. These kids were going to have trauma one way or another in these circumstances."

"How am I supposed to go on knowing I killed someone? How can I look the people I love in the eyes, knowing I killed someone?"

"Maggie, you didn't go and pull a gun out on this kid. You defended yourself and your students. What would've been the outcome if you didn't fight? Death." He shook his head. "The people who love you will not see you as a murderer. Instead, they are going to see someone who fought and survived."

"That was the thing I didn't want!" I shouted. "I don't want to be looked at differently. I just want to be me. I want my life to be the way it was before that morning." I shook my head and wiped the tears coming down my cheeks. "I was finally happy, and now it is all gone."

Dr. Loggin reached out, grabbed my hand, and squeezed it. "You still have those people; you still have your home. You now just have another scar or wound that needs to be healed."

I ripped my hand away from his. "I don't want any more scars!" I shouted again. "I am sick and tired of having demons and fighting. I am tired of all this fuck up shit that keeps happening." I shook my head and sobbed. "Why did it have to be me?"

"Because you're a fighter, a handpicked fighter." I looked over at him. "You have a strength that most don't. I believe people who have these demons of mental health and trauma are marked for a reason."

I scoffed, "Yeah, what reason is that?"

"They are the people who have an unmatched strength. They have a love that's unmatched. They're fighters, survivors, and voices." He looked up at me, then smiled, "You remind others that there's so much good in this world, but also the dark side of life."

I curled my lip, "So I remind others that aren't as fucked up as me that their life is good? That they could be like me?"

"Yes and no. You bring out the good in others because you struggle with bringing out the good in yourself." He stood up and grabbed his clipboard. "Maggie, do you view doctors or victims of violence who have lost a patient or defended themselves as murderers?"

I frowned, "No."

He smiled: "You are a victim of violence; you are not a murderer, Maggie Kensinger. Not even close, so don't label yourself as one."

Dr. Loggin left without saying another word. I know Skyla and Jackson had lost patience. Calvin and my family had, too, but that did not make them murderers. Women and men who are fighting for their lives in violent situations aren't murderers. Why was it that when it came to me, all I could see was a murderer and nothing more?

Jackson

My shift had ended five minutes ago, but I stood frozen in the lounge, staring out the window at the night sky. She had refused to talk to me, and she wouldn't even look at me. She was barely eating or acknowledging that anyone was there. I always figured that if she ever was in the hospital, she would be a stubborn patient, but I never thought she would shut everyone out.

It broke me to see life in her beautiful eyes vanish. She looked broken; it was as if the protection she had for herself had crumbled apart. She looked like a lifeless person. Now I understood what it must feel like to watch her father diminish into just a body. I didn't want that for her. I wanted her to get help. I wanted to do anything I could, even if that meant I had to leave her alone; if it helped her, it would help me.

To distract me from the idea of Maggie not being in my life, I picked up extra shifts. I had not been out of the hospital for three days, and neither had Skyla and Calvin. Skyla lived in that room with Maggie, even if they didn't talk. Calvin refused to see Maggie and really took time to train the interns, something to distract him. I understood why he was doing it because a part of me was doing it as well.

During a break on my night shift last night, I decided to stop and see Maggie. Her room was dimly lit, and the TV was on, playing some basketball games. Skyla was lying on the bed with Maggie, and both were fast asleep. They both looked so peaceful and unbothered. Maggie's heart rate was a steady beat of 71. I gave a small smile before leaving the room to leave them in peace.

I checked up on a few patients and settled myself in an empty lounge on the fourth floor. The stars were out, and they were shining brightly. My mind went back to that night when Maggie and I sat out on the dock. The way she looked up at the stars reminded me of how I looked at her: speechless. I remember each moment with her so clearly, as if it were in HD. My heart raced at the thought of her; chills ran through my body when she looked at me, and the warmth and color she brought to me with that smile, I didn't want to lose that. She had given me a reason, and she had given me a chance at a life I never knew I could have.

She was everything, even if I wasn't hers, and I owed my life to her for giving me life.

Standing there, I finally felt myself crumble. I covered my mouth as I began to sob loudly. I lowered myself to the floor and let myself break. All the emotions of seeing those kids with gunshot wounds, the sickening fear of Maggie being dead, and the sight and sound of her pain. I wiped my eyes as the tears kept falling down my face. I was finally letting myself feel, letting myself bleed out the emotions.

As I was squeezing my eyes shut, I heard the door close. I felt my body tense up and my face flush, embarrassed to be caught in the state that I was in. Calvin walked over to me and slowly sat down next to me. Instead of trying to hide, I felt my body shake as I leaned my head back and cried. Calvin reached out, grabbed my forearm, and squeezed it. I felt the tears coming down harder and sobs escaping me. Calvin just sat there with me, staring out into space while I wilted like a flower. It was then that I understood what Skyla meant about presence: sometimes, all you needed was their presence.

I don't know how long I sat there, sobbing, but when the wave of fatigue hit me, it stopped. Calvin stood up, helped me up, and embraced me with a hug. He then, without a word, gestured for me to lie down on the couch. I knew sleep was what I needed, and Calvin would take care of my shift. And as soon as I lay down, my fatigue won.

The day was cloudy, snow flurries sprinkled the air, and the temperature was close to freezing. The weather seemed to match everyone's mood in Bemidji. Still shocked at the horror that had happened and the permanent scars that would be left. I slept through the night and day and was finally woken up by Calvin sometime around five that evening. He told me I could go home, and the Chief had Skyla, Calvin, and me take a few days off to clear our minds.

I didn't want to go home; going home would mean I would be in a gutted house. Going home would remind me of the throbbing pain of losing Maggie. As I was walking out of the lounge, Skyla stopped me.

"Calsen, you good?" She was in her scrubs, hair a flying mess.

I nodded, "Yeah, just trying to decide what to do."

Skyla smiled, something I hadn't seen in what felt like forever, "She's talking. Dr. Loggins from the freak floor came to see her yesterday. We ate lunch together, and she finally got up and took a shower."

"What did he-"

She shook her head, "Whatever he said, it seemed to bring a little bit of life back. Maggie asked about any major celebrity news she had missed. She even asked about you."

I frowned. "What did you say?"

"You look like hell, and that watching you waste away was killing him, whether he wanted to admit it or not."

"Gee, thanks."

"You can't say I am wrong." She fired back. "Seeing her like this is eating you alive. It is eating Calvin alive. She just vanished in front of us."

I ran my hands through my hair, "You don't seem phased by this."

Skyla sighed, "That is because I have seen her like this before." She mumbled. "The time I found her nearly dead, she shut off like this. I think it is her way of coping with the demons."

I closed my eyes, "I don't know what she would do without you."

Skyla laughed, "I honestly don't know what I would do without her." She grabbed my hand, her hands freezing. "Go on up. I know she wants to see you." She stood up and stretched. "I have to go home and take a personal day, so go!"

The whole way up to Maggie's room, I was nervous. I had changed and showered, taking my time. I used the stairs, going one step at a time with my head filled with constant thoughts. What was she going to be like? How was I going to react? I wanted her to talk about it with me if that made her feel better. I just wanted her to be better, and no matter how much I think psych floor is a freak show, I would be forever grateful for whatever was exchanged with Maggie.

When I got to her floor, I smiled at a few of the nurses I saw and carefully slipped into the room. Maggie was lying there, her eyes closed, and the TV screen glowed on her face. On the

TV, there was an NBA game that was playing, and the sound was muted. Her room smelled like lavender, her hair was wet, and she had just recently taken a shower. I smiled; it was a step in the right direction for her, even if it seemed like a small step.

Moving carefully to the chair, I noticed that someone must've brought stuff from the house. My guess was Calvin, as there was no way in hell Skyla would have left. I could see her lavender lotion resting on top of a set of clean clothes. Maggie had that famous green blanket she always slept with tangled up in her hands as she took shallow breaths. Delicately, I moved the bag to the floor, barely making any noise. I settled back in the chair, laid back, and focused on the NBA game.

"You know, Calsen, people usually knock before they enter." Maggie's voice was sluggish. "At least, that is what is taught here. I don't know what rules they've got in the land of California."

I turned to look at her; she was still blinking her eyes, coming out from a deep sleep. She wore a weak smile as she stretched her body, careful not to move her legs. It felt like it had been weeks since I had seen that smile. A wave of relief washed over me as I scooted the chair closer to the bed.

"Harsh, Kensinger." She reached out and squeezed my hand, just as cold as Skyla's hand was. "Can I ask why the NBA is on a Wednesday night?"

She looked up at the screen, "Because that is when I get to see Shaq and Charles bicker with each other."

I laughed, "That is the only reason?"

She picked up her phone and showed that she had a timer set. "I was going to sleep through the first half and listen to them bicker during the halftime show."

"I guess they do bicker like a married couple." I wondered out loud.

"Clearly, Shaq is the dominant one, and Charles is his bitch." Maggie said casually.

I smiled, "I can't really disagree there." Her eyes were focused on the TV. "I am glad to hear you talking." Her eyes did not leave the TV. "Are you okay?"

She took her time, eyes darting down to her hands, which were clasped together. Her uninjured leg was bouncing at a fast pace. She kept biting down on her lip as she contemplated her answer. I knew better than to push it, so I waited until she took a deep breath.

"It is going to be a while before I can say I am okay." She closed her eyes, and a tear fell down her face. "I understand that I am safe and that I protected my students. I took an unspoken oath as a teacher to protect them at all costs. I just never thought that I would be put in that position." She looked over at me, clearly trying to hold off sobs. "I killed a person trying to do so. I killed a kid. I took away someone's child. It isn't just something I am going to be able to brush off."

I reached out and gripped her leg so it would stop shaking, which it did instantly. "I know this really isn't the same, but when

I lost my first patient, it was a fifteen-year-old boy." Her eyes immediately stopped filling up with tears, and she focused on me. "It was the first year of my surgical residency, and I was covering the pit when a gunshot victim came in. I immediately went to the OR and got scrubbed quickly. He looked so young on the table. In the end, he had lost too much blood as the bullet nicked a few arteries. It was a surprise he made it as long as he did." I took a deep breath, remembering this night so clearly. "He had been walking home from a friend's house that was a block away when he got caught in the middle of a drive-by shooting. The intended target was already dead on the scene.

"After declaring him dead, I went to the scrub room and cried. I had sunk down to my knees and let myself cry. I didn't know anything about this boy other than that he was a fifteen-year-old boy. I sat there for a good five minutes, letting myself feel the pain. The head of trauma, Dr. Hendrick, sat down next to me and let me sob, but reminded me that we had to pull our shit together to do the worst part of our jobs.

"I dried my eyes and looked as presentable as I could. I had been the lead, so it was my job to deliver the news. The mother stood up, eyes so hopeful that her son had made it. Somehow, my voice remained strong, and I kept a straight face as I delivered the news. I watched her crumple to the floor like I had.

"I walked away feeling like there was a part of me that had died going through that. It is a fucked-up part of the job, and the pain doesn't get any easier. Xavier Edden was the boy's name, and his mom was a single mom named Addison."

This time, Maggie reached out and held my hand. "Maxwell Fath was his name." She whispered. "His father is named Lucas Fath, and his late mother's name was Treasa Fath."

"Do you know when you'll have to go back to work?" I asked her as her eyes locked with mine. "Or do you think there is no way in hell you can go back this school year?"

She shrugged, "As far as I know, school is closed as the whole area is a crime scene. All these kids are going to have to go to therapy. I know I am going to go to therapy." Saying out loud seemed painful for her. "Those kids are never going to be the same; they are never even going to be able to look at me the same way. I killed someone right in front of them."

I squeezed her hand, "You protected them, and if I had to guess, they would look at you as someone who is going to protect them. They are going to be bonded to you."

"I have to go to therapy," she said again, her voice quieter this time. "Two times a week, to begin with." Her eyes were now focused on the TV. "I have to start on medication again."

I rubbed my thumb in circles on her hand. "I am glad you're going to get the help you need."

"We're going to get through this, right?"

She looked at me, and I nodded. "We're going to get through this."

Chapter Twenty-Two

The Light Always Returns and Vanishes

Maggie

It had been twenty-one days since the shooting. Out of those days, fifteen had been out of the hospital. I had been to two therapy sessions; Dr. Kelly Roder was her name, and she let me call her Kelly. I had been prescribed a few different medications. I was on day eight of them, and I felt okay. It was a challenge walking on crutches as they didn't want me to put a lot of weight on my leg. I slept in my room; Jackson and Skyla were always there to help me get from my bed to the bathroom or help me shower.

Over time, it was getting easier for me to walk on my own, but I was still very unstable. I had fallen the few times I had tried, as it was a searing pain and a heavy flashback to the day. I have been going to physical therapy three times a week as well.

The first few nights at home, I didn't sleep very well. I kept waking up to flashes or the sound of gunshots. I would scream and thrash around, causing more pain in my leg. Once the medication started, the night terrors happened only a few times.

In our first few sessions, Kelly was blunt with me: PTSD was going to be hell. The first session was about getting to know each other, which felt hard, but I knew therapy and medication were the only shot I had at moving beyond this. During the second session, she let me talk about my feelings and the night terrors. We even touched on the abuse I'd gone through with Daniel. I never said his name, and she didn't ask for it.

My mother had been taking me to all my sessions, sitting out in the waiting room for me. Every day, she would bring me lunch, or we would go out for lunch. She kept me distracted by telling me about my aunt's drama, Anika's residency, how Dad was doing, and how much she liked Jackson. I would chime in with a few words, but I made her do more of the talking.

I hadn't seen Calvin, and I know Skyla hadn't been to his place, but as far as I knew, he hadn't been to ours. Jackson said he was swamped by taking on interns. Skyla just shrugged and said that she wasn't worried and that when he was ready to grow balls and talk to me, he would.

As for what I did during the day to keep myself busy, I would do the exercises given to me by the doctor. I took a shower and ate all three meals. I did my best to look at myself in the mirror, which wasn't working. I slept a lot during the day, and at night, I found myself watching stupid infomercials and *The George Lopez Show*. I didn't usually fall asleep until three; that seemed to be when the medicine would kick in.

There had been a decent number of people who wanted to talk to me about the shooting, mostly news people. That all got shut down after it was clear I wasn't going to break. The shooting had become an old topic in the country; some other shooting or war had taken over its spot. I avoided the news like the plague; instead, I would watch the NBA or college basketball. Jackson had made it a point not to work Wednesday nights so he could sit and watch Shaq and Charles bicker.

Things between Jackson and me were odd. I relied on him to help me stay steady, making me embarrassed. He didn't push me to talk, but was very adamant about me taking my medication and eating. He would hold me and kiss me, but didn't dare to do anything else, which was nice. He had a hard time looking at the wound, and Skyla was usually the one who helped me clean it, especially when it got infected a week ago.

Skyla went about like everything was normal, brought me ice cream on Thursdays (the day of the shooting), watched TV with me, bitched about the people at work, and she braided and washed my hair, claiming I looked like a train wreck. There were days when she would kick Jackson out of bed, and she would sleep with me while he was banished to the couch downstairs. There were days when she would join my mom and me for lunch.

It was very strange not to work. I had no contact with anyone from the school, and I was told that I was not to have contact with the students. I found it hard not to want to know how my students were feeling and what they were going through, but at the same time, there was so much I was going through that I couldn't take on the burden of the pain others felt.

The weather had turned cold again, meaning there was snow back on the ground, which meant a higher chance of my slipping and falling. Luckily, because it seemed I was never alone, there was always someone to help. The only time I was alone was when I was with Kelly in my sessions or the bathroom. It was great that I had all this support and these people, but sometimes I found it very overwhelming.

It was on day twenty-one after the shooting that I finally saw Calvin. He was in the kitchen, grabbing a cup of coffee, as I had met my challenge of walking down the stairs without someone. Skyla stayed at the top of the stairs, watching me like a hawk. Once, I was at the bottom when I saw him, and he looked like shit. There were dark circles under his eyes; he had lost weight, and he had not shaved in a while. He gave me a weak smile as I hobbled over to the couch without my crutches.

"You look like shit," I stated.

He laughed and sat down by me, "You're one to talk."

I rolled my eyes, and then silence washed over us. His eyes were fixed on my wound, and I was watching him.

"Why haven't you talked to me?"

His eyes didn't leave the wound, "Because I figured you didn't want more people up your ass. If I know anything about you, Maggie, you like to be left alone. I have also been reassured that Skyla has corrected me."

"That's a very detailed excuse."

Calvin finally looked at me, "What am I supposed to say? I am sorry. I know that you're tired of that. I know you would rather do all these things on your own: driving, walking, showering, and such. I know it is killing you that you never have a moment alone."

"Why do you think I want to be alone?" I whispered.

Calvin sighed, "What you went through is something none of us can relate to. Not to mention all the other shit you've dealt with, sometimes your head is just swimming, and just for a Goddamn second, you want everything to shut off and be silent."

"That's how you felt when Kara and Heather died, didn't you?" I asked. "You just wanted to be left alone, but you never said anything because you knew it would kill those who loved you if they couldn't help."

He gave a sad smile, "But also being left alone for too long will get you thinking, and not the good thinking."

"Can I ask you a fucked question?"

Calvin shrugged, "Knowing you, you're probably going to ask me anyway."

"Would you have stayed that night?" I watched the color drain from his face. "Would you have done that whole moment differently?"

Calvin knew damn well what I was talking about. He looked away and out the window towards the back. I knew, remembering the life he once had, but remembering them was a whole different kind of pain. The type that you lock away in your brain and shove it in a corner so it can be forgotten.

"Of course, I would've, but who knows what would've happened? If there was anything I learned in rehab, it's that you can't change what you did. I know it sounds fucking cheesy, but unfortunately, it is the truth." He finally turned to look at me. "I can't change what I did or what Kara did. What I do in reaction to it is what I can control."

I looked down at my hands, "Do you think it is fucked up of me to wish I hadn't killed him?"

"No," Calvin said immediately, "killing someone, whether it was in self-defense or intentional, leaves a mark."

Closing my eyes, I forced the tears to stay in, "Is taking one life worth the dozens I saved?"

"Yes, Maggie, he went there with the intent to kill all that he could. Shit, even when you were fighting him, he still tried to kill you. I know you know that if you had not stopped him, all of those kids would be dead. I also know that you know that he still had a little time to go to other rooms and kill more." He swallowed and looked down at his coffee cup. "Maggie, they found a suicide note pinned behind his computer."

I felt my heart sink. "When?"

Calvin sighed, "A few days after the shooting. Maxwell had been battling depression, clearly seen in the journals they recovered from his room. He wanted others to feel the pain he was feeling, and that the end goal was for him to be either shot by the police or himself."

My heart rate began to rise. I let myself sink back into the couch as my hearing got all muffled. He was battling, just like me, and was ready to be done. My vision got blurry as the flashes of his terrified face came to mind. The way his body looked after beating him to death. My hearing was filled with gunshot sounds and the cry for help outside my classroom door. Then, it was followed up by the ear-screeching sobs of mine.

Maxwell Fath had suffered from undiagnosed depression. How long had he been battling? Why hadn't he reached for help? Why did he choose to kill others to end up taking his own life? Why did he have to do that? Why didn't he just move on to the other classroom when he realized my room was locked? Why? Why did he have to destroy other lives?

My hearing and attention came back to life, and there in front of me were Skyla and Calvin. I blinked my eyes a few times before mumbling that I was thirsty. There I remained, on the couch, staring off into space, my mind circling with the same question: why? Why? Why? Everything could've been avoided. But the selfish thing that was eating me alive was the fact that I wished he would've just taken his own life, and not anyone else. How fucked and thoughtless of me to think that?

"Why does it make a difference?" Kelly asked.

I sat on the gray couch, my hair pulled into a messy ponytail, and I wore sweats and one of Jackson's T-shirts. I had not showered in the last two days, and I had barely talked to anyone.

My mind was stuck on the fact that Maxwell was selfish enough to kill others just to take his own.

"It makes all the difference in the world," I stated bitterly. "I felt all this pain for killing someone when, in the end, that was what they wanted."

Kelly crossed her legs. "If you had known, would it have changed anything about what you did?"

"No," I said slowly, "but I keep thinking, why did you have to go and fuck up more lives?"

Kelly gave a sad smile, "Because he had been in pain and was so tired that no one else could feel it."

"That still doesn't make it right."

"Correct, but I want you to think for a moment: how hard is it to tell others you have depression?"

My eyes looked at the hourglass sitting on the table in front of me. "It is not something you broadcast."

"In his mind, he had given up because the world or system had failed him. I believe he was angry and decided to show that anger." Kelly said.

My leg was bouncing, "Sort of like flipping off the system for failing to help him."

Kelly sighed, "That is what I would assume, as I never met the kid or know what was recovered from his room, but that would be my best guess."

"Why does the system fail in mental health?"

She smiled, "Because it is something that can't be cured with just medicine. It is a sign to people that they are damaged."

"Obviously, no one wants to be damaged," I mumbled, "so people are afraid of it."

Kelly nodded, "People who have not dealt with or coped with it are afraid of it. Because once they are told they have a mental illness, no one will look at them the same."

"It is fucked."

"Indeed, it is, but you have the strength and courage to admit and battle. I know therapy and medication aren't your way of coping, so I applaud you every time you are here and when you take your medication." I rolled my shoulders back uncomfortably. "I have told you this before: none of this is going to be easy. None of what you've been through should be something you are ashamed of. Don't let it be the thing that destroys you."

I bit down on my lip, "Then let it be what?"

She leaned in: "Let it be the thing that drives you."

It had been thirty-four days since the shooting. My daily routines stayed the same, with mom coming over for lunch and taking me places to Skyla to bring me ice cream. I had even gone and seen Jackson's house, which was gutted entirely, to my surprise. He told me that he had held off on any further plans because he wanted to do this with me. I didn't say much other than smile and nod.

To get my mother off my back, I agreed to see my dad. I had been avoiding him. My mother said he was lucid at times and understood what had happened to me. However, listening to my mom chat all the time, I knew the times when my father was lucid were far and few between.

Skyla said it might not be a bad thing to talk to someone who wasn't aware of their surroundings. Someone who might not remember what was said. In a fucked way, Jackson agreed with her, and even Calvin. It took me a few days and confirmation from Kelly that it probably was the right thing to do all along.

My mother had taken me to PT and was now driving to the facility. She told me she would drop me off and pick me back up in an hour, giving me way more time than I wanted with my father, especially if he was lucid. I knew the last time he had a full, lucid day was back at Thanksgiving, so I highly doubt today would be the random day that he decides to be lucid.

My leg had been getting better; I had been able to put more weight on it, and I could hobble around more smoothly. I had gotten a lot of my balance back, so I didn't need the crutches anymore. The scar was an ugly thing, making me self-conscious about it being seen, especially by Jackson.

Walking into the facility, I was greeted by the fake smiley nurses. They led me up the stairs at a very slow pace. I had been used to the stares and fake smiles when Mom had taken me out to lunch. It wasn't an unknown fact about what went down in that school, and some footage had even been revealed. Of course, the buzz had died down, but the people in Bemidji were still invested and curious as to what happened in the school.

Skyla had taken me a few days ago to the graveyard. I got to see all the graves for the twenty-one lives that were lost. There were so many flowers, balloons, and photos at each grave. I felt pain radiating down my leg at each picture I saw. Each face I had seen every day at work now lay on the ground. Skyla helped me lay pink roses down at each grave. I swear I saw tears in her eyes, but I knew better than to mention or ask about it.

Once I reached my dad's room, the nurse let me in and closed the door behind me. As usual, my dad was sitting in a chair facing out towards the lake, which oddly looked gray from this view.

"Hey, Dad, Mom brought a box of cookies. She said you had been asking for them," I said as I set them down on his bed. "She said you had been asking to see me; how have you been?'

I had just settled myself down on the seat next to him when I noticed. His eyes were still open, but clearly, there was no movement.

"Dad?" I whispered. I reached out and touched him, but he was stone-cold. "Dad?" I said a little louder as I checked for a pulse. "Dad, wake up, please." I whimpered as I grabbed his face. "Dad, DAD!" I screamed.

There wasn't a lot of feeling left in me, but whatever was left was now gone. I held on tight to him, begging for him to wake up. I shook him and kept checking for a pulse, but nothing. Tears rolled down my face, fast and uncontrollable. He was gone. My father was dead. He died alone. He was gone. Dad was dead. People were dying.

My brain suddenly felt a considerable throb, and my heart was racing. I fell back onto the ground, my hands shaking violently. My father lay there in his favorite pajamas, green bottoms, and an old Dartmouth t-shirt. His hair looked like he had just rolled out of bed and planted himself there on the chair. He was dead. He was dead, like all those children and adults from school. Dad was dead.

There were sharp pains that shot down my leg as I had landed back on it awkwardly. My head was pounding, making it hard to focus. My vision was going in and out as flashes of my father throughout my life appeared. He was dead. No heartbeat. He died, not knowing the reason why I had broken his heart. He died not knowing his best friend had raped and abused his daughter. He had died alone, here in this room.

Sweat was coming down my back, and my heart hurt as it pounded just as loudly as my head. Death. Then, something snapped inside me, like the last glass cup being dropped and shattered. I tried to scream, but nothing came out. I tried to talk, but there was nothing left. I tried to breathe, but it was hard. I wanted to remind myself of all the good memories, but the flood of images of Maxwell, the kids, my father lying there, and the blood.

My eyes began scanning the room until I caught sight of my graduation photos. I awkwardly got to my feet and hobbled over to it. I grabbed it and dropped it onto the floor, the glass shattering just enough to have a few shards fall out. I grabbed the biggest one and fell back down on the ground next to my dad. I reached up and grabbed his cold hand and squeezed it, begging for a light squeeze back, nothing but ice.

I fell away from him and pulled up the sleeve of my sweater on my left arm. You could see my veins pulsing as my head and heart were still racing. Closing my eyes, and in that moment, everything stopped, the pounding and pain. Everything was just silent and still. This was comfort, the sound and feeling of nothing.

Opening my eyes back up, using all the force I could, I dug the shard of glass through my skin from my elbow down. The vibrating red began to spill down my arm, and a wave of soft pain ran through my body. Using my mauled left arm, I pulled up the other sleeve and repeated the process, watching the blood spill out onto my jeans.

Dropping the shard of glass, I pulled myself up onto my father's lap. I carefully closed his eyes and sobbed into his stiff shoulder. It wasn't too long until I began to drift out of consciousness, and I could feel the deep sleep crossing through me. I couldn't lose my father, not now, not after everything that had just happened. My brain cannot take another blow.

I had reached my breaking point. There was nothing left but a lifeless body. I had given up, just like Maxwell Fath had, only I had chosen to go out, eliminating only myself. This way, I didn't take life away from someone else. I was just there, lying in my dead dad's arms, beyond shattered.

Jackson

I had received an urgent page from Skyla down at the pit. My heart raced, afraid that it had to do with Maggie, but I reminded myself she was with her mom. Maggie had been taking her time coming back to life. She had been able to regain her balance and independence to walk and shower alone. It wouldn't be long before she would be able to get back to her everyday life.

The therapist seemed to be helping, along with the medication. Maggie was sleeping better and had regained her appetite. She had even been willing to talk a bit more about what was going through her head. The only thing she asked that I do was remain quiet and let her speak.

Somehow, her mother had convinced her to go see her father, which I was nervous about but not opposed to. It had been a decent time since she had seen him, and usually, she would spiral out of control after a visit with him, but I guess Kelly thought it might be a good thing for her. I even thought showing her the house would bring more smiles and ideas out of her. Instead, it was met with silence and a few nods.

Once I reached the pit, Skyla met me right at the elevator doors. Her scrubs looked dirty, and her hair was a rat's nest. There were dark circles under her eyes, as this last month had taken a toll on her, whether she wanted to admit it or not.

"What's up?" I asked as I followed her out the doors to the ambulance bay. "What did you need me for?"

Skyla shrugged, "Ask the Chief; he told me to page you."

I followed her eyes to where the Chief and Calvin were standing. The Chief looked pale in the face, bringing back the memory of Maggie being brought in on the ambulance. I took a deep breath and reminded myself where she was, with her mom, seeing her dad. She was safe. She was okay.

"Okay, the three of you," the chief eyed all of us, "prepare yourselves for this. I need you all to promise me that you won't freeze."

"What the hell is going on?" Skyla snapped.

The chief shook his head, "I just need you guys to prepare for what is coming in."

My heart rate sped up, and I could clearly see the panic rising in Skyla's eyes. Calvin looked just as pale as his uncle. Sure enough, the ambulance pulled into the bay, lights off. The Chief glanced back at the three of us before making his way to meet the EMT at the doors. When they opened the doors, there was the lifeless body of Dr. Mitch Kensinger. Calvin stood there frozen, eyes fixed on his father. He was covered in a considerable mass of blood, but I did not see any sign of a wound. Skyla jumped into action, checking for brain function.

She looked up at the EMT, "Why the hell did we bring him here?"

The EMT looked at the chief, "In Dr. Kensinger's will, it was asked that his body be brought here and donated to science."

Skyla began examining the body. "Where did all this blood come from?"

Just as the words from her mouth left, there, coming around the corner, was another ambulance with its lights on.

"I was informed it was just my brother who was coming." The chief yelled at the EMT. "Who else?"

I felt the ice rush through my veins as there was shouting and yelling. Skyla reached out and grabbed my hand as we braced for what was going to come out.

"Twenty-eight-year-old female, Maggie Kensinger, in critical condition from self-inflicted wounds."

My stomach dropped, and that is when Calvin sank to his knees, finally realizing that his father was dead and now his sister was back in critical condition. Sure enough, there was Maggie, and there was a male EMT on top of her performing CPR. The wounds on her arms were bleeding through the bandages, staining everything.

I didn't know what to say or do. I didn't know. I grabbed Skyla and pulled her into a hug as she let out a hollowing scream. I squeezed her tightly as I felt myself beginning to break, and tears formed in my eyes. Maggie was not okay. Once again, she was not safe.

Chapter Twenty-Three

The Return of the Unwanted

Maggie had been in the ICU for several days before being moved to the psych floor. Even then, she refused to talk to anyone, including Jackson and Skyla. She had lost a decent amount of blood, requiring her to have a few blood transfusions.

Mitch Kensinger had died about an hour before Maggie found him, his battle with dementia finally coming to an end. Maggie did not attend his funeral as she was not allowed to leave the hospital, but Skyla and Jackson did go.

While the funeral was wrapped up and the reception began, Maggie was visited by someone. She sat in her room, staring out the window at the falling snow. Her mind was still foggy with all the images of death and blood. She barely even heard the door open and close, as all she could hear was herself screaming and sobbing. Maggie was getting lost in her head, and she was losing herself in the process.

Jackson was worried, but even more worried because Skyla was deathly scared. Calvin refused to go and see Maggie, as it was all too much for him. Julia Kensinger was battling the feeling of losing the love of her life and the fact that she nearly lost her daughter to self-harm. She remained at the house, surrounded by family and different kinds of casseroles and desserts.

Anika Kensinger had flown in for her father's funeral and was stuck to her mother's side. She wouldn't acknowledge that Maggie was in the hospital. She wouldn't even talk to Skyla or Jackson. As soon as the funeral was over, she was back on a plane going back to her residency.

Maggie refused to turn and see who had walked in; she just assumed it was a nurse or Dr. Loggins. When she didn't hear anyone asking questions or feel any movement to check her vitals, that is when she finally turned around.

Daniel Dobson had heard of Mitch Kensinger's death and had been on the next plane out to Bemidji. He was sad, of course, about his friend's death, but he was more excited at the thought of being able to see Maggie after all these years. It had been too long, and he wondered if she still smelled like lavender. There had not been a day she hadn't crossed his mind. He was always waiting to see if she would speak out, but as the years went by, he became more curious about how her life turned out.

At the funeral, he kept himself in the shadows, only talking to Julia and Anika before dipping out. He found out that Maggie had been the one to find her father and that she had attempted to kill herself by slicing her arms open. He also heard that she had been the one to stop and kill the school shooter a month and a half ago.

Knowing that he was still well respected in the psychology community, it was not going to be a huge deal to get on the floor. It also wasn't going to be a shock that he was here to talk to the floor's VIP patient. He was excited to see her, and he was even more thrilled that she was going to be in a position where there was nothing, she would be able to do.

Entering her room, she sat staring out the window. Her hair was still beautifully golden. Her eyes were still that stunning blue, and her skin pale as always. She had aged beautifully, reminding him a lot of what Julia looked like at her age.

"It has been too long, Maggie." He said as he watched her turn to look at him, fear filling her eyes. "I was afraid I was not going to be able to see you."

Maggie's heart rate soared as she made her hands into fists. "Get out." She said weakly.

Daniel just smiled and came closer to her, and she still smelled like lavender. There was something about the fear in her eyes that turned him on.

"We will be seeing more of each other." He leaned in and whispered to her. "I might find a job here, and we can resume our little fling." Chills were running down her spine. "I know you miss me."

Daniel smiled and backed away from Maggie, whose hands were now violently shaking, and her leg was bouncing. He shot her with a wicked grin before exiting the room. Right at that moment, Jackson Calsen slammed right into him.

"Sorry," he mumbled, "are you one of the night shift doctors?"

Jackson was positive that he knew all the freak doctors on this floor. This man was older and not dressed in hospital attire.

"I am actually one of Kensinger's older friends, and I wanted to see Maggie before I headed out." He said with a smile. "Keep an eye on her; she is a real troublemaker." He joked before patting Jackson on the back and making his way down the hall.

Finding this interaction odd, he noticed that no one on the floor seemed to be alarmed by the sight of this man. In fact, a few of them waved at him as he left. Jackson shook his head and entered Maggie's room to find her hyperventilating, trying to get out of bed, and shaking uncontrollably.

He raced over to her, grabbed her shoulders, and told her to breathe and focus on her breathing. He eased her back onto the bed, and she was still shaking. It took a few minutes, but Maggie was finally able to breathe, and she slowly stopped shaking. Her eyes were wide and filled with fear.

"That was him." She whispered. "That was Daniel."

Jackson's heart skipped a beat as tears began to fall down her face. He climbed into the bed with her and held her as she began to shake again.

"He's back." She whispered again. "He's back for me."

Maggie hid her face into Jackson's chest as fury rose through him. The man who had broken Maggie had been right there. The man who had shattered the woman he loved was back to do more damage. For once in his life, Jackson didn't know what to do. He was afraid that he couldn't protect her.

As for Maggie, she was preparing herself to fight another battle, just as if it were any other day. This time, she wasn't going to lose. She was going to come on top.

To be continued.